WINTER CIRCUIT

Also by Kim Ablon Whitney

The Perfect Distance
Blue Ribbons
Summer Circuit

Winter
CIRCUIT

Kim Ablon Whitney

Winter Circuit © 2015 Kim Ablon Whitney
www.kimablonwhitney.com

This is a work of fiction. While references may be made to actual
places or events, all names, characters, incidents, and locations are
from the author's imagination and do not resemble any actual
living or dead persons, businesses, or events.
Any similarity is coincidental.

ISBN : 1517669928

Cover by Littera Designs
Cover photos by Betsy Smith and Fotolia
Text set in Sabon

For Jenny—a faithful first reader from the very start

Chapter 1

IT DIDN'T SEEM POSSIBLE that a day could be grayer. Gray sky. Gray buildings. Gray snow. Gray was beautiful on a horse—dapple or steel gray was coveted in the hunters. I'd heard someone talk about a gray horse once, saying if he were bay he wouldn't be anything special. Even an old flea-bitten gray had its charm. But in the rest of the world, gray was a depressing, blah color. Which, of course, fit my mood perfectly.

I headed across campus, trudging by the President's Lawn on my way to the Health Center. It was the week after Thanksgiving and there had been an early snowfall the Sunday after Thanksgiving, the day before classes resumed. What had been a pretty white layer over campus on Sunday had turned to ugly gray by Monday when the temperature thawed and a little frozen rain fell. Nonetheless, a few students were attempting to sled down the slope of the lawn on rectangular cafeteria trays—fulfilling what was a Tufts tradition. I watched apathetically as I walked by them. Three guys and two game, sporty girls—hair poking out adorably from under their cute snow hats complete with pompoms—laughed as they jerked down the lawn. One of the guys pushed another to give him more momentum, but it ended with them both rolling into the snow. They stumbled to standing, jeans soaked, laughing even harder. Like it was one of the funniest things that had ever happened. Like it was the best day they'd ever lived. One of the guys made a snowball and tossed it at one of the girls, who smiled like she was loving every minute of college.

And then there was me. Miserable me. All around me kids seemed to be reveling in college life. They walked in packs to classes, went to the gym to work out, formed study groups, pre-gamed before hitting the frat parties. They hooked up with people they wished they hadn't the next day and seemed to love their ability to do so. They slept little, ate late at night, and generally were imbibing college life.

I'm sure I wasn't the only one who wasn't happy at Tufts. There had to be others or else there wouldn't be a Counseling and Mental Health Center. There wouldn't be others walking across campus to talk to a psychologist when they could be sliding down a slope of mushy snow on a cafeteria tray. But, surrounded by all the I'm-Finally-Here Kids, I felt dreadfully alone.

The voices of the happy sledders faded as I made my way to the Counseling and Mental Health Center. Chris was probably getting on his third or fourth ride of the day by now. Maybe teaching a lesson. We had texted that morning and he'd said he had a busy day ahead. Of course I was happy for him. But I was also sad for me.

The Health Center was warm, nearly too warm, the air overheated and dry. I checked in and then sat down in the waiting room to wait for Dr. S. She came out to get me after a few minutes and we went into the non-descript office that I'm sure she shared with the other staff psychologists. Dr. S (I'd given up trying to pronounce her incredibly long and consonant-filled last name) was not what I had expected when I'd decided to go to the Health Center. She had beautiful, natural blond hair. The kind that all the people who dye their hair blond wish they had. She didn't wear much make-up—she was naturally pretty. She looked like she belonged at a country club, not in a student mental health center. But I liked her even more for that—I made up in my mind that she'd had the most perfect upbringing filled with everything she'd ever wanted and still she'd decided to help people. Then she'd gone and married a foreigner with a crazy last name.

"Hi," I said, after I sat down.

"Hi," she said.

I always hated this first part of our sessions. It must be protocol for therapists not to ask something like, "How're you feeling today?" or "How's it going?" But I always wished she would. Instead, I would have to start things off. Well, our first session ever she had started things off by asking why I had come to see her. That had opened the door for me to recount everything: how until July I'd lived a quiet existence. I'd been a good student, but had few true friends or life experiences. I'd ridden horses but hated my trainer. Then, my father had decided I should go to the seven-week horse show circuit in Vermont and that I should take care of my horse—all by myself. I had learned over the weeks of the circuit to love caring for Logan. I had learned that I was good at it. I had gotten better as a rider but the most important thing I'd gotten out of the experience was seeing myself as capable of taking care of a large, living, breathing, needy animal.

The other important thing that had happened last summer was Chris Kern. Chris and I had fallen in love and while most people on the show circuit couldn't believe a gorgeous, accomplished, rising-star grand prix rider like Chris would fall for me, he did. We were still together, but we hadn't seen each other since the circuit had ended.

"Thanksgiving was okay," I told Dr. S to start us off. "I went to my father's in California. I guess it was good to see the sun. I got to see my brother, which was great. But the whole time I was thinking of Chris."

"What did Chris do for Thanksgiving?"

"He was with his family."

"Do you have plans to see him?"

"We're working on it but not yet. It's like nearly every second of every day I'm thinking about him. I know I shouldn't miss him so much but I think about the summer and how happy I felt. Here, nothing's right."

I explained how I had passed the kids sledding on the President's Lawn, how they seemed to be living the quintessential college life. And that by contrast I felt aimless and disconnected.

"Are you able to do your course work? You said you were worried about your expository writing class?"

"I've been getting the work done. I guess that's one of the

only things that keeps my mind off Chris for a while. It's not like I'm killing it in my classes, but I'm probably getting Bs. I used to care more how I did, though. That's bad, right? That means I'm depressed?"

Dr. S crossed her athletic legs cloaked in their black tights. She had a deep purple skirt on over the tights. "There's no one thing that means someone's depressed."

"Yeah, but I am, right?"

"It's how you feel."

I looked at my fingernails. God, I wanted to bite them. It would feel so good to chew them down to the bare, fresh, pink skin underneath. But I hadn't done that in a long time and I'd promised myself I wouldn't do it again.

"Do a lot of college students have a hard time first semester? I mean I thought I wouldn't have homesickness or whatever because, well, first of all I didn't grow up that far away from here and second of all, living with my mom wasn't exactly wonderful so I figured I wouldn't have any of that feeling like I was missing my old life. But now what I'm missing isn't my life before the summer but my life during those weeks in Vermont." I smiled, thinking of the horse show, the quiet town of Weathersville, of Chris. "Oh my God, I think of how great it was . . . it was like my life was finally happening. And now it's back to . . . I don't know . . . nothing."

"So you say you think about Chris a lot?"

"All the time. Sometimes it's good memories. Other times I obsess about his ex-girlfriend."

"Mary Beth?" Dr. S said.

Sometimes it amazed me that Dr. S could keep track of all

the details and names. It wasn't like she was looking back in her notebook. There had to be countless mothers, fathers, husbands, wives, friends, and exes to remember. I guess you had to have a good memory in order to do this job.

"Mary Beth, yeah. I don't think they've seen each other that much but they *are* at the same shows together and when the winter circuit starts, they'll see each other practically every day."

Dr. S asked me to tell her a little more about the winter circuit. I tried to sum it up quickly, explaining that from January through April, the top riders in the sport on the East Coast went to one of two winter circuits, The Winter Equestrian Festival in Wellington or Horse Shows in the Sun in Ocala. WEF, near ritzy Palm Beach, was the biggest circuit—with twelve weeks of competition and the wealthiest competitors. For the jumpers, there was serious prize money and FEI classes. It had become such a premier circuit that even some of the top European riders came for the winter. Chris would be there all circuit, continuing to rebuild his business. He'd lost his sponsor during the summer, but he still had a few good horses, including Logan, and he had picked up several clients too. Chris would be in Wellington, and so would Mary Beth. While I was stuck in Boston in the grayest weather known to man.

"So you're worried something will happen between them?" Dr. S asked.

I leaned forward in the uncomfortable, low-budget chair that must have been all the university could afford. "What if he realizes she's better for him than I am?"

Dr. S cocked her head. "Why would she be better for him?"

"Because she's a grand prix rider too so she fits into his life better."

"But when you were in Vermont, you two fit together pretty well?"

I blushed. Dr. S certainly hadn't meant it like that but Chris and I had fit together well indeed.

"Yes, but that was in Vermont and we're not in Vermont anymore. He's in Pennsylvania and soon he's going to be in Florida and I'm stuck up here. Mary Beth was the one who broke up with him. Well, he found her with another guy—or that's what I heard anyway. So he probably still loved her and if she's sorry maybe he'll forgive her."

"Do you think he could? If she cheated on him?"

"I don't know. Maybe, or else I wouldn't be worried about it."

Dr. S folded her hands on her lap. "But your worry is keeping you from living your life here, it seems."

"Yeah, I guess so."

We were silent. I looked at the clock, which was positioned so it was kind of hard for me to see and I always felt rude looking at my phone for the time. Our session was halfway over.

"Lots of people at college are in long-distance relationships and still have friends and fun on campus. Maybe you need to let yourself have a life here—worrying isn't going to change what you and Chris have."

Every time I went to see Dr. S, I felt a little better because of reasonable, sane statements like these that righted my world a few degrees. But then I'd leave her office and any plans I had to change faded away. A part of me thought maybe if I could just make it through to Christmas break, things would get better. I could go see Chris over break and maybe that would be enough to give me confidence in our relationship. I could spend a week or two with him in Wellington and maybe I'd go back to school in January feeling like Mary Beth wasn't a concern. Would that make me able to go out to frat parties, or partake in any part of regular college life? I wasn't sure.

I asked, "Do those long distance relationships work out? I mean in your experience? Or do they fall apart and the people go their separate ways eventually?"

"I don't think there's one pattern for long distance relationships."

"Because it feels like the high school boyfriend-girlfriend who vow to stay together at college don't make it through freshman year."

"I'm not sure that's true."

"Okay, maybe they do, if one transfers to the other's school."

"Maybe the problem here is not Chris and you being together, but who you are apart from Chris?"

I looked out the one tiny window at the gray snow and sky outside. Who was I away from Chris anymore? Was I that girl before Vermont again? No, I couldn't ever go back to being her. That was impossible. So then who was I?

Chapter 2

As I left the Health Center, my phone rang out the song of the summer, MISSION. The song of Chris and me, as I had come to think of it. Now MISSION only played on the radio sporadically and on my ringtone for Chris. Chris's face popped up on my screen.

Immediately, instead of feeling happy, I felt intensely worried. He'd said he had a busy day. Why was he calling? Was something wrong with Logan? Or worse, was he calling to break up with me? I shouldn't have been considering this as an option. I had no reason to believe he was breaking up with me, but lately I often found myself imagining scenarios where he would tell me he couldn't do the long distance thing, or he'd slept with someone else. More often than not, in my imagination, that someone else was Mary Beth. It was kind of like imagining your own funeral. Imagining things going wrong with Chris must have served some emotional purpose that I didn't know about. As I answered the phone, I tried to make a mental note to ask Dr. S about it next time we met.

"Hey," I said, making my voice upbeat. I never let Chris know how down I was. Whenever I talked to him I raised my voice those all-important few octaves. I filled my texts with happy-face emoticons. I forced myself to smile when we Face-Timed. He didn't ask all that much about college life—maybe because he didn't know what to ask since he'd never gone to college himself, choosing the horse-life out of high school instead. I might casually mention a paper due or a fake party attended just to keep up the front.

"I thought you were super busy today," I said. "I didn't expect to hear from you."

"I know. I've only got a few seconds, but I had to call you because I have great news."

"Yeah?"

I hoped his great news—about a new horse, a great jump session with Logan or Arkos, a new client, maybe even a new sponsor—would fill me up enough to get me through the day.

"I'm coming to visit you!" Chris said.

"Seriously? Why? When?"

"I hadn't wanted to tell you and get your hopes up but I'd put out a few feelers back in October about maybe doing a clinic. I just heard from one of the barns—Maple Valley? It's in Littleton. They want me to do a clinic the second weekend of December. They're paying my gas and it's not bad money. They were going to put me up at a hotel near the barn but I said I'd take care of it. I made us a reservation at a place in Cambridge—The Charles Hotel? Have you heard of it? I think it looks nice."

I had vaguely heard of it and it didn't matter what kind of

hotel it was. I would stay anywhere with Chris. I guess a tiny part of me wished he'd at least mentioned the possibility of staying in my dorm room. Even if it was half-hearted like, "I know I could stay with you but I think this will be much better . . . We'll get to be alone together. No roommate."

But I got over his not mentioning it pretty quickly. Because he was coming to Boston. In two weeks. In two weeks we'd be together again. We'd look into each other's eyes. We'd have dinner together. We'd talk in person. We'd have sex.

"Isn't that great?" Chris said.

"Oh my God, so great. I barely have words it's so great. I can't wait."

"Me neither," Chris said.

I heard someone calling him in the background. It sounded like Dale, his barn manager. I wondered how Dale felt about Chris arranging this clinic and visit to me. It wasn't like Chris would be missing anything during the second weekend of December. December was the one down-month before everyone headed South. Sure, if you really wanted you could find grand prix classes to compete in. There was a pre-circuit in Wellington and classes in other parts of the South. The European indoor shows were still in full gear with Olympia in London and Mechelen in Belgium. If Chris still had the top horses he'd had at the beginning of summer, he might have been competing abroad. But his number one horse, Nova, had gotten hurt at Devon, and then both Nova and his other top horse, Titan, had been pulled out from him by his sponsor, millionaire tycoon Harris Delaney.

I was definitely a contributing factor in Harris pulling his horses, since my former best friend Zoe had posted a fake online journal, supposedly written by me, that detailed my sex life with Chris. I'd learned that top grand prix riders had to have impeccable reputations—or at least that some owners tolerated debauchery more than others did. Because, of course, where there were top classes, big prize money, cocky men, and pretty girls there was debauchery aplenty. Harris might have also pulled his horses because his second wife told him to, after Chris declined her advances. But either way, by the end of the summer, Chris was down to two horses—one of which was my Logan, a recently reformed children's jumper with possible potential.

"Sounds like you have to go," I told Chris. I didn't want to have him tell me he had to go and the longer I stayed on the phone with him, the more likely it was that I wouldn't be able to hide my true state of emotions.

Two weeks. I had to hold it together for two weeks and then I'd see Chris.

Chapter 3

I WAS SUPPOSED TO GET MORE EXCITED about Chris coming as his visit grew nearer. I imagined I'd also stop obsessing about Mary Beth. But the opposite happened—and I couldn't figure out why. I stalked Chris's Facebook page and Instagram account and Mary Beth's too. Sometimes I just stared at photos of her. Most of the photos she posted were of her competing. Soaring over impressive looking jumps, often in Europe. Lush green grass fields paired with primary colored jumps. There were shots of her walking the course and on the medal platform after a Nations Cup class. Then there were the occasional what I would call, "Stars—They're Just Like Us" photos. A picture of Mary Beth's top horse curled up in his stall with Mary Beth's adorable rescue dog snuggled up beside him. Mary Beth grazing her horse under a beautiful sunset. If I looked back far enough on her timeline I could find Chris. Them standing next to each other on the medal platform, caught smiling at each other while walking a course, and my least favorite photo and the one I stared at most: Chris, in the middle of the ring after the Central Park Horse Show, spraying MB with a bottle of champagne that must have been given as a prize. Chris had won the grand prix and Mary Beth had come in second.

From looking at her timeline you wouldn't necessarily know that she and Chris had been a couple. And not just any couple but the circuit's young royal couple—show jumping's Will and Kate pre-marriage and babies. It would have been a lot worse if Mary Beth were a regular twenty-something woman. Then there would be the obligatory photos of her and Chris, lips plastered together, or totally drunk. There would have been the inane postings of "Feeling grateful for my boyfriend today, who always brings me my favorite coffee" and the heart emoticons. But Mary Beth and Chris were professional athletes and so their Facebook pages and Instagram accounts were for promoting an important, successful, and mature image.

Mary Beth came across as pretty, talented, and driven. And looking at that persona as I sat hunched over on my bed, tablet on my lap, blanket pulled half over my head, made me feel even more worthless. Why would Chris be interested in me when he could have her? Everything that had happened between us in Vermont seemed fake, like it was a figment of my imagination. Or at the very least like it was only possible because Mary Beth had been away in Europe and Chris had been desperate. Maybe he'd picked me on purpose. Maybe I was just the kind of disposable interval girlfriend he needed until he and Mary Beth realized they couldn't live without each other a minute longer. If he had dated another grand prix rider, when it ended he would have still had to see her every day. But with me, it could be over and he'd never have to see me again. It wasn't like I had a role in the sport. So maybe he was coming to Boston to tell me that he didn't see any future for us. Maybe he wanted to do it in person so he didn't feel like an asshole for dumping me over the phone. He could clear his conscience and head to Florida ready to get back together with Mary Beth.

My roommate Van startled me out of my stalker-depressive behavior when she opened the door and pretty much fell onto her bed. It was eleven o'clock in the morning—she'd been out all night.

Without sitting up she said, "You're doing it again, aren't you?"

"Doing what?"

"Looking at her page. You're sitting there, sucked into the vortex of jealousy over someone he's not even dating. You are obsessing over a self-created non-drama. I can feel the vibe in the room and it's toxic."

Van and I got along well, even though we led completely different lifestyles and she probably thought mine pathetic. But she was never mean about it. She seemed to have a soft spot for me, like I was an injured creature she'd found out in the woods but didn't quite know how to care for.

It seemed to me that there were two kinds of kids at Tufts—the kind that never left campus and formed their college life around frat parties and the dining hall and at the very most ventured into Davis Square for dinners out or frozen yogurt. Then there was the kind like Van, who spent as much of their time as possible off campus. Van attended what classes she had to and then rode the subway all over Boston, mostly to hang out in cool coffee shops and hear indie bands. Van wasn't exactly a groupie because she didn't follow just one group, but she did spend all her time seeing indie shows. The less discovered the band, the better. Secret shows were her Holy Grail and if she wasn't in Boston she could be found hopping on the train, the Chinese Bus, or into the dilapidated incense-smelling car of a near stranger to Providence, Portland, or Manhattan to catch a show. She had dated a lead singer in a band but from what I could tell that had ended.

"You're right. I'm obsessing," I told Van. She was perhaps the only one I could tell the truth to. I had nothing at stake with her. It didn't matter what she thought of me and I also knew she wouldn't judge me. She didn't care what people did, as long as it made them happy. But it didn't take a genius to see that I wasn't happy. I couldn't even tell Dr. S exactly how bad things had gotten because I was worried she might do something extreme like insist on calling my parents.

Van sat up and surveyed me with bleary eyes. She'd probably only slept a few hours on a friend's couch, if at all. She had a short haircut—probably chopped by another friend who professed to have experience with hair cutting. It was uneven in places and a part of it was dyed blue. It would have looked awful on someone else but it worked on Van.

"Okay, you've got to stop. Put down the iPad. We need to save you from yourself."

I did what she said and placed the iPad next to me. "He's coming, actually."

"Chris? Here?"

"Well, not here, not like to our room. But he's coming to Boston. He's giving a clinic nearby—a clinic's kind of like a master class or something like that. He got us a hotel room in Cambridge."

"That's so great," Van said. "But—" She stopped herself.

"What?"

"You kind of look like shit."

"What about you?" I said. "You probably haven't slept in days."

Van tossed back her head, shaking her angular pixie cut. "But it kind of works for me, you know? You, not so much. You need to clean up. Get your shit together before you see him."

"You're right." Of course she was right. I had been able to pretend to Chris on the phone but I wouldn't be able to do it in person if I didn't pull myself together. And if I didn't pull myself together for his visit, then he'd most certainly be running straight back to Mary Beth.

* * *

I spent the next few days getting myself back together. I realized that I hadn't done much personal upkeep since I'd arrived at school. I walked into Davis Square and got my hair trimmed. Just an inch or so to snip off the split ends. It felt great to have the woman wash my hair and give me a mini head massage. I thought about getting a cool, new haircut.

Maybe something short like Van. But I decided it was best not to change anything too much from the me Chris had inexplicably fallen in love with during the summer.

There was a small nail salon, Kim's Nails, next to the hair place and I decided to have my nails done too. Picking out my color I couldn't help but think of Zoe. For the first few weeks of the summer circuit, we'd been best friends and she'd taken me along with her to get her nails done. The wild child that she was, she'd picked Come-to-Bed-Red. Being the naïve, inexperienced virgin that I'd been, I'd picked a light pink color with some sickly sweet name that I couldn't remember now. I felt a small stab of pain thinking about Zoe because by the end of the summer, she had betrayed Chris and me. I knew that it wasn't all about me, or Chris. That she had heaps of problems, stemming from growing up on the circuit. An orphan rider, Chris had called her at one point. She drank way too much—she was probably an alcoholic. She was a sad case, but that didn't mean it didn't hurt me that I had lost one of the only close friends I'd ever had. It did.

Now, here I was, getting my nails done alone. The only friend I'd made at school was Van and that wasn't really a true friendship. What few friends I'd had in high school, I'd pretty much lost touch with. We'd never been close anyway. I hearted their posts on Instagram and occasionally mustered a comment or two, but it was clear they were doing what we all were supposed to do at college—grow, bloom, achieve. While I was shrinking, freezing, floundering.

I picked a purple hue—it wasn't Come-to-Bed-Red, but it wasn't sickly sweet pink. Maybe the purple would help me channel someone else.

My last stop was a small boutique clothing store with an eco bent—Gentle Goods—where I bought a really cute sweater. Maybe spa and retail therapy actually worked because I felt better than I'd felt in weeks as I walked back to campus.

Tomorrow I would see Chris.

Chapter 4

CHRIS CAME TO PICK ME UP at campus in the mid afternoon. He had driven all the way from Pennsylvania. He
probably should have flown but like many horse people he
was used to logging lots of miles in a day. He had told me his
cars lasted only a few years since he often put fifty thousand
miles on them in a given year between driving to horse shows
and going to look at horses. He listened to audio books in the
car and said he liked the time to just think.

He called from downstairs. Van had gone to New York
for the weekend in search of some secret show so Chris could
have stayed in my dorm room. But as I glanced around it
before I went to meet him, I knew we'd made the right decision.

I came around the bend by the rows of mailboxes, a few
always strangely flung open, and saw him out the window of
the door before he saw me.

Yes, he was still as amazingly good-looking. He was still
Chris. He had on jeans and a black North Face puffy down

jacket. The perpetual tan he had from working outdoors had faded somewhat in these late fall months but he still had a healthy color, unlike my skin which had quickly turned pale.

I took a deep breath. It didn't seem possible. Chris Kern, who had competed and won at some of the country's top shows, was standing outside my college dorm. Chris Kern, who was probably one of the most desirable straight men in the sport of show jumping, had traveled over six hours in a car to give a clinic to riders, most of whom would never compete over three-six, in order to spend one night with me. Me. Hannah Waer. Previously a virgin until this past summer. Still a not-very-talented rider. Pretty, but not model-gorgeous. Nice, but not volunteering-for-Doctors-Without-Borders-selfless. So why me? It was a question that had plagued me over the summer but somehow I'd been able to get past it. I was able to convince myself that he craved normal to balance out his crazy life. Why me and not Mary Beth? I had told myself he needed an anti-superstar girlfriend.

Now, as I saw him here—at Tufts—those same questions started drumming all over again with more urgency. This made no sense. Why me? Why not Mary Beth?

Chris saw me and his face lit up. I opened the door and he immediately pulled me to him. I snuggled into his puffy coat, trying to ignore the voices in my head chanting, *why me, why me, why me?*

"So this is it? This is college," he said when we let go. "What I saw of the campus driving in looks great. Beautiful."

I felt like either he was lying, or he was seeing a different vision from what I saw on a daily basis. Probably the latter because I knew Tufts had a pretty sloping hillside campus, complete with attractive buildings and views of the Boston skyline. But to me everything looked gray and lifeless. The only thing that was in color was Chris.

Chris asked to see my room, which was sweet of him. We walked past the room of one of my hallmates and I wished the door had been shut. It was the prototype Pinterest college room. She had the super cute sheets, duvet cover, and throw pillows. The practical expandable shelf organizer. The artfully hung funky mirror. The precious string of twinkle lights suspended across the room.

Then there was my and Van's room. Van had stuck up a few vintage posters from '80s punk bands like the Dead Kennedys and Social Distortion. Otherwise the walls were blank. We each had our bed. Mine had pink bedding that made me look like I was ten. The only thing worse would have been if it had horses on it. Van's bedding was an ugly beige color. We had no cute lamps or wastepaper baskets. There was nothing homey about it.

Chris sat down on my bed. He must have known mine was the pink one.

"I know what you're thinking," I said.

"What am I thinking?"

"How can I live like this?"

"Isn't this college-living?" he said.

"Did you see the room we passed? With all the cute décor?"

"So that's college-living?"

"I don't know what college-living is, that's the problem," I said.

Chris cocked his head at me. "Are you okay? You seem kind of . . ."

I was glad he couldn't find the right word. I shrugged. "I think I just haven't seen you in so long and I've been imagining this moment since we left Vermont."

Chris gave me a seductive smile. "Me too. Come here."

I stood in front of him. He put his hands on my hips.

"Did you say Van's gone?"

"Yeah."

He moved his hands around to my backside and then pulled me so that I was straddling him on my bed. I was glad I'd closed the door behind us.

"I've always wanted to make it with a college girl," he said.

His words hit me in a way they shouldn't have because he had made it with a college girl many times—Mary Beth. Unlike Chris, she'd gone to college. She'd spent most of her time commuting to the barn and horse shows but she'd completed her college course work and had a degree. But I guess he meant a real college girl—one who wasn't also a standout grand prix rider.

We started kissing and I forgot about Mary Beth for a while. I forgot to wonder, "Why me?" I just lost myself in kissing him. We lay back on the bed, shedding our clothes. I rolled on top of him. Once his shirt was off, I pulled back so I could stare at his chest for a few moments. I knew that besides the many horses he rode daily, Chris also found time to go to the gym and it showed in his body. He did it because he took his profession seriously and knew that to be the best rider he could be, he had to be fit, strong, and as resistant as possible to many of the aches, pains, and strains that came with riding.

I followed the small trail of dark hair leading from his bellybutton downward with my eyes and hand. He breathed deeply while I took hold of him.

"I've missed this," he said.

I leaned over him and kissed him again, this time in a quick, teasing way. "Yeah?"

"Been getting a little too familiar with my own hand," he said, smiling.

"Well, let me take over for a little while," I said, as I ran my hand up and down his dick.

After a few moments, he put his hands around my back and somehow expertly flipped me over so he was on top of me. My shirt and bra were already off and he peeled off my jeans and underwear, kissing parts of my body as he went.

"You said you went on the pill?" he asked as he tossed my jeans and underwear onto the floor.

"Yeah, right after the summer." I had done it because I had thought I was a college girl now and it was something college girls should do. I'd made an appointment with the women's health group on campus and had a full exam and consultation—something I should have done in high school. I guess it hadn't really mattered because until Chris I'd never been sexually active, besides one time messing around with one of Ryan's friends. But now that I was in a relationship with Chris, an older man too, it seemed like I should be on the pill.

With his hand on one of my knees, he parted my legs. He

touched me first, and listened to me moan. Soon, he put himself inside me. I swallowed hard at the first thrust, getting used to the feel of him again. I loved it. I loved the feel of him inside me. He lay over me, resting much of his weight on his forearms. It didn't last all that long. Movies always made it seem like people had sex all night but it was probably only a few glorious minutes. It started to feel good for me too as he moved inside me, rubbing up against what I guess was my clit. I hated that word—clit. It sounded so illicit. But I thought maybe I should try to love that word. Because that word was all about female pleasure and what could be dirty about that?

I was surprised that I quickly found myself climaxing. I hadn't ever climaxed before while we were having sex—only when he was touching me or going down on me. But there must have been something about the angle or the pressure because today it felt amazing. I always liked sex with Chris but in a different way than when he got me off.

He came soon after and then rolled off me.

"I came," I said.

"I thought so but I wasn't sure."

"I did," I said, still surprised.

He looked over at me. "I'm sorry if I practically jumped you. I hadn't planned on that or anything but when I saw you, I just couldn't stop myself."

"I'm happy you didn't stop yourself," I said.

It was as if somehow having sex had been an easier way for us to reconnect after the time apart than talking. It was normal to be awkward with each other after the months that had passed since we had seen each other. And maybe if we hadn't had sex within the first twenty minutes of seeing each other, that awkwardness would have naturally dissipated. It didn't make sense that stripping off our clothes and participating in life's most intimate act would be easier than just chatting until we got reacquainted with each other again, but somehow it just was. There was a muscle-memory in our movements, a familiarity in our lust for each other.

Now, as we lay next to each other, naked, on my pink sheets, it was like those months apart had disappeared and we had only just been together in Vermont.

"What are we doing for dinner?" I said.

"I made a reservation. There are supposed to be a few good restaurants right in the same building as the hotel so I figured we'd try one. I didn't want us to go too far because basically all I wanted was to get you back in the hotel room and fuck you."

I giggled. "Well, we already did that."

"Once," Chris said. "Only once."

I gave him a little smile. "You ready to go again?"

"Okay, maybe not right now," he said. "But definitely later."

* * *

In fact, we messed around again after we checked into the hotel room. This time we didn't have sex but instead he made me come again, and then I gave him a hand-job. I thought that would be it for the night but we went at it again after a delicious and leisurely dinner at the restaurant Chris had chosen. After dinner, we had sex. It took longer, perhaps because Chris had already come twice in one day, and I didn't come this time but I loved looking at his face as he moved on top of me. It was like those moments when we were connected—physically—were the moments when the voices inside my head quieted the most. I could no longer hear the, "Why me?" or the "Why not Mary Beth?" that kept returning and infiltrating my brain the rest of the time.

Chapter 5

WE OVERSLEPT AND DIDN'T HAVE a chance to have sex that morning before going to the clinic. Chris was not the type of trainer who would ever be late to a clinic. There were plenty of trainers who rolled in twenty minutes after the start time or were unprofessional in other ways—taking phone calls during lessons or showing up with their high-maintenance dogs and demanding someone babysit them—but Chris was not one of them. He made it his goal to be professional in every part of his business.

I stayed in bed while he jumped in the shower. His phone rang and I grabbed it from the bedside table. I looked at who was calling and I think I had planned to go into the bathroom and see if he needed to take it for any reason. I recognized the name of the caller—it was one of his new clients, Lily Teller. After Chris had lost Harris, he'd had to find a way to make his business profitable again, which meant taking on clients. He didn't want to build a large training stable but he thought a few, decent clients could help generate income and also might translate into a future ownership stake in a grand prix horse. He'd been lucky in that he'd picked up Lily. She was nineteen, a sophomore at Princeton, and a decently talented rider. She also had beaucoup buckage. Chris was charged with keeping her horses, which included two very nice international level mounts and two younger jumpers, in shape and tuned up so Lily could fly in on her father's private plane to show them. It was semi-rare that Lily would pick a trainer only a few years older than herself but Chris said he figured her family wanted undivided attention and also didn't want to deal with the blustery attitude of some of the more experienced jumper trainers.

Instead of bringing Chris the phone, I kept it cradled in my hand. When the call had gone to voicemail, I found myself punching in his passcode and going into his texts. I hadn't planned it. It wasn't, as they say in murder trials, premeditated. But there I was scrolling down over the names and numbers. There were plenty of texts from me, of course. There was his mom, his brother, clients, other grand prix riders who were friends or whom he was doing business with.

I stopped on the name I was looking for. Mary Beth McCord. Okay, I tried to tell myself, no one says he can't text with her. Of course he's going to come in contact with her because they work in the same industry. They were going to see each other all the time once circuit started. That was just the way things were when you dated someone on the show circuit.

But . . .

I read the stream of texts that started with Mary Beth asking, *Hey, when do you get down here?*

December 28, why? Chris wrote back.

Have a horse I want you to look at.

Which one?

Moxie.

Don't know that one.

Got her in Europe. Tons of scope but I can't ride her to save my life.

That's ridiculous. You know you ride great.

Smiley face emoticon. Then another line from Mary Beth: *You always did know the right thing to say.*

That line right there killed me. She was flirting with him. Straight-out dead-on flirting. And trying to rekindle old feelings by bringing up their shared past.

No reply from Chris. Then Mary Beth again: *Will you come look at her when you get here?*

Can try.

Not sure I can wait . . .

That was the end of the string of texts. Not sure I can wait . . . For him to see the horse, or for her to see him? And what exactly did that ellipsis mean? Didn't an ellipsis mean that there was more to come, something she was saying without saying it? Like what she really wanted to happen when she saw him?

Zoe had said on the last night in Vermont that Mary Beth wanted Chris back. I'd told myself that was just Zoe trying to make me jealous and stir up trouble. Only now it sure seemed like Mary Beth did want him back.

Chris hadn't exactly taken the bait. He could have written back any number of things. But he did tell her she was a great rider. Why did he have to flatter her like that? And why didn't he say something that made it clear how things stood between them now. Like, Not sure I have time to look at the horse. Things are really busy for me.

I still had his phone in my hand when Chris came out of the bathroom, wearing only a towel around his waist. A very good look for him. Of course Mary Beth was after him again. Who wouldn't be? Chris was gorgeous, he was successful, he was kind. She must have realized she had been insane to cheat on him and she'd do anything to get him back.

"Did someone call?" Chris asked. "I thought I heard my phone ring."

"Yeah, it was Lily. I was going to come get you but then I figured we couldn't waste any time and you could call back in the car."

He came to the bed and took the phone from me. If he was mad I didn't come get him or suspected me of snooping, he didn't let on. Instead, he leaned over and kissed me, making me feel guilty. "Better get going yourself. You sure you want to come with me? It's going to be cold."

"Don't they have a heated viewing room?" I asked.

"I hope so but you never know. Changing your mind?"

"No way," I said. "I'm coming."

I didn't care if I froze my butt off. I wasn't saying good-bye to Chris eight hours earlier than I had to. If it was up to me, I'd never let him out of my sight again. Because if I wasn't keeping an eye on him, there was no telling what Mary Beth would be up to.

We didn't get too far from the hotel when Mary Beth

came up in conversation. Or, to be more accurate, when I brought her up.

"Have you talked to Mary Beth?" I asked as Chris followed the GPS directions his phone was issuing. "Or seen her?"

His car smelled deliciously horsey. A combination of horse and tack. One of his saddles was in the back seat and there was plenty of white hair from his dog, Jasper, whom I realized he must have left with Dale for the weekend.

Chris gave me a confused look. "What's that about?"

"What's what about? I'm just asking a question, and you're not answering it, which seems kind of, I don't know, suspicious?"

Siri spoke, prompting Chris to stay left to go onto Route 2 West toward Concord. He glanced at the screen of his phone to double check the route and I felt like he was also giving himself a moment to figure out how to respond to me. Was he trying to figure out how to hide something?

"I'm not answering it because it feels like the question is not really what you want to ask. It seems like what you're asking is really something else, like do I still have feelings for her, which I think I answered pretty clearly this summer."

"Why can't you just answer the question?" I couldn't stop jabbing at him. It felt very un-me. Chris and I had never had an official fight. There was the time he'd abruptly cut me out of his life when he'd thought I had posted online about our relationship and sex life but that seemed understandable.

"Why are you picking a fight?" he said.

"I'm not," I said, even though I knew I was.

"I haven't seen her. I've texted with her. And no, I don't have feelings for her."

Chris's hands looked tight on the steering wheel and he was going pretty fast on what was a small two-lane highway. Part of me hated myself for annoying him. Was I trying to ruin this trip? But I couldn't stop thinking about the flirtatious nature of her texts.

We drove the rest of the way in near silence. There was no traffic and soon we were driving through historic Concord, passing stately colonials bearing historical society plaques, on the way out further to Littleton.

"I'm sorry I said anything about Mary Beth," I told him as the GPS told us the destination would be ahead on our right. I wanted to get back on good terms before we arrived at the farm.

"Okay," he said, but he didn't look convinced.

I put my hand on his arm. "I shouldn't have. I just miss you, that's all. Don't let what I said ruin this trip."

We turned up the long driveway passing a few pastures and a fenced outdoor ring covered in snow. Chris angled into a spot in front of the barn. He started to get out of the car and I followed him, quickly putting on my jacket. He zipped up his jacket and we went inside the barn.

Oh, the smells. If the car smelled deliciously horsey, I could have eaten the barn up in one big bite. The sweet hay. The musty horse blankets. The sooty footing in the indoor arena, which was attached to the barn. I missed all the smells of the barn, not to mention the horses themselves. One had its head over the stall door and I went and played with him, while Chris talked to Ginny, the trainer who had arranged the clinic. His nameplate read MILO. He was a chestnut and he was friendly, playfully poking me with his nose and breathing on me. His breath was hot and grassy, I guess from hay since the pastures were blanketed in snow except for small patches where brown grass poked through. His muzzle was unclipped with long spiny whiskers unheard of for any of Chris's horses.

"You are cute," I told him, missing Logan terribly. I'd heard people talk about the delicious smell of babies but babies had nothing on horses. Horses were the most beautifully smelling animals on the planet and if you didn't believe that, then you weren't a horse person. Even the manure in the barn smelled good to me.

Chris and Ginny—a solid woman in her fifties—came into the aisle.

"Making friends?" Chris said. He had either moved past our tiff in the car, or wanted to act like he had in front of Ginny.

"He's really sweet," I said. "Makes me miss Logan."

Chris introduced me to Ginny. I knew her from some of the Massachusetts shows I'd gone to with my old trainer, Jamie. She ran a solid program but mostly stuck with the A shows in the area, not venturing much beyond Connecticut. I think she did a week or two at Vermont each summer, but that was Maple Valley's one big show of the year. If riders who trained with Ginny got really good and wanted more, they usually left for other barns. She gave them good basics and foundations, but for whatever reason wasn't interested in the life you had to live in order to have students who were competitive at the biggest shows.

I was sure Ginny had no idea who I was. Chris introduced me as his girlfriend. "She goes to Tufts," he said.

"Oh, do you ride for the team?" Ginny asked. "One of my students is on the Tufts team, Jenna Ramsey?"

"I'm not riding this semester," I said. It wasn't much of an explanation but I left it at that. And why wasn't I riding on the Tufts' IHSA team? Maybe I wouldn't be so miserable and friendless if I were going out to a local barn once a week for a lesson, and competing at IHSA shows on some weekends. But after being taught by Chris, I felt like I didn't want to ever be taught by anyone else. I knew that sounded—and probably was—ridiculous. But after so long of having Jamie scream at me and put me down, it was a revelation to have Chris teach me. He had made me feel like I could ride a little, and like I was worth teaching. I was sure the Tufts coach was nice but I hadn't wanted to risk it. The end of the summer had been perfect—I had finally made progress with Logan and ridden well. I didn't want to tarnish that.

Ginny pointed me toward the viewing room and took Chris into the ring. I sat with a few other riders and mothers in the viewing room, which was heated but not exactly balmy. Still, it was warmer than it must have been for Chris in the ring. I couldn't hear what he was saying because there was no intercom in the viewing room so it was sort of like watching TV without the sound. I could generally figure out what was going on but it felt like I wasn't getting the whole story. Still, I observed Chris being Chris. I could tell, even without hear-

ing him speak, how he was kind and encouraging to the
riders. He taught four riders in the first session and three in
the next session. The first session, I learned from some of the
others in the viewing room was three-feet, and the second session was three-foot-three. None of the riders or horses was
amazing. In fact, many trainers of Chris's caliber would have
turned up their noses at teaching at a barn like Ginny's where
horses' whiskers and coats grew long. As I watched him, I felt
a pang of guilt and love. Chris was doing all this for me.
There was nothing he was getting out of this experience. He
was only breaking even on the trip or making enough for a
new pair of breeches. He wasn't going to find his next grand
prix horse here. He had come all this way and was teaching
this clinic solely so he could see me. That was how much I
meant to him. Again, I was plagued by the feeling of *Why
Me?* How could I mean that much to him that he'd be willing
to do this? I didn't feel worthy of his love.

He gave the riders his full attention, working them solidly
on the flat, before moving on to jumps. He called them in
sometimes to talk to him and I could see him asking them
questions about their horses and he would nod along with
them; he was truly listening to their answers. He would then
explain something about how he wanted them to ride. He
would use his own body to show them how to look in the air
after a jump, or turn their hips in the saddle. And when they
got it right he clapped his hands and cheered as if they had
just put in the winning ride in a jump-off in a big class at an A
show.

We broke for a quick lunch and I overheard the riders in

the barn saying how great their lesson had been and how thrilled they were with Chris. I stood listening, letting the praise for Chris wash warmly over me. I felt like someone was complimenting me and I felt my admiration for Chris well up inside me in the same way it had when I watched him compete in Vermont.

"He's good," one rider said to another. "I didn't think he'd be that good at teaching. He zeroed right in on what Rio needed with keeping her shoulder from popping out."

It was true that often some of the best riders weren't the best teachers and vice-versa. Chris was good at both.

"I thought he might throw up all over our horses," the other rider confided to the first. "But he told me Paddy's great. I think he really liked him."

After the break, Chris taught two more sessions—both at three-foot-six. The combination of the small indoor and the sparsely decorated jumps—most were just rails, maybe the odd gate or box wall—made three-six look big. These were the best riders Ginny had in the barn and to give her credit they were really good. They might not have had the most expensive tack, the best horse, or the best style in the saddle, but they could ride, which was more than could be said of many of the people on the A circuit now that big shows included endless divisions under three-foot. I could tell Chris enjoyed teaching the higher groups, although he had given his all to the less experienced riders too. I felt so proud to be associated with Chris. So many Big Name Trainers were snobs and gave the horse show world a bad name. Not Chris. Chris truly loved horses—not just the horses that could jump the big jumps, but the common-folk blue-collar horses that taught people to ride, the ones he'd seen today with their trace clips, fuzzy ears, and blanket rubs on their shoulders.

Ginny thanked him profusely and told him she'd love him to come back any time. In the car, Chris upped the seat warmers and put the heat on high. He took out the envelope Ginny had given him and transferred the checks and twenty-dollar bills into his wallet as the car warmed up.

"It looked cold out there," I said.

"It was freezing."

"You looked like you were having fun, though."

"Would I have rather been teaching the same clinic in seventy degree weather? Yes. But it was fun. It's always fun to teach people who're hungry to learn."

I smiled and shook my head.

"What?" he said.

"You're perfect. You're just perfect. I feel like I suck in comparison to you."

In the barn I'd been so self-satisfied that Chris was who he was, making me fall in love with him all over again. But now, the two of us alone, I nearly wished he had more faults. I didn't understand myself.

"Is that supposed to be a compliment? Because it doesn't feel much like one."

"I don't know what it's supposed to be. It's supposed to be how you make me feel."

Chris gave me a confused look. "I thought I was pretty good at making you feel good. Judging from last night . . ."

"Of course you make me feel good. But I just feel like I can't compare to you in real life."

"Why do we have to compare you to me, or me to you? Aren't we supposed to compliment each other? That's what the best couples do."

"See, even just saying that, that's . . . that's, like the perfect thing to say."

Chris shook his head. "I'm missing something here. You're upset because I'm saying the right thing?"

The car had warmed up and he reversed out of the parking spot, and headed out the barn driveway. It was already getting dark.

We didn't really conclude that line of discussion. It was like there wasn't much else to say really. I felt inadequate next to Chris, not to mention worried that he'd wake up and realize he could do better than me. But I loved him for being so great all the same. The qualities I'd seen in him today were why I'd fallen in love with him.

He drove me back to campus and we sat outside my dorm in his car for a time. He should have been kicking me out of the car because he had the whole entire drive back to Pennsylvania. But, of course, he didn't say a word about having all those hours in the car alone ahead of him.

We kissed for a while and he told me he was going to miss me. Sometime while we were kissing I started crying.

"What's wrong?" He lifted my chin and looked at me carefully. "I feel like I'm missing something that's going on between us. Like I'm a step behind."

"Nothing's going on," I said through my tears. "I just miss you, that's all. You've got this whole life going on—"

"So do you," Chris said.

But he didn't know that I didn't, not really. Not like he

did. And I wasn't going to tell him. He'd think I was turning crazy, like my mother. Something I had begun to worry about myself.

"I just miss you and I love you," I said.

"I love you too. I'll come back and give another clinic. Or you'll come to Florida for a weekend right after I get down there, okay?"

I nodded, afraid that if I spoke, I'd start crying again.

We kissed again and I climbed out of the car. I watched him drive away. As I saw his tail lights go out of view, I knew seeing him sporadically wasn't enough for me. That what we were doing wasn't working. That I couldn't live with it. I wouldn't survive continuing to feel this way. Something had to change.

Chapter 6

I CALLED RYAN AFTER I'D STOPPED crying and pulled myself together. If I had been like a normal nineteen-year-old I'd be on the phone with my best friend, but my older brother would have to do. And Ryan was always great about thinking through big issues—he was mature beyond his 22 years and could be logical and unemotional, always giving the best advice. It might not always be the advice I wanted to hear, but it was the best advice I would get on the subject.

I caught him between meetings. In addition to going to college, Ryan was running two start-ups.

"Hey, do you have a minute?" I asked when he picked up.

"For you, always."

I loved my brother. I knew a lot of siblings had strained relationships but Ryan and I had always been close. Although we'd never said as much to each other, something about having lived through our parents' divorce made us both realize that we had to hang on to each other. That parents could divorce but that your sibling was with you for life.

"So you know how Dad dropped out of school to start his business . . ." I began.

I'm sure that wasn't what Ryan had expected me to launch into. "Yeah?" he said in a tentative voice.

I wouldn't mince words or give some big build up to what I'd been thinking of ever since I watched Chris's car pull away. I announced, "I'm thinking of taking a semester off."

"To start a business?" Ryan asked.

Unlike Dad and Ryan, I'd never been particularly entrepreneurial. Besides the occasional lemonade stand of my single-digit years, I'd never had a job. Taking care of Logan this past summer was the closest I'd come to a job, and I hadn't been getting paid for it. But Logan had depended on me and that had to count for something.

"No, to go to Florida. The winter circuit starts in January and goes through April. Logan's going to be there."

"And Chris'll be there." Ryan pointed out the obvious.

"Yup."

"So what will you be doing there exactly?" Ryan asked.

"Um, I don't know. I haven't thought through that part yet."

"Well, you better."

I was relieved Ryan didn't tell me I was crazy. But he wasn't saying it was a brilliant idea either. He was pointing out how my plan was flawed and needed further consideration.

"Do you think Dad'll go for it?" I asked.

"No," he said plainly.

"Why not? He dropped out of college. I'd just be taking a semester off."

"He dropped out of college to start a business that made him millions. Right now it sounds like you want to take a semester off to be with your boyfriend."

"And Logan."

"I'm sorry, your boyfriend and your horse. Sounds like an old Tom Petty song to me. I'm sorry to be harsh but you know I don't sugar-coat."

I was silent for a few moments. Then, I admitted, "You're right."

"So what are you going to do about it?" Ryan said. "If you really want to go, you have to make it sound better. You have to make it something Dad will understand."

"You mean I have to get a job. A real, paying job."

There was nothing our dad liked more than kids having real jobs and responsibilities. It was why he loved Ryan, who had been holding jobs and starting companies since he was nine and founded his own sneaker customization business. He hired two kids who were amazing artists but were basically dorks to decorate sneakers and took a fee for arranging their bookings. Dad's feeling that kids needed to strive and claw their way through childhood was why I drove him crazy. It was why he'd sent me to Vermont last summer on my own. He had this whole theory on how America was killing its future generations by setting them up in cushy dorm rooms complete with PlayStations and cable TV, too many choices at the dining halls, and abstract think-tank classes that introduced no practical skills. I had to appeal to that line of thinking.

"Thanks, Ryan," I told him. "I'll let you get back to running the world."

"Haha," he said. "Catch ya later."

I clicked off with Ryan and looked around my dorm room. Maybe my dad was right. We college students were too spoiled for our own good. Our lives were too comfortable. Look at Chris. He had chosen a profession where if you didn't have gobs of money you had to work hard, really hard. He was up at the crack of dawn every day, riding and teaching, all so he could perhaps get back to having a top horse again. He was willing to pay his dues and climb the ladder if it got him to the top. If he got knocked down again, he'd just start back up. How many people did I go to school with that I could say that of?

So I needed a job. And it was late in the season to be finding one. I was certain most everyone had their Florida plans all buttoned up. Grooms, exercise riders. What could I possibly do for work? Could I work in a mobile tack store? Could I get a job in the office at the horse show? But who wanted to be stuck inside when I could be working with horses somehow? I wasn't a good enough rider to get a job riding—that was for sure. But I had proven myself to be a pretty good groom. And I had come to love taking care of Logan. But that was one horse. Would I really cut it if I had four horses to take care of?

I didn't have a ton of contacts in the horse show world and I didn't want to ask Chris for help. If I pulled this off, I would surprise him with the amazing news that I was coming for circuit. Jed was enjoying college life at NYU and he'd said a few weeks ago he didn't think he was going to show at all this winter. Zoe and I weren't talking, of course. Jamie hated me. So that pretty much left Mike. Mike was Jamie's head groom. He and I had become unlikely friends in Vermont. He'd taught me all about taking care of a horse and was always there to bail me out of trouble.

I texted him right away. *Hi Mike! I'm thinking of coming to WEF for the winter. Catch is, I need a job!! I know it's late to find one but I thought you might know of someone looking for a groom?*

A few minutes after I had pressed send, my phone rang. Mike's voice was deep and grainy when I picked up, "Hannah! What the hell happened to college?"

I laughed. Classic Mike. Mike was one of the only white grooms left on the circuit anymore, having been replaced first by Mexicans and then by Brazilians. Mike was burley and brusque but underneath that exterior he was a sweetheart.

"Nothing. I'm still in college. But I miss the show world. I miss Logan."

"You miss Chris," Mike said.

"That too."

"So what are you going to do about college?"

"Take a semester off. Like a work-program thing. Maybe I can even get partial credit."

That last part was a total fib. There was no way I'd get credit for working in Florida but Mike might not know that and it sounded good.

"You don't want to groom," Mike announced.

"Why not? I loved taking care of Logan and I got pretty good at it, right? Didn't I?"

"You did," Mike said. "But you're not a groom. Grooming's tough and circuit is like the worst. The longest days. So much pressure. Trust me when I say you don't want to groom."

Part of me wanted to rise to the challenge, to prove I could do it. But selfishly I didn't want to be so physically exhausted each night that I couldn't spend time with Chris. I also didn't want to be so busy during the days that I could never watch Chris ride.

"Okay, I believe you," I told Mike. "So is there anything else I can do, something with the horses in some way? Like a barn manager maybe, even though I don't know the first thing about that?" I hoped Mike wasn't offended that I thought I could be a barn manager when I had only weeks of experience taking care of one horse, my own, to his years caring for multiple horses at a time.

"Hmmm," Mike said, seemingly unoffended. "Let me make a call or two. I heard about something—I'm not sure the position's still open. Let me see."

"Okay, that would be great," I said. "Thank you so much, Mike!"

"It's good to hear from you, kiddo."

Mike wasn't that much older than me but to him I guess I was a kiddo. He was a horse show groom by trade, working endlessly for little pay. I was a spoiled college girl who could play horse show when she wanted.

"Hey," I said. "One more thing. How's Zoe?"

I couldn't believe I was asking about her after the way she'd burned me. But I knew that she was troubled and I still worried about her sometimes. She hadn't done nearly as well at the eq finals as she'd hoped to. She'd only finished fifth in the Medal Finals, and didn't place in the Maclay, Washington, or Talent Search, when she'd been thought of as a contender to win at least one of the finals. It was her last chance at the finals and the win or a top ribbon would have helped as she moved into the professional ranks. I had no idea what she was doing now.

"Haven't seen her in a few weeks. After the National, she went back home to Virginia. I'm trying to keep my distance, if you know what I mean."

In Vermont it had been clear to anyone with eyes that Mike was in love with Zoe. He would be good for her too. But Zoe thought he was beneath her and spent the summer flirting with him only when she needed to feel good about herself and then sleeping with a dirt-bag Irish grand prix rider.

"Is she going to work for Jamie this winter?"

"I don't think so. She said she had some job offers but I don't know if any of those were real or just her talking," Mike said.

Mike and I finished up our conversation. He said he'd call me back when he knew more. I just hoped there was a job out there with my name written all over it. A job that would bring me three glorious months with Chris.

Chapter 7

CHRIS AND I HAD RESUMED our "everything's-fine" long distance relationship but I think he now knew everything wasn't fine. I blamed my picking a fight, overall moodiness, and crying jag on the stress of my classes and upcoming finals, and maybe he believed me.

Mike got back to me a few days later. He had only dug up one job and he said he had to warn me that, although it sounded good, it was working for a difficult family. The job description wasn't exactly concrete—more like a smattering of responsibilities. One part babysitter, one part extra set of hands around the barn, one part exercise rider. The job was with a family whose daughter had just moved out of the ponies. They had a private trainer, whom I'd never heard of, but that didn't mean much since I didn't know that many trainers. Mike said the trainer was in her early thirties and nice. She hadn't been working for the family for that long, just over a year. The parents were okay, Mike said, but they weren't around much. It was the girl who had a reputation as spoiled and difficult, a regular pony princess.

"They have a farm off the show grounds, totally gorgeous, with housing there. They want someone to live with the girl when the parents aren't there—make sure she gets to the ring on time, gets to tutoring, maybe even help her with her homework. I thought you'd be good at that part. You also will probably help the trainer flat the horses, and pitch in around the barn. You get free housing and a salary."

"It sounds perfect!" I told Mike. Somehow I tuned out the part about the girl being difficult. I mean how bad could a thirteen-year-old be, anyway? I was perfect for this job and it was perfect for me. I'd get to be at the ring, at the barn, even ride a little. And I would be good at homework help.

Mike gave me the contact info of the trainer, Linda Maro, and said to tell her he sent me. I called her immediately and was hired after she asked a few simple questions, one of which was, when can you start? I told her I would have to get back to her because of course there was the minor detail of getting my parents to say yes and getting whatever paperwork filed for school.

I texted my dad asking if we could talk. This was a conversation I thought would be best conducted with a little advance warning. He told me he'd call me that afternoon. I had to say one thing about my dad—he always had time for me, or made time for me. There was never a time that I could remember when I'd needed to talk to him and he'd said he couldn't that day. No matter what was going on in his business life—and there were certainly always big things going on with him—I was important to him.

"What's up?" he said when he called me.

"Um, well, I wanted to talk to you about school . . . and life."

I was sitting in my sadly decorated dorm room. Van was out. Again. Through the thin walls I could hear the girls in the room next door, in the perfectly decorated dorm room. Their names were Jenny and Jen, or Kate and Katie, something like that. Becoming roommates seemed like their dream-come-true and I always saw them together in the halls and in the cafeteria. They seemed in love with college, in love with their friendship, in love with life. And it practically killed me. Now they were playing music and singing along and then bursting into peals of laughter.

"That sounds ominous," Dad said.

"I'm not having a good time here," I said. "I don't know what I thought college would be like but it's like I'm not getting what I'm supposed to out of it. You know how once you said that you thought college might be wasted on the young?" It was always a good idea in my opinion to try to quote my dad to my dad when setting up for an argument. "That you probably would have gotten a lot out of college if you'd worked for a few years first?"

"Oh God," Dad said. "Just lay it on me. You want to drop out? You want to join the circus? I thought you were my kid that was going to do everything by the book. Ryan was the one who was going to turn the world on its head, break all the rules. What happened to you?"

"What happened was you sent me away to a horse show and made me take care of my own horse," I said.

"That was supposed to prepare you for college life."

We were both quiet for a moment. Then Dad said, "So what do you want? What are you asking for here?"

What was the ask? What terms was I looking for? Dad always saw things through a business lens. Most people who approached him wanted him to invest in their business. They had a strategic plan, a profit-sharing idea. He wanted to know what mine was.

"I don't want to drop out. I want to take the semester off. I've got a job offer in Florida. It's working for a family whose thirteen-year-old daughter rides. It would be taking care of the daughter, helping with the horses, exercise riding. I'd also be able to watch Logan. I miss him so much and I want to be a part of his development."

"And you'd be with Chris," Dad said. Everyone I'd pitched my idea to—Ryan, Mike, Dad—had been quick to point that out.

"Okay, yeah, that's true but this isn't all about him," I fibbed.

"I don't care if it's all about him or not," Dad said. "Your mom's going to flip out and say she doesn't want you making decisions based on a man. But I'm not like that. I'm a realist. If this is what you want to do, I'm not going to come up with all the reasons why you can't. I'm certainly not going to support you as you do it but if you want to pay your own way by having a job and you can make this work with the university, fill out whatever needs to be filled out, etc. then fine. You have my go-ahead."

I swallowed. So my salary would have to pay for everything I needed down there. Dad didn't need to say as much but if I was hurting for money or anything, I couldn't come to him.

"Ask all the right questions when you do the paperwork," Dad said. "If you lose your spot at school, I'm not going to step in and get it back for you. You'll have to reapply or take some time off."

"Okay, I get it," I said.

"You're old enough to make decisions like this for yourself but you need to make them in the stark light of day," Dad said. "You need to realize what you're getting yourself into and if you do, then that's great."

"Okay." I breathed a sigh of relief. I had gotten what I wanted. So why didn't it feel like more of a victory? "Will you talk to Mom for me? You said it yourself, she's going to flip."

"I'll email her to tell her what we've discussed. But you'll still have to hear her flapping her wings about it."

Flapping her wings. Dad's choice of words made me cringe, for Mom's sake. Mom was a dedicated bird-lover. Birds were all she cared about, besides Ryan and me. Mostly it was a way to deal with her terrible, pervasive anxiety. Flap her wings felt like a horrible insult.

I hung up with Dad and immediately walked over to Academic Services to fill out the necessary paperwork. I had to fill out a Request for Personal Leave of Absence Form so that I would still maintain my matriculated status. Next I texted Linda to tell her I could start by the end of December. I'd spend Christmas with my mom and then head to Florida, getting there only a week after Chris.

I would talk to my mom soon but before I did, there was a more important person to call.

"Hey," Chris said, when he picked up.

"What're you up to?" I asked.

"I'm actually on Logan. Just schooled him and he was super."

"Aw, I miss him so much," I said. "But I have really good news. You're not going to believe it, actually."

"What?" Chris said.

"Well, I decided I want to be there with you in Florida this winter, watching Logan, and I just miss the horses and everything so much. So I found out about this job—with the Pearce family? Dakota Pearce? I don't know if you know her but she's apparently a pony rider just moving up to the big eq and junior jumpers. Linda Maro is her private trainer. They need someone to look after Dakota, make sure she does her homework, help out in the barn sometimes, help flat the horses."

"I know her a little and I know who Linda is," Chris said.

"I'm taking the job!" I blurted. "I'm starting after Christmas."

"Wait, but what about school?"

"I've submitted forms for a leave of absence—a semester off. It's not a big deal—people do it all the time." I had no idea if people did it all the time. Riders did take gap years fairly often. A year between finishing high school and college to concentrate on riding. "This is kind of like taking a gap year," I said. "But I didn't know I wanted to take a gap year till too late in the summer."

"Till you met me," Chris said.

"No, this isn't only about you. I mean, of course, I'm going to love being with you all winter."

"Where are you staying?" Chris asked.

"On the farm—they have housing on the property." Was Chris worried I was going to stay with him? Was he not excited I'd be in Florida this winter? He was supposed to be overjoyed.

I said, "You seem . . . I don't know, skeptical. Like, not entirely happy."

"I'm in a little bit of shock, I guess. I just never thought you'd drop out of college—"

"I'm not dropping out! I'm taking a semester off. That's it. Not dropping out."

Chris's voice was tinny in the acoustics of the indoor arena. "Okay, I never thought you'd take a semester off because of me."

"This isn't because of you. It's everything. I miss everything. Logan, the horses in general, the shows. I haven't been happy here at school."

"Okay, but I can't help but think that if you'd never met me this wouldn't have happened. You'd have gone off to college and been a regular, happy college student. Maybe we should have broken up at the end of the summer. Because I feel like you're not living life there because of me."

"You wish you'd broken up with me?" I said.

"No, I didn't say that."

"That sounded like what you were saying."

"I just don't want all this to be because of me," Chris said.

"It's not, I promise."

"Your dad's really going to be happy with me now. I wouldn't be surprised if he wants to find a new rider for Logan."

"No, he's fine with it. He is, I swear."

Chris was quiet. I could hear the fabric of his jacket as it moved while Logan walked. I could picture him on Logan, his reins in one hand, the other hand holding the phone to his ear. I couldn't wait to be there with Chris and Logan—to see them myself.

"Give Logan a mint for me," I said. "I can't wait to see him. This is going to be good. Trust me."

Chris still didn't speak.

"Be happy," I pleaded.

"I'm happy," he said, his voice sounding loud coming out of the silence.

"I love you," I told him.

"I love you too," he said.

He might have been a little shocked, or not sure about the idea, but I knew he would change his mind once I was down there and he saw how great it was to be together all the time again.

Chapter 8

THE DAYS PASSED ACHINGLY SLOWLY as I finished out the semester and went home for Christmas. It was weird to pack up my stuff from my dorm room. I didn't have all that much to bring home, but it felt—and *was*—premature. This wasn't May when Kate and Katie, or Jen and Jenny, would be lovingly packing their cute dry-erase boards and shoe-racks, exchanging hugs and shedding the occasional tears. This was me, alone, packing up like I had been kicked out or cracked up. Van was packing too, but just for winter break. She stuffed a few things into a nondescript gray backpack and that was it. She was getting a ride to the airport. She wasn't thrilled that I was leaving her with what would probably be a new roommate. If she got really lucky, she'd have a single for the rest of the year but it was more likely she would get someone who couldn't get along with her first semester roommate and had requested a room change.

Christmas day was quiet. We watched a movie in the afternoon and ordered take-out. Ryan had decided to stay in

California—he had a lot of work to do on the next round of venture funding for one of his businesses. Mom and I got along fine. My plan wasn't what she would have chosen for me but she seemed to have gotten comfortable with the idea. She turned any anxiety she had into helping me online shop for clothes I'd need for Florida, which I wasn't complaining about since, as Dad had made clear, I was going to be paying my own way down there. In fact, I'd gotten a letter in the mail while I was home saying my credit card that Dad paid for had been canceled. Yup, financially this one was on me.

If my mom were a normal mom we would have gone to an actual store to shop. But my mom was different and had been since I could remember. She suffered from serious anxiety, which limited everything about her life: where she went (hardly anywhere), what she did (only bird-watching and blogging about it), and whom she did it with (basically no one). But you wouldn't be able to tell she had so much anxiety from looking at her. She didn't have any of the telltale signs you'd associate with anxiety. She didn't look like she hadn't showered in days; she didn't wear sweatpants; her nails weren't bitten to the quick. No, she looked good. Even though she didn't go out much, or ever, during the day, she wore nice clothes that she bought online. She had become a champion of online shopping. The UPS guy knew her by first name and she knew exactly which sites had solid return policies with bags that you could easily repackage and send back with said UPS guy, equaling no trips to the post office.

Today she had on nice jeans and an open front cardigan. Her hair was a rich brown color and she kept it shoulder length. She hosted a haircut and color club with a few women from the neighborhood every six-weeks at our house. Mom did well at home—it was out in the real world that she came to pieces. She had crafted a workable life for herself as long as, for the most part, she stayed home.

"Ooh, look at these colors," she said, as she clicked on a pair of breeches. "How about one in the blue, one in the brown, and one in the dark gray?"

"Three pairs?" I said. "I don't even know how much I'm going to be riding."

"It's better to have a few extra," Mom said. Sage advice from the woman who never wanted to run out of anything that would force an unplanned trip into the outside world.

She moved the breeches into the shopping cart and deftly auto-filled the necessary information. Once we had finished shopping for breeches, she clicked over to Vineyard Vines and picked out polo shirts. Then, on to Patagonia for a raincoat, and a down vest for the chilly mornings.

"Mom, what was it like when you met Dad?" I asked. Totally random out of the blue question.

"What do you mean? When I first met him, like the day I met him when he came into the store?"

"No, I mean like when you were first dating and falling in love."

Mom drew back from the computer. She smiled a nostalgic smile. "It was perfectly lovely."

"Because you two seemed right for each other?"

"Clearly we weren't right for each other," Mom said. "But being in love . . . well, I don't have to tell you, do I? It's like the world is a sunnier, happier place when you're in love."

I nodded. I did know what she meant. Or I used to know. Now my days were anything but sunny. I hoped the color would come back to them soon.

"And then you fell out of love?" I said.

I hadn't talked to either of my parents much about their divorce. In a way it seemed like ancient history, a kind of family story that had been told so many times there was nothing else to add to it. Of course, I hadn't told it that many times to people in reality. But I'd probably told it to myself again and again in my head, trying to make sense of it. They'd fallen in love and quickly after getting married had Ryan and me, then realized they were all wrong for each other, and my father had asked for a divorce. Somehow I knew that part, but I couldn't remember being told it. I couldn't remember any TV-like scene where the parents sat the kids down and told them they were splitting up and one kid cried and the other yelled, "I hate you both," and ran out of the room.

"One of us fell out of love," Mom said sadly. "But I guess I understand why."

The "why" that she was alluding to was her anxiety, which she'd had somewhat under control when she met my father. But it had surged back, and he had left her. But had more happened that I didn't know about? I thought about Mary Beth.

"Did Dad . . . I mean was there someone else?"

"It wasn't because of someone else," she said.

But that didn't mean there *wasn't* someone else. I wanted

to know more but I also didn't want to upset Mom, making her relive painful memories of when Dad left her.

"We were too different," Mom said. "We lived in different worlds. Your father's life is the business world. I couldn't be more different than that."

So that was why they'd divorced? It made sense in a way. Dad's relationship with Monica seemed to work because they both lived business lifestyles and understood the sacrifices that way of life involved.

Mom returned to the computer. She opened her email, reviewing the confirmation emails from the stores. "You are going to have such a good time in Florida. It'll be so nice to have good weather. I always thought Ryan was smart to go to college in California. Maybe you might want to transfer to a warmer climate. That might make school better for you?"

We hadn't really talked about why school was bad for me. But I guess it didn't take a genius to figure out it wasn't going swimmingly if I was suddenly taking a leave of absence and heading to Florida.

"I don't know. We'll see." I couldn't think beyond April right now. Getting to Florida and getting my relationship with Chris back on track was about the only thing on my radar. "Do you think you'd ever move somewhere warmer?" I asked her.

More than anything, she loved being out in our yard, with all her bird feeders and roosting boxes, watching birds. But in the winter there weren't as many birds to watch. Somewhere warmer she'd have more varieties of birds all year round.

"I don't think I could move," she said.

I understood why she wasn't the type of person who

could pick up and move across the country. But not much beyond birds made her happy so it was hard to hear that she couldn't move even if it would mean two times more happiness.

"What about coming to Florida to visit me?" I spoke the words before I'd had a chance to really think about them, to think about how insane what I was proposing was. Mom had a hard time going to the grocery store. She wasn't going to be getting on a plane.

"I would love to see a purple gallinule," she said.

I had expected her to say no. To come up with the usual excuses. "So come. You could see the horse show, meet Chris, watch Logan . . . and see birds. Tons of birds, I'm sure."

Mom smiled. "Maybe I will."

I felt a flutter of hopefulness. Of excitement. Would she actually come to visit? Maybe her desire to see me, or even to see birds, would outweigh her anxiety.

She clicked over to her blog, Feathered Friends, to look at the comments other bird-crazy people had left her. "Oh, look what BirdLover89 said . . ."

I stood behind her and watched her for a few moments. She leaned close to the computer, chuckling at some comment by another bird-friend. Did these other bird people leave their homes? Did they have lives?

I knew that Mom would never come to Florida. She couldn't handle the airport, the flight, even if she would get to see spectacular birds. I felt sad for having thought she would ever be able to come—and stupid too. Wasn't I old enough to know that things didn't change just because you wanted them to?

Chapter 9

I TOOK AN UBER TO THE AIRPORT and boarded the plane, leaving behind the frigid New England weather for sunny Florida. Twelve weeks with Chris lay ahead.

The grayness was gone even before the plane landed. Out the small oval plane window were a blue sky and plump white clouds. Actual blue—pretty, charming, hopeful blue. No more blocks of sky the color of smog. And there were rays of sun! As we started our descent some people pulled on their sunglasses. I was sitting near the wing and the sun was glinting off the metal. Then, as we came closer to landing, I saw green. Grass, trees. No monotonous layer of dirty snow. The first palm trees I saw were along the runway as we touched down.

"Welcome to the North Pole," the steward cracked over the PA, fulfilling that newly-found need for airlines to live up to their zany commercials and also offer in-flight comic relief.

Everyone chuckled. This was far from the North Pole.

Linda had asked whether she should pick me up at the

airport but I told her Chris would. I came down the escalator to the few obligatory men in suits holding placards with the names of the people they were waiting for. I guess a part of me that had seen one too many romantic comedies hoped that Chris might be waiting for me with a sign that said HANNAH or even I LOVE YOU HANNAH! But that was pretty silly. In fact, Chris texted me and said he was in his car waiting outside. I wasn't even worthy of parking, which I guess was legit.

I got my huge bag from the carousel and headed out. I wouldn't exactly say a rush of hot air hit me but the air was temperate. I found Chris right away. He hopped out to help me with my bag and we kissed. I had arrived.

The first part of the drive was four-lane highways bordered by scrub grass. Nothing scenic. But after fifteen minutes, the roads got smaller, turning to two lanes and then one. The grass on the side of the roads became greener and trimmed. We began passing one development of condos after another. Each had a prominent sign that fronted the road and each seemed to have a nature-themed name: The Shores, Treetops, Meadowland Cove, Greenview Shores, Emerald Forest.

"Is this where all the horse show people stay?" I asked Chris.

"All the horse show people who don't own their own beautiful farm," he said. "These are actually kind of the down-scale condos. If you really have money you either have your own farm complete with gorgeous house, or you live in Palm Beach Polo."

I nodded as I stared out the window. Wellington was all

new to me. I was trying to get a handle on it, to get my bearings, but I had the feeling it would take a while. "Where do you live?"

Chris pointed as we drove past another development. "In there. I'll take you later."

He showed me Palm Beach Polo with its prominent sign and gatehouse. We continued down the road, called South Shore, and came to a stoplight. We turned right onto a road called Pierson. Now things were starting to look distinctly horsey. For one thing, alongside the sidewalk was a bridle path and I could see from the hoof prints in the sand it had been recently ridden on. Alongside the road on the right were paddocks, complete with horses turned out. I could see barns on the other side of the paddocks and the occasional ring or jumping field.

"Wow," I said.

"Just wait." Chris pointed to the left. "That's the main entrance to the horse show."

I could see a security gate but not too much more beyond it.

"And this," Chris added, taking a left, and pulling up to another gate, "is Grand Prix Village."

"Is this where all the grand prix horses live?"

Chris chuckled. I guess my naiveté was kind of cute to him. Thank goodness. To most people I'd just seem like a clueless idiot. He punched a code into the keypad and the gate swung open. "No, it's just called that. It's the closest set of farms to the horse show so it's basically the most exclusive and expensive. Just look around."

What I saw was farm after gorgeous farm. Chris told me

that most of the elite trainers and riders owned their own stables within hacking distance to the show grounds. If a rider
couldn't afford his own second barn in Wellington, he rented
stalls at one, which is what Chris did. Trainers and riders usually kept a set of stalls on the show grounds as well for when
they were competing, but otherwise they could train their
horses at their home base, where they had all the necessary
amenities like beautiful wash stalls, treadmills, hot-walkers,
and turnout—not to mention rings and even grand prix fields
full of jumps to practice over. There would be no fighting over
jumps in the schooling ring; no watchful eyes of USEF stewards.

Each farm had its own fence, often beautifully sculpted
hedges surrounding it, and its own stately gate. Some of the
gates were made out of rich cherry-colored wood, others were
a mix of wood and black wrought-iron. Still more had metal
shaped intricate patterns.

Chris turned into a driveway, pulling up to a giant castle-
like gate with two bronze lion faces on each side. The corre-
sponding bronze sign read MORADA BAY FARM.

"Do you know the code?"

I scrolled through my emails to find the four-digit code
Linda had given me. Chris typed it in and the giant gate
swung open.

"Oh my God," I breathed as we pulled into one of the
most amazing barns I'd ever seen. Every blade of grass
glowed bright green and had been coifed to golf-course per-
fection. As we got out, I bent down to touch the grass, certain
that it was fake.

"It's real," Chris said.

There were smaller, sculpted hedges and rows of pink flowers. In front of the barn was a giant hedge horse on its back feet with its front knees up in jumping form.

"Do you want me to go in with you?" Chris asked.

"What do you think?" I said, suddenly slightly nervous. I wanted to make a good first impression on Linda. Did that mean coming in with my grand prix rider boyfriend, or not coming in with him?

"I think I should see you later," Chris said.

I felt for a split second like he was less my boyfriend and more older trusted advisor. I wasn't sure how I felt about that. But I had the inkling he was right. This was my job. I didn't need him coming in with me.

He pulled my bag out of the car and kissed me. "Text me later."

I waved as he pulled out. I took out my ponytail and redid it to buy myself a little time. I was nineteen and about to start my first job. I didn't feel ready at all.

Chapter 10

THE BARN WAS STUCCO with a red roof. I picked up my bag by the handle and rolled it over the cobblestones into the barn. To my left an artfully distressed antique table stood against the wall with two large tasteful urns poised on either side of it. Two decorative, vintage pairs of dress boots, a huge gilded mirror, and two glass lamps completed the picture. Down here, it appeared, people used decorators for their barns.

I rolled my bag further into the barn.

A groom with a blue heeler dog following at his hip walked by leading a gorgeous horse with an impeccably banged tail.

"Hi," I said, feeling dumb standing there with my bag.

He nodded and smiled.

The barn was a semi-circular shape with stalls on each side, all opening to a courtyard with more manicured grass and cobblestone paths. It was open and airy, the complete opposite of the New England barns I was used to that were built sturdy and nearly claustrophobic to withstand the snow and wind. This barn felt more like a spa for horses. I even thought I detected a slight smell of lavender, mixed with the usual thick smell of manure and fly spray. A pretty fountain bubbled in the middle of the courtyard. The aisles were matted and the stall doors were all that rich cherry color again. Each stall had a V-shaped screen so the horse could hang his head out but wouldn't scrape an eye on the halters or the hooks they hung neatly on. A wrought-iron stairway led from the courtyard up to what I assumed was where I'd be living.

I looked around, wondering where Linda might be. I should have asked the groom with the dog where she was.

I abandoned my bag and walked down the aisle, looking in at the horses. Their stalls were large and filled with loads of clean shavings. Each stall had a window that looked out the back so the horse could hang his head out either way—into the barn aisle or outside to get some sunshine. At the end of the aisle I came to a few doorways. I peeked inside the first and saw a petite blond sitting at a desk that looked like it belonged in a corner office rather than in a barn office. Sunglasses were propped on her head.

I knocked on the side of the doorframe, which gave off the appealing, deep thwock of knocking on quality wood, and then felt stupid for knocking and just opened the door.

Linda pushed out her chair from the desk and spun—the chair was on wheels—to face me. On the broad desk sat a laptop, a large printer, and a bunch of horse-supply catalogs. A small, furry dog with a bejeweled collar looked up from its dog bed.

"Hi there, you made it!"

Linda's friendliness put me right at ease. *I will be fine working for her*, I thought to myself. I bent down and patted her dog, Taffy. She showed me around the barn, pointing out different horses of Dakota's. Soon enough I'd know each one by sight and know nearly every little thing about them—what tack they wore, what supplements they got, how they went in the ring—but right then it all seemed a bit of a blur. Should I have been taking notes? One of the horses had an adorable miniature donkey as a companion. The donkey lived in the stall with him.

"He used to destroy his stall, his blankets, injure himself," Linda explained.

She strode around the barn with her shoulders back and chin slightly jutted out, the sunglasses propped on her head. "Now he's happy as a clam."

I took in everything she said, nodding I was sure too often and too eagerly, and hardly saying anything. I figured it was preferable to talking too much. She showed me the tack room with its bridles and saddles neatly organized on their racks. There was a stack of sparkling white saddle pads, a stack of half pads, and a rack of fleece girths. Everything was in perfect order. The horse boots, ear plugs, extra bits and other miscellaneous tack were stowed in floor to ceiling dark wood cabinets, like those you'd see in someone's mansion. She showed me the laundry room, complete with four industrial washers and dryers. She smiled as she said, "I'm a clean freak."

Even the barn bathroom was spotless and fancy, with a

marble countertop, tile floor, and monogrammed hand towels. The barn opened onto a good-sized ring with colorful jumps surrounded again by gorgeous hedges. Adjacent to the long sides of the ring were paddocks. At the end of one of the barn aisles was a patio area with wicker lounge furniture, a bar, and a grill.

Linda asked me where my stuff was and I told her I'd left my bag in the front of the barn. She said she'd ask Fernando to bring it over to the house. I assumed Fernando was the groom with the blue heeler.

"I'm not staying above the barn?" I asked.

"That's the grooms' apartments. You're in the main house . . . since you'll be taking care of Dakota when her parents aren't here."

"Right," I said. "Where do you live?" I was surprised Linda didn't live in the house too. Or somewhere nearby.

"Over in Bedford Mews. I own a condo there. Wanna see the house?"

"Great," I said.

If the barn had impressed me, I was blown away by the house. It wasn't so much the size, although it was plenty spacious, but it was how it was decorated. Gorgeous, bright colored wallpaper and tile in hues like pink, clementine, and turquoise. Funky sconces and light fixtures that looked like birdcages. Transparent kitchen stools and abstract art on the walls.

My bedroom was good-sized—especially compared to my dorm room. It had white furniture with a little desk in one corner and a queen bed with an ornate headboard and a lime colored bed skirt and matching accent pillows that just screamed Lily Pulitzer.

"Nice, huh?" Linda said.

It was all very nice. Incredibly nice. And this was just a home that the Pearces spent some time in during the winter months. I couldn't imagine what their real home was like. Linda showed me the sliding glass doors that opened to the oval-shaped pool. As we walked back through the house, I was a little worried about what essentially amounted to me living with the Pearce Family. I had just assumed I'd have my own separate space. I hoped I'd like the Pearces. I didn't really mind living with a kid but living with Dr. and Dr. Pearce might be kind of odd. I shook off the thought—it would work out. And plus, I could spend most nights they were here with Chris if I wanted to. I glanced around the kitchen with its gleaming gourmet appliances one more time—this was not a house to bemoan having to live in.

"So when do the Pearces get here?" I asked Linda.

"Probably next week. So you can just settle in, get used to things."

"Great," I said. "Do I, um, have to stay here, or can I stay with my boyfriend some nights?"

She shrugged. "Fine if you don't stay here when Dakota's not here. Just as long as you're here in the morning when I need you."

"Of course," I said.

The last thing Linda showed me was the car and golf cart at my disposal. The car was a black Jeep. She handed me the keys and told me to keep my receipts for gas to get reimbursed.

"Okay, take the rest of the day to settle in. Tomorrow morning you can start getting up to speed on the routine with the horses and I could use your help running errands."

"Of course," I said. "Great."

I texted Chris that I was through for the day and that I'd love to come over to see his barn. He gave me directions via golf cart. His barn was not in Grand Prix Village, a fact I was slightly surprised by.

I found my way, passing other golf carts, cars, and a few riders on horses. I went slow, looking at every gorgeous barn I passed. There were paddocks by the road and occasionally I could see through to a ring or grass jump field. There was one huge jump field that I had a good view of with the fences set incredibly high. A few riders were cantering around and a very famous trainer that even I recognized from afar was standing in the middle teaching. His voice reverberated over a microphone system.

Once out of the back gate of Grand Prix Village, the farms didn't look as impressive. They didn't have formidable gates and weren't as landscaped. I felt sort of like I'd crossed the proverbial tracks to the place where the other half lived. I knew I had found the right barn because Jasper came running out barking. I would have been scared of him if I hadn't known it was all bluster.

"It's just me, Jas," I told him.

He gave me a small tail wag and slight nuzzle, which was a pretty warm reception for the dog whose sun set and rose on one person only: Chris. At least he remembered me.

To be honest, compared to the Pearces', Chris's barn

looked pretty shabby. It was just a simple one aisle barn with ten stalls and a ring. There were patches of sand where there should have been grass and the ring itself had only a calf-high fence around it—no impressive hedges. A giant mirror stood on one side of the ring, which seemed odd. But, of course, the barn was still immaculate. Chris ran a tight ship. It might not be a fancy ship, apparently, but it was still a tight ship with blankets folded neatly on stall doors and the aisle swept clean.

As excited as I had been to see Chris at the airport, I was almost equally as excited to see Logan. I hadn't seen him since he'd gotten on the trailer in Vermont. The horse I had almost detested at the beginning of the summer circuit had become my greatest friend.

Dale was organizing a tack trunk that probably didn't need to be organized. But Dale didn't sit still. Ever. I tried to be cheerful, hoping he'd give me even half as warm a reception as Jasper had. "Hi, Dale," I chirped and then wished I'd sounded a little less chipper.

He moved his chin a millimeter in my general direction. Didn't even speak. I didn't warrant enough breath to make words. Why did Dale hate me? Was it because I was a complete outsider to this sport? Had he been as chilly to Mary Beth?

"What's with the mirror by the ring?" I asked.

He shook his head like I was a total idiot for not knowing. "Used to be a dressage farm."

Chris must have known I'd want to see Logan because he took me right to his stall. Jasper followed us faithfully. Logan was eating his hay. I opened his door and said his name. He swung his head to look at me as he chewed. Did he recognize me? If only horses were like dogs and could wag their tails, do happy dances, or lick you. But that was the enigma of the horse. You weren't ever truly sure how they felt about you. It wasn't like I'd spent my whole life caring for him, either. Before Vermont, I'd only ridden him a few times a week. Then in Vermont I'd been his sole caretaker and from my end I'd felt we'd formed an amazing bond. We'd come together in the ring and around the barn and I'd grown to love him like I'd never loved any animal before. But now I didn't even know if he remembered me.

I'd heard stories of horses remembering their owners years after they'd last seen them and certainly all horse movies made it seem like every horse would gallop up to the pasture fence, whinnying, when its owner came. But how many horses really did that?

"It's me," I told Logan, as if that would jog his memory.

His ears flicked at my voice but that was it. He kept chewing.

I put my arms around his neck and hugged him tight. I breathed in his wonderful smell. Maybe it didn't matter if he remembered me. Maybe all that mattered was how much I loved him.

Chris poked his head over the stall door. "I have to call Craig back. I'll be in the office."

I knew Craig was Lily's father.

I had no idea where the office was but I was fine hugging Logan for a while longer. I ran my hand over his neck and stepped back to take a look at him. Then I ran my hands down each leg and picked up each hoof. His legs felt tight and cool, not at all puffy or hot. His hooves looked strong too. Wow. He looked amazing. He was more muscled along his topline and hind-end, and his coat gleamed. Under Chris's care he got things I couldn't have given him—time on the treadmill for fitness, time spent standing on the vibrating pad, and wearing the magnetic blanket. Most of all, though, he looked happy. I was so lucky Dad had agreed to send him with Chris.

I stayed in his stall a few minutes longer. As I was closing the stall door behind me, I turned and found Dale blocking my path. We stood closer than I had maybe at any other time before. Abnormally and uncomfortably close. I could see the lines around his eyes and mouth. For someone who rarely smiled, he had a lot of laugh lines. Probably from too much sun exposure and squinting. I wished I could go right back in the stall, or that Logan would swing his head over and save me.

"This is a big winter for him," Dale said.

At first I thought he meant Logan, and I was confused because I didn't think Dale cared that much about Logan. But then I realized he meant Chris. Dale had a quiet voice—he never talked loudly. But it was a serious voice. He continued, "Losing Harris was huge but he's making out okay. He's recovering from it. He's got a few clients. This is the big stage here. It doesn't get any bigger. Do you get that?"

I nodded, even though I hadn't really thought about it. To me, Florida had always seemed like just another horse show. But judging from what I'd already seen in terms of the farms and the pure wealth, it was very different.

"This is where he lands another sponsor and gets a number one horse. This winter is when he gets back in the game."

I wasn't sure what I was supposed to say to Dale. I wanted all that for Chris too. We were on the same team—Team Chris.

"He can't have any distractions," Dale added.

"I'm a distraction?" I said.

"Before you he had Harris."

"That wasn't because of me," I said. "Or we don't know it was just because of me."

I knew Chris had told Dale about Harris's wife making a pass at him and Chris rejecting her. Chris told Dale everything. They were more like uncle and nephew or big and little brother than rider and barn manager.

"Don't ruin this for him," Dale said.

"I'm not going to," I promised him. "I want everything you want for him." As much as I felt like Dale was out of line, his intentions were good. He wanted Chris to be the best in the sport and I didn't get the sense it was because it would promote Dale or get him something he wanted. Sure, if you're the barn manager for an Olympic Gold Medalist you get more attention and accolades. But I'm not sure your pay gets any higher really. Dale loved Chris and wanted him to reach his fullest potential. Which was what I wanted too, but Dale couldn't see that we were actually aligned in that goal, and I didn't hold out much hope of convincing him. At least not today, my first day in Welly World.

Dale turned and walked off. I leaned back against Logan's

stall door and let out a breath. I hadn't even been in Florida a few hours and things were already more complicated than I had thought they'd be.

Chapter 11

THAT FIRST NIGHT we went out to dinner at a place Chris liked called Oli's. Apparently you couldn't go anywhere in Wellington without running into people you knew. Or people Chris knew, anyway. On the way to our table, we passed Tommy Kinsler and his girlfriend. Chris stopped and chatted innocuously. Instead of talking about the weather, they exchanged thoughts on the footing at the show. Maybe footing was the horse show equivalent of weather for a common conversation piece. They were civil to each other, but not as chummy as they'd been in Vermont and Chris cut it short by saying we'd better go sit down.

"What's that like?" I asked Chris when we were seated. "You and Tommy?"

They had been close until this past summer when Harris had pulled his horses from Chris and given them to Tommy.

"We're both professionals—we can still be civil to each other," Chris said, picking up a menu.

"That's it? That's all you feel about it?" Sometimes Chris

could be almost too controlled in his emotions. He was always so levelheaded. But underneath it seemed impossible that he wouldn't have the same emotions that we all did.

"Are you still friends?" I asked.

"Definitely, but I'm not going to lie . . . it's hard to watch him ride my horses."

"Just hard?"

Chris placed the menu to the side. "No, it nearly kills me. Each time I watch him go into the ring on Titan I think I might die."

He said this with a straight face and little emotion and I couldn't tell if he was joking or not. I gave him a confused look. "Are you serious?"

"Yes, totally, completely, undeniably, thoroughly, utterly, unconditionally, unreservedly serious."

I burst out laughing. Most people would show their emotions with a slew of passionate swearwords, a raised voice, or a pounding fist. But it was so Chris to convey his emotions in a calm and composed, well-spoken, cerebral manner.

"What was that again?" I teased. "Completely, thoroughly, totally . . . ?"

"I think it was: totally, completely, undeniably, thoroughly, utterly, unconditionally," he said with a smirk. "Oh, and unreservedly, at the end."

The waitress came and filled our waters. Chris ordered a beer. She said she'd give us a little more time with the menu, since I hadn't even opened mine. Having been here before, Chris already knew what he wanted.

He continued, "That was my horse. I brought him along.

And now he's Tommy's. It's not Tommy's fault. Tommy's a good guy. And this is a business and this kind of stuff happens but it kills me to watch them. I don't know how long it's going to take for that to go away, or if it'll ever truly go away. Maybe it'll be better when I have a horse for the big ring again."

"But in the meantime it nearly kills you."

"Yup."

I loved how Chris had gone from seeming like somehow he was above emotion to admitting just how much it hurt him to see Tommy ride Titan.

We had a nice dinner. The food was good, the restaurant was quiet enough for us to talk, and it felt great to be with Chris and not to be worrying about when I'd see him next or how much time we had left together. All of Vermont had seemed to be lived under somewhat of a ticking clock as the circuit inched toward its end and we went our separate ways. Of course, the Florida circuit wasn't forever either but it was just starting and we had months together ahead of us.

Tommy and his girlfriend must have come in shortly before us, because they were heading out the door at the same time we were. This time, Chris introduced me to Tommy as his girlfriend.

"Sure, I remember you from Vermont," Tommy said. He introduced his girlfriend who was willowy and slightly exotic looking.

"Did you hear what happened to Louie?" Tommy asked Chris.

"What?"

"His tack room was broken into. A whole bunch of tack including five saddles stolen."

"When?" Chris asked.

"Last night. Cleaned him out. It was like twenty grand in tack and saddles."

In the car I asked Chris whether things like what happened to Louie were common on the circuit.

"I wouldn't say common but I wouldn't say totally uncommon either."

"But how can whoever stole the stuff make any money off it? Wouldn't people find out if suddenly five saddles show up on ebay or something?"

"I'm not exactly sure but I guess it's like stolen art. You don't sell it right away, or you sell it through black market channels, or to other countries or something."

We talked a little more about Tommy. He said Tommy's girlfriend owned an upscale, boutique clothing store at the show, real clothes, not riding clothes. Chris told me that Harris had bought Tommy another top grand prix horse after he'd told Chris he couldn't afford another one.

"Where's Harris's farm now?" I asked.

"Now?"

"I guess I assumed last year his horses were with you at your farm?" I realized as I said the words how off my thinking was. Harris would never tolerate a barn like the one Chris was using this winter.

"Harris owns the most amazing farm in Grand Prix Village," Chris said.

"And that's where you were last year and where Tommy

is this year." Now I truly understood what a step down his current situation was for Chris. There were certainly no dressage mirrors at Harris's farm.

"You want to come over tonight?" Chris said, changing the subject.

"Most definitely." When Dakota was at the show, I'd have to spend my nights with her. But until then, I could do what I wanted, and I wanted to be with Chris.

I imagine that most men think they make a girl want them with what they do sexually. They think it's the way they press their lips against yours or probably more likely the way they thrust their hips or the size of their dick. I guess maybe I had assumed as much too before I'd started having sex with Chris. But now I realized that for me anyway, something tiny could turn me on to him. Some little thing he said, or a quick touch. That night it was when I walked by him in his kitchen and he reached out and grabbed my wrist. Something about how quick and predatory it felt, his hand tight on my skin, telling me he needed me. Maybe he needed me to make him feel good and powerful again after seeing Tommy. I got that sweeping burst of excitement in my stomach. Without a word he was saying he wanted me. Right then. And it made me want him back badly.

We started kissing. Before much longer, our hands were all over each other's back and chest. Then, I took the lead and pulled him by the hand into his bedroom. He removed his own shirt in that sexy way guys do—one hand over the back, pulling it over his head. He lay back on the bed and I crawled on top of him. I kissed him for a while and then sat up, moving my weight a little bit further down his thighs, so I could undo his jeans. I had to move to the side so he could pull them off and his boxers too. He told me once that since so much of his time was spent in constricting breeches and in the saddle, he liked to wear boxers at other times. I loved his boxers. They seemed to represent a different side of Chris—a more relaxed, playful side.

I took off my shirt, pants, and underwear too. When I had first started having sex with Chris, it had seemed like such a big deal to be naked in front of him and now here I was taking off my own clothes. We did it with me on top for the first part. We'd never done that before. In fact, we'd only done it missionary. I felt a little self-conscious but I liked watching him look up at me. Toward the end, though, he rolled on top of me again and I realized how much I'd missed the weight of his body against mine. So much time was spent talking about a man's dick and it being inside of you. But for me, a good part of sex was also about the rest of his body and the rest of mine. It was about how good it felt to have his weight thrown against mine. It was about our skin touching. It was about his breath on my neck as he came.

"Was that good for you?" I asked after we were done.

He answered, "It was totally, completely, undeniably, thoroughly, utterly, unconditionally, unreservedly good."

Chapter 12

THE FIRST WEEK was still pre-circuit and Dakota wasn't there yet. She and her parents were on a volunteer vacation in Peru, which is apparently where you go somewhere exotic but spend your time digging wells or building huts. A week without Dakota was perfect because it gave me time to get to know Linda, the grooms, and the horses. Dakota had six horses, which seemed like an incredible number for a thirteen-year-old just starting out in the three-six. She had a really nice equitation horse they'd just bought from Rob Renaud. He'd won the finals three times and had also placed a million other times. The horse was older, 15, so he needed endless care and management, but he'd be just the horse to get her started in the eq. They also had a green equitation horse that had done the finals this past year with a working-student type rider. He was only seven and gorgeous. The most scope and style in an eq horse I'd ever seen. Dakota probably wouldn't show him at all yet, though. Other, better riders would bring him along until he was ready for Dakota.

Then she had two jumpers. Again, one was a been-there-done-that old pro. In fact, in another life Tizmo had been to the World Cup with an Argentinian rider. The other, Sonny, wasn't as green as the eq horse but was still on the younger side. Dakota would be able to show that one, though. Finally, she had two small junior hunters. Neither of the hunters were big winners that cost a fortune. They probably weren't cheap—still a buck-fifty at least. But they weren't the top-in-the-country junior hunters that cost upwards of half a million. Linda and Dakota's parents had decided that she wouldn't concentrate on the hunters but that doing the hunters would still be good for her overall development. They didn't care if she won; they just wanted her to have the extra rides and get the experience of learning to put in smooth rounds.

The first week, Linda had me ride the hunters most of the time. I think she was trying to scope out whether I could ride. I had learned a lot from Chris in Vermont and I'd never been terrible so I did a fine job of flatting them. I wasn't improving them or schooling them but I was doing what I was supposed to be doing—exercising them. She took me out along the canals, pointing out different amazing farms. Stork-like birds whose names Mom would have known stood near the canals and flapped their wings occasionally. The horses took little notice, used to them already. One time she also had me flat the old pro eq horse. Oh my Lord. I swear on that horse I felt like I could have won the finals. He was that amazing.

Besides riding, I got to know the set-up of the barn and the grooms. The most senior groom was Fernando, whom I'd seen the first day. His English was amazing so communicating with him was no problem. His dog, Rudi, was the best-trained dog I'd ever known. Rudi not only sat and stayed, but did things like fetch polo wraps or brushes on command.

Linda had me run a bunch of errands, picking up supplies for the barn and for Dakota. I didn't mind going to Publix to stock the fridge, hitting Farm Vet for supplies, or picking up numbers at the horse show office.

One day she sent me over to the show grounds to pick up a new saddle that had come in for Dakota. Linda told me it had been ordered exclusively for the old pro eq horse—he had a sensitive back and needed the proper fitting saddle to keep him sound.

I drove the golf cart over to the show grounds. I was getting better at knowing my way around. Unless I had to go out into the real world and go to the drug store or supermarket, or drive over to Chris's condo, I could have lived for weeks with just the golf cart to get me around. Golf carts were a regular sight on the actual car roads around Grand Prix Village and then there was a whole network of smaller routes along the canals that traversed between all the farms and the horse show. I passed a groom leading a fully tacked up horse to the show with a scrim sheet on it and a number tied around its neck. It was a long walk on foot and I'd noticed that many of the grooms led horses back and forth multiple times a day. Sometimes I'd see a groom, who clearly wasn't a rider, on a horse. I guess it depended on the owner, whether they were comfortable with their groom riding the horse.

Arouet Sellier was set up in a tent by the International

Ring schooling area. Beautiful saddles in soft, deep brown leather were arranged in rows on each side of the store. The store reminded me of a museum with its uncluttered space. Honestly, the Arouet saddles looked like works of art, especially without stirrups on them. They were so perfectly, simply designed. I was a bit mesmerized by the beauty of the saddles and startled when I heard someone ask, with a slight European accent, "Can I help you?"

I turned to see a somewhat grungy but good-looking guy in his twenties. He was medium height and had dark hair that fell past his ears. He also had a few days' stubble. He was wearing jeans and a white V-neck shirt that showed a little dark chest hair at the V. In some ways he was the totally wrong guy to be working at Arouet. The beautiful saddles probably deserved a perfectly styled and outfitted person. But then again, there was something sexy and natural about him that fit with the sensual beauty of the saddles.

He introduced himself as Étienne. Even his French name fit. I told him I was here to pick up a saddle for Dakota Pearce.

He went in the back to get it and I turned again to admire the saddles. My saddle was fine—it was a Butet. But a Butet was nothing like an Arouet, which cost thousands.

"Here it is," I heard Étienne say.

I turned to find not just Étienne, but Zoe. I took a short breath, the air catching in my throat.

I knew I would see Zoe at some point. In fact, I knew I'd cross paths with her at times. But since we hadn't started showing yet, I hadn't prepared myself for running into her. I guess that was stupid since all of Wellington was filled with horse people. Whether you were at Publix or the dry cleaner, you were bound to run into someone from the horse show.

I should have planned out what I would say to her. She wouldn't have known I was in Wellington unless she'd heard somehow through Linda, but I had no reason to think that Linda and Zoe knew each other.

Zoe was likely surprised to see me too but of course she wasn't at a loss for words like I was. "Hannah," she said, casually draping an arm around Étienne. "What are you doing here?"

"Here like in Wellington? Here like here at Arouet?" I said, sounding like a complete idiot.

"Either I guess," Zoe said.

She and Étienne were standing close, indicating a shared intimacy. Zoe looked beautiful as always, her hair pulled back in a messy knot with tendrils whispering against her neck. She wore a pink scoop neck shirt that revealed her tanned shoulders and the top of her chest. The pink flattered her tremendously. Clearly they were sleeping together. Of course, Zoe was sleeping with Étienne, the gorgeous, foreign, slightly greasy guy. Zoe always went for the guy with the accent, sexy but with a slight slime factor.

"I'm here for the circuit. I'm working for Dakota Pearce and her family."

"Wow," Zoe said. "So you just couldn't stay away from Chris? What, did you drop out of college?"

Étienne was standing there breezily, like he didn't have a care in the world, holding Dakota's beautiful saddle, with Zoe's arm looped around him possessively. He didn't seem at all uncomfortable with what was playing out in front of him. It seemed like he was the type of guy who could have sex in front of a roomful of people and feel totally at ease. His ease only made me feel more uncomfortable.

"No, I'm taking a semester off."

"To be with Chris?" Zoe said. "Worried about Mary Beth?"

"No, that's not it at all," I said, probably too quickly.

Zoe raised her eyebrows. "Well, I would be if I was you."

I reached into my pocket. I'd brought a receipt for the saddle but now I couldn't find it. I checked my other pocket. Nothing. I must have left it in the golf cart. Flustered, I looked at Étienne. "Is there something I need to sign to take the saddle?"

"No." He offered me the saddle, a slight grin forming on his lips. "It's yours. All paid for."

He handed me the saddle and I turned to go. "Have a good circuit," Zoe said.

I made the mistake of looking back at her. I should have just kept going.

"And be careful you don't get your little heart broken." Her voice was singsong sweet, but then it fell a few octaves as she warned, "This isn't Vermont. You are so in over your head."

I put the saddle in the golf cart probably too hastily for a six thousand dollar custom saddle. I drove too fast back over to the Pearces', bumping and lurching over the divots in the sand. Why did I let Zoe get under my skin? What the hell was wrong with me when it came to that girl? I told myself to put her out of my mind. I knew just what I was doing. I had a plan that was solid. If I had stayed home while Chris was here with Mary Beth, well, then I would have been worried. But I was here and there was no way MB was taking him away from me.

On a whim, I decided to go by Jamie's barn and see Mike. I just hoped Jamie wasn't around. It was the end of the day so chances were she'd gone home. She had never been one for logging long hours if it wasn't necessary.

I found Mike sitting on a tack trunk having a beer.

"Hannah!" he bellowed as he saw me drive up.

I got out and gave him a big hug. He smelled like sweat and a little bit like B.O. Of course he did—he had worked hard all day. He was wearing a white tank-top and jean shorts that fell below his knees.

"Wanna beer?" he asked.

"No, thanks," I told him.

He shifted over on the tack trunk to make room for me.

"Is Jamie here?"

"Are you kidding? It's after four."

I sat down next to him.

"How's the job?" he asked.

I shrugged. "Good so far but Dakota's not here yet. It's just been me and Linda and the horses."

"Nice horses, huh?"

"All for a thirteen-year-old." I shook my head. In the horse world we were all privileged. Well, all of us riders. But within the ranks of us, there were clear levels. Those who had no horse of their own and were working students were nearly extinct. Those of us who had only one horse lined the bottom of the barrel. Then there were the riders with two or three good horses. They were the upper middle class of the show circuit. Lastly, there were the über-rich like Dakota who had upwards of five horses, private trainers, their own barns and grooms. They were the children of rock stars, software moguls, CEOS of country-wide chain stores. It was probably ridiculous that I was bemoaning Dakota's wealth to Mike, who had no assets besides his Harley.

"Linda seems really nice," I said, trying to change the subject. "Thanks again for getting me the job."

"I didn't get it for you, and don't thank me till you've been there a little longer and Dakota's been showing."

"She's a handful, huh?"

Mike elbowed me. "Nothing you can't handle."

"You have a lot of faith in me," I told him. I thought about telling him that he seemed like one of the only people here who believed in me. Dale thought I was going to do nothing but harm Chris's career; Zoe said I was in over my head and would lose Chris to MB. My dad was humoring me but he probably thought—or at least hoped—that Chris and I would break up, I'd run out of money, and go running back to college.

"I've seen you handle some hard things," Mike said. "Most riders dropped at a horse show who'd never picked out a stall wouldn't buckle down and learn how to take care of a horse."

"You're forgetting when I made Logan colic, or the time he got loose and ran around the show grounds."

"Good times." Mike chuckled and took a swig of his beer. "Good times."

"I never told anyone this but the first time I got on Logan, that first day, I didn't tighten my girth enough and when I went to get on my whole saddle swung around under his belly."

Mike and I broke out in peals of laughter. It was a pretty funny image and now I could truly laugh about it. "Luckily only a few people saw me and no one that I knew or cared about."

Mike had a deep, almost phlegmy laugh. His eyes were watering. It was probably even funnier if you were a groom and spent your life dealing with rich girls who didn't know the first thing about horse care.

"I also couldn't put on a running martingale. I knew it belonged on Logan somehow but I saw it in my trunk and it looked like some kind of Rubix-Cube-slash-spider-web."

"And now look at you," Mike said when he'd finally stopped busting a gut over my previous ineptitude. "You actually got a job working with horses."

"You never asked why I wanted to come here," I said, turning serious. "Everyone else, that's the first thing they want to know."

Mike tightened his grip on his beer can, making the aluminum squeak. "I figured you had your reasons."

"Everyone else figures it only has to do with Chris."

Mike crushed the empty and tossed it into the open cooler in front of him full with half-melted ice and one or two fresh beers. "One thing I've learned about this business is not to spend too much time worrying about what other people are thinking. It'll bleed you dry."

"Good advice," I said.

Chapter 13

THE FIRST THING DAKOTA SAID to me was, "Can you get my water and bring it to the ring. I like to hydrate halfway through my rides."

Hydrate? What kind of thirteen-year-old used the word hydrate? Dakota Pearce. Dakota was disgustingly, disturbingly pretty. Weren't thirteen-year-olds supposed to have braces, acne, and frizzy hair? Not Dakota. She had beautifully highlighted blonde hair, Neutrogena-commercial-worthy skin, and delicate features. She was tall and skinny and had straight white teeth. She didn't look thirteen—she looked fifteen or sixteen. She looked like she should have been starring in a Disney Channel pre-teen show.

I had been over at the show grounds picking up Dakota's two new coats from Charles Ancona when the Pearces must have arrived. Now, Dakota was pulling a hairnet over her beautiful hair, securing a hair elastic to create a long ponytail, and sliding on her Samshield helmet so the ponytail stuck out the back and the little hairnet ponytail she had created did too. It was the exact style top juniors used when schooling and Dakota could have done it with her eyes closed. At the same time, Fernando was taking Dudley, the seasoned eq horse, off the cross-ties. I hadn't seen Dr. or Dr. Pearce yet.

I run-walked back into the barn to get her bottle of water, then sat by the ring watching Linda teach her. Dakota was a decent rider. She looked good in the saddle and found most every distance but somehow she looked a little disembodied. Technically everything was right and maybe that was even the problem. She had no individual style, no minor personality trait to her position like a certain way she held her neck or her elbows. She was too perfect—the product of endless super-vised rides on superb horses where she never had to improvise or scramble. She was a singer who hits all the notes but has no character to her voice, nothing that distinguishes her.

Halfway through, Dakota motioned for her water.

"I'm Hannah, by the way," I said as I handed it to her.

She rolled her eyes like she couldn't have cared less who I was. I still hadn't seen her parents. Somehow she had just ap-peared at the barn, dressed to ride.

It was only later, after the lesson, that I met them.

"So good to meet you," Dr. Pearce told me in a British accent. "Call me Audrina." She was impossibly glamorous in dark jeans and gorgeous boots that went over her knees. Her hair was long and stylishly tousled. It was terribly stereotypi-cal but it was hard to believe she was a doctor, let alone a leading heart surgeon who dedicated her life to the less fortu-nate. I had assumed she'd be dowdy with a practical haircut and unstylish glasses.

The other Dr. Pearce was good looking too for a dad. Tall and well-built, wearing a baseball cap which gave him an air of youth and approachability. Audrina introduced him as Winston. What a bunch of names: Audrina, Winston, and Dakota.

"We are so happy you'll be looking after Dakota," Audrina said. "It's dreadfully important to have the right minder."

Minder—I guessed that was British for sitter. I didn't mind the label. In fact, it seemed to make much more sense than sitter or nanny since Dakota was a teenager.

"I'm really looking forward to getting to know her," I said, even though after our first meeting I wasn't feeling too positive about it all.

We small-talked. Where I was from. How cold it had been in the Northeast. I explained how I had a horse with Chris Kern. I thought I saw Audrina's eyebrows go up at that, like she was impressed. Then, when I could, I asked, "What will your schedule be like?" What I really wanted to know was how many nights I could spend with Chris.

"Yes, well, I'm glad you asked," Audrina said. "We just signed on to the most tremendous opportunity in Guatemala." She rubbed her hands together. "We're opening our own clinic. The funding just came through."

"Oh my goodness, that's amazing," I gushed, even though I didn't know what it meant exactly.

"We'll fly back and forth when we can," Winston said, and I noticed he played second fiddle to her. "But we're really going to be depending on you this winter."

"Of course," I said. "Totally." I liked the word "depend."

Not many people had ever depended on me. But it scared me a bit too, since it essentially meant I was going to be stuck with Dakota, who I was pretty sure might be as difficult as I had been told.

"Here's the thing," Audrina said. She stepped a little closer to me, giving me a sense that we needed to pull together. "You can't let her out of your sight. We've had some . . . problems with her."

I must have looked shocked—this hadn't been in the job description—because Audrina immediately tried to minimize, gesturing with her hands. "Nothing that bad, just regular horse show stuff she's gotten into. But we want her to focus on her riding and not get distracted."

Distracted. I didn't want to hear that word again. And how was I going to keep tabs on Mary Beth and spend time with Chris if I was glued to Dakota?

"Basically pretend you're her shadow," Winston said.

I couldn't tell if he was trying to inject some humor or comment subtly and ironically that his wife tended toward the overprotective and dramatic. I looked at him meaningfully to try to tell but his face was unreadable. Maybe he was serious. My stomach started to ache—what had I gotten myself into? Should I quit right now? But I needed a job. Audrina probably *was* being dramatic. I had plenty of experience with dramatic mothers. I needed the money and a reason to be here in Florida. Dakota was tough on the outside but surely she would warm up to me. Wasn't that what kids did, tested limits at first? Taking care of her couldn't be as hard as taking care of Logan had been in Vermont when I didn't know the first thing about horse care. Like Mike had said, I was tough. I'd bond with Dakota over TV shows and music. Soon she'd think I was cool. I was dating Chris Kern—that had to count for something. She'd become like my younger sister . . .

"No problem," I told the Pearces. "It's going to be a great circuit. So when are you leaving?"

Audrina's hands fluttered around her throat. I felt uneasy—this situation was seeming weirder by the moment.

"Tomorrow morning," she said.

* * *

Audrina and Winston left on a seven a.m. flight the next day to go back to New York so they could "pack, prepare, and whatnot" before they left for Guatemala. Talk about a quick turnaround.

Dakota slunk out of her room at 8:30 and I asked what she'd like for breakfast. Audrina had given me the rundown of what Dakota ate but I wasn't sure what Dakota would *want* to eat. I thought maybe I could be the one to let her get away with snarfing down coffee and a donut, at least at first, so we could build rapport. I could be the cool babysitter who let her be a kid in the way her parents didn't.

"Didn't my mom tell you? A four egg-white omelet with spinach and tomatoes—no cheese. A bowl of blueberries and strawberries. No raspberries. I hate the seeds."

"Okay," I said, taking out the eggs. "Yeah, I know, the seeds always get stuck in my teeth."

I was trying to be funny—to bond with her—but she

didn't even smile. Instead of feeling funny, I felt uncouth, like Dakota never got anything stuck in her teeth, ever. I tried to remain hopeful as I cooked. I had to give her time. Her parents had just dropped her and ran, and that had to suck, even if they were going to help the world be a better place. Maybe that was even worse because then she couldn't hate them. If they'd just ran off to be together in Bora-Bora or were workaholics for the sake of making millions, she could full-out hate them and not feel the slightest bit guilty about it.

"I guess your parents were really needed in Guatemala," I said, thinking I might get her talking about the subject. Maybe she could admit to me, and only me, how she really felt about them going.

Nothing.

"It must kind of suck to have them leave so soon."

Still nothing.

"I mean you must be super proud of the work they're doing over there . . ."

Continued staring at her iPad.

I slid the omelet onto a plate and brought it over to her. I glanced at her iPad. It was open to a website and I swear I picked off Chris's name.

"What are you looking at?"

"HorseShowDrama."

Well, at least she'd spoken. "What's that?"

She positioned the iPad so I could see it. I stepped closer to have a look. It appeared to be a bulletin board with threads about different subjects to do with the horse show world. There were no ads. It wasn't a fancy site, just bare bones.

"This is like a gossip site?"

"They're gossiping about your boyfriend. Is he still your boyfriend?" Dakota smirked at me. She pointed to a thread entitled "Chris & MB."

Re: Chris & MB
By Equitate37:
Is Chris Kern single again? Or is he back together with MB?

Re: Chris & MB
By Ridingmyassoff:
He's still with the girl from the summer. And I say girl because I think she's 16.

Re: Chris & MB
By Luv2Gossip:
She's definitely not 16. I heard she went to college and they're still together. But can't imagine that will last long.

Re: Chris & MB
By HJPrincess:
Can totally see him getting back with MB. They were cute together.
Re: Chris & MB
By Wankie23:
Who is MB?

Re: Chris & MB
By Ridingmyassoff:
Wankie23, have you ever been to a horse show? Or are

*you 60 and used to show in the 80s? Find another site to
bother with your lame-ass posts. Everyone knows who
MB is.*

Re: Chris & MB
By HJPrincess:
*MB is Mary Beth McCord. Ridingmyassoff, you don't
have to be so angry. Wankie23 might just not know who
MB is.*

Re: Chris & MB
By Ridingmyassoff:
*I'm sorry but if you have the screen-name Wankie23, you
are asking to be shit on.*

Re: Chris & MB
By Dapplegray:
Chris is so hot. One of the hottest guys out there.

Re: Chris & MB
By Love2gossip:
*Are you kidding, HJPrincess? MB is a raving bitch. Re-
member when she reamed Chris out for not watching her
go in a grand prix? It's all about her with that girl. Chris
deserves better.*

Re: Chris & MB
By Doublecombo:
Yeah, but she has $$$$$.

Re: Chris & MB
By Love2gossip:
You think she'd buy him horses? Puh-lease.

Re: Chris & MB
By HJPrincess:
I'll bet you they're back together by week 3.

Re: Chris & MB
By Love2gossip:
Probably right.

I tried to act like what I'd read wasn't confirming every worry I'd had about Mary Beth. "You read this stuff?" I said to Dakota.

She sliced her omelet delicately. "All the time. Everyone does."

"Do you post on it?"

She made a bored face. "Are you going to give me a lecture on Internet safety?"

"No," I said. Maybe I had been, but I covered by saying, "You could post that Chris and I are together and really happy."

"No," Dakota said dismissively. "I don't think I'll be doing that any time soon."

Chapter 14

I EXPECTED TO GET LOTS OF TEXTS from Audrina and Winston checking on Dakota. I had figured from the whole speech they'd given me about her, they'd constantly be asking whether she'd gotten her schoolwork done, how her riding was going, and generally whether she was behaving. But I received only one text the first week, telling me they were in Guatemala and to contact them if I needed anything.

The week went by quickly as we amped up to show the following week. Linda and I went over the plan for what classes each horse would be doing and what preparation they would need to be ready, whether they needed lunging, flatting, a serious school in draw reins. There were final lessons and final jump-schools by Linda and last minute tack changes. Linda had a good sense of humor and liked to imitate the foreign trainers that were in abundance at the show grounds. "First we dressage, then we do jumping," she would say in a heavy accent as she and Dakota headed out to the ring.

When she wasn't riding, Dakota did her schoolwork, met with her tutor, and spent time with her friends—other privileged teenage girls like her who spent their winters in Florida. They hung out at the horse show or at the pool at Dakota's house, taking endless selfies and posting them to Instagram.

I couldn't stop thinking about what I'd read on Horse-ShowDrama and went back to the site to see whether people had written more about Chris and Mary Beth. I wondered whether Mary Beth had asked Chris again to help her with her horse. I kept wanting to ask him but I never found the right time to bring it up.

I decided that Mondays would be Chris and my couple's day. A day for us to sleep late, have sex, lounge around his condo. It would be our day for escaping everything and everyone horse show and focusing on us. Our connection to each other. No matter what had happened during the week, we would have Mondays.

This Monday would be the first of these perfect days, and we would continue to have them throughout the circuit—a day for us to reset our relationship.

Audrina told me that for the Sunday nights and Mondays that they weren't there, Dakota would sleep over with a friend of hers whose mother was staying for the whole circuit. It seemed like a good sign that Audrina realized I should have an official day off—either that or she knew I would need a break from Dakota or else I'd quit.

I woke up at nine to find Chris had already gotten out of bed. So much for lingering together under the covers, half-asleep. So much for waking up and finding him watching me

sleep or something incredibly romantic like that. Nope. He
was at the kitchen counter with his laptop, watching videos of
horses. I came out of the bedroom, stretching and yawning.

"How long have you been up?" I asked.

"I don't know. A few hours. Long enough to watch every
animal that might have a future as a grand prix horse and
figure out they don't have a future as a grand prix horse."

"Did you eat anything?"

"No."

"Well, I'm making pancakes," I declared cheerfully. This
was part of my carefully constructed plan. I'd bought the ingredients and some fresh fruit and brought them over to
Chris's last night with the rest of the stuff I'd said I would
pick up for him to make us dinner, which he had done.

Chris kept his eyes glued to the screen as I took out the
strawberries, blueberries, milk, butter and eggs from the
fridge. I selected the dry ingredients from the cabinet and
whisked together the proper amounts of flour, sugar, baking
powder and salt that the recipe I'd gotten off Rachel Ray's
website called for. I combined the necessary wet ingredients
and then added them together with the dry. After they were
whisked, leaving the few small lumps that Rachel said were
fine, I heated up a skillet. The whole time I was working, I'm
not sure Chris even looked up once. I'm not sure he registered
I *was* cooking. He'd been distracted during our dinner last
night too, intermittently answering texts. I'd been so concerned he might be texting with MB that while he was in the
bathroom later I'd taken another look at his phone. I felt terrible that I'd done it—and I hadn't turned up anything except

texts with his clients—but I had needed to know if something was going on.

I sliced up the berries and put them in a bowl on the table. My first pancake came out a little underdone so I threw it away and made a second, which was perfect. I wasn't sure if Chris liked blueberry pancakes so I'd left the blueberries out of the mix. I scurried around setting the small table in the open living-room-dining-room between flipping the pancakes. Chris's condo wasn't fancy but it was satisfactorily equipped. He didn't own it; he rented. When I had a good stack of pancakes ready and the table was set, I announced proudly that breakfast was served.

Chris looked up like he was surprised to even find me there and had no idea I'd just cooked a full breakfast in his presence. "Oh, okay," he said. "Wow."

We sat down at the table and I put a pancake on his plate and mine. "I hope you like pancakes."

He reached for the butter and set about spreading a thin layer on his pancake. "Definitely."

I slid the maple syrup toward him. "Do you cut yours first and then put on the maple syrup or the other way around?"

"I put on the maple syrup first."

"I cut mine first."

"I didn't know it mattered."

"It doesn't. It's just something I've noticed when people have pancakes. My dad likes to make pancakes. It's like his one thing that he likes to do for people close to him. And Ryan and I have this theory about putting on your maple syrup first versus after you cut them."

Chris took a bite of his. "What's the theory?"

"If you cut them first like me," I said, slicing my pancake into neat squares. "It basically means you have to do things the traditional way people are supposed to do things, like everything in the perfect order, and then because of that you don't get the big payoffs in life. But if you do it like you—" I motioned with my fork to his plate. "See how you're cutting them now with your fork since they're all soft and gooey from the maple syrup? That means you go for things you want and you don't care if you're not following certain procedures. In the end, according to Ryan, you get the better bit of pancake and by translation, more out of life."

"So Ryan puts his syrup on first?" Chris said.

I nodded, my mouth full. When I'd swallowed, I added, "My dad does too."

"I guess I'm in good company," Chris said.

He had finished his first pancake and I served him another. I smiled as he spread a little butter on it, smothered it in syrup, and carved out a piece with his fork.

"I feel like I passed some test," he said.

I laughed. "Not really. But I guess I'm not surprised you cut it after."

"Why? What about me screams that I don't do things by procedure?"

"Well, you do certain things by procedure but you don't let what other people think, or what you're supposed to do, stop you. Like even the way you started teaching me in Vermont."

"And the way I kissed you that time in the tent?"

I broke out in a huge smile, remembering our first kiss in Vermont. We'd both been so uncertain about our feelings but we also knew that there was something between us. Chris had finally been the one to act on it. "Yeah, that too."

This was so perfect right now. This was what our Mondays were supposed to be like. The breakfast I'd made was delicious. We were talking again. His mood, away from the endless horse videos, seemed to have lifted.

"Do you know about this site, HorseShowDrama?" I asked him.

"Vaguely. Why?"

"It's just got all this stuff about so many people. Dakota reads it religiously."

"I wouldn't get drawn into it," Chris said. "There are a lot of haters out there."

I wondered whether I should tell him about what it said about him and Mary Beth. I decided not to. Instead I said cheerfully, "So what are we going to do today?"

I would have been fine with him saying, absolutely nothing. That we'd stay home all day and go back to bed, binge-watch some episodes on HBO. Or propose something fun like going out to lunch at a new place, going into Miami, or going to the beach. I'd heard people at the show saying those were some of the things people did on Mondays, besides sleep.

"I have to get to Athlete's Advantage," Chris said. "And then to the barn."

"On Monday?" I asked.

"I can't work out as much during circuit so it's really important that I at least do it when I can."

I knew Chris had personal training sessions at the place every grand prix rider who cared about their physical strength and longevity went to. He had told me about all the other professional athletes that worked out there—some major league baseball player I couldn't remember, a former NFL player, lots of collegiate athletes and wealthy people who wanted to feel like real athletes. The sessions were tailored to the sport you did. Chris worked on exercises of short bursts of intensity like you'd get in the ring, and building his core. Athlete's Advantage I could handle. But couldn't he take a day off from the barn? Wasn't that what Monday was for?

"Can't you come back after working out?" I envisioned him in his workout clothes and all sweaty. That could be nice or we could shower together.

"No, I've got a lot of paperwork to catch up on with Dale. We have to send out bills. The farrier's coming."

"On Monday?"

"Yeah, on Monday."

I must have looked pouty because Chris said, "What's wrong? What's going on?"

"I just thought that in Vermont Mondays were like our day to do whatever. Remember when we went to the quarry?"

"Yeah, and I'd love to just hang out but I can't. Back then I had one client. Bills were easy—just send them to Harris. Ordering supplies? Just charge them to Harris. It's completely different now. I'm running a business."

I looked down at my half-eaten pancake, trying to get myself together. Intellectually I totally understood how things were different for Chris now. I got it. But emotionally, it still hurt. I wanted to hang out with my boyfriend, to get to know him more outside of the horse show, to play house a little. "What time do you have to go?"

"I'm working out at eleven, meeting Dale at twelve-thirty."

"Maybe I could bring lunch over for you guys?" I asked.

Chris offered me a smile. "That would be great."

"Okay, cool. Do you want another pancake?" I was being so mature. I wasn't letting my disappointment ruin this.

"One more," he said.

Chapter 15

THE FIRST WEEK OF WEF BEGAN. Twelve rings suddenly burst into action. The horse show practically hummed with activity starting from six-thirty in the morning often till five or six at night, sometimes even later.

Each ring was like its own country. It had its own in-gate guy, often its own announcer, its own schooling area, and its own subset of people who showed there, based on the type of classes held. The pony ring was filled with fluttering hair ribbons and absurdly expensive, but often still recalcitrant, ponies. The trainers there acted half like trainers and half like mothers, and kids burst into either smiles when they rode well or won a class, or tears when they forgot the course or missed a distance.

There was the grand hunter ring where riders who made their living from dealing horses tried to make a sale in huddled talks with other trainers at the in-gate.

There was the International Arena where one could hear several different languages and accents and the riders looked serious because they knew they were the gods of the horse show.

The in-gate person became the unofficial leader of each ring, setting the tone. There were the professional in-gate guys who ran their ring like they were running a small company. There were the diplomatic in-gate guys who ran their ring like they were a politician trying to represent every person's interests, even the disenfranchised. There were the cowboy in-gate guys who ran their rings like the old west with back-door-deal making and vigilante justice.

Some trainers bobbed and weaved between rings. Others spent the majority of their time at only one or two rings. What went on at the other rings was of no concern to them. Put together, all of these individual countries that were the rings made up the planet of WEF. And it did indeed feel like a busy, spinning planet—a blur of colors, and sounds. Somewhere out there in this spinning planet was Mary Beth but I hadn't met her yet. I kept looking for her. I thought I would recognize her. I'd had a few false sightings—someone who I thought might be her, my heart beating fast and my palms growing sweaty.

Chris took Arkos and Logan over to the Turf Tour during Week 1 of WEF instead of competing at the show grounds. Arkos hadn't shown since the summer and Chris wanted a low-pressure situation to start him out. The Turf Tour was run by a grand prix rider and her course designer husband out of their farm in Grand Prix Village. Sometimes it alternated locations between other really nice farms with grand prix fields. The idea was to offer an alternative to WEF and to give riders a chance to show on grass. The in-gate was open all day; you could come and show whenever it suited your schedule.

Dakota lessoned in the morning so I had a break in the afternoon and I took the golf cart over to The Ridge, the farm where the Turf Tour was happening that day, to watch Logan go. Chris had texted me he was heading over. So far Linda seemed really cool about letting me take time to go watch Chris if she didn't need me.

I pulled the golf cart up to the field. I spotted Chris on Arkos in the schooling ring. Arkos was such an impressive-looking horse that it was hard to believe he hadn't lived up to his potential. There were some grand prix horses that didn't look the part. They were small or wormy-looking but somehow they jumped the moon. Maybe they jumped in unorthodox fashion but they cleared the top rails. Arkos looked like he was meant to be a grand prix horse, especially with Chris on him. But all last summer he'd have four or even eight faults each time out in the grand prix classes. Nothing would ever go overtly wrong—he just seemed like he wasn't careful enough. Like he didn't care enough. Chris couldn't understand it because when he'd picked him out in Europe it was *because* he was so careful. It was like Arkos had become a different horse. Chris had all the possible tests done on Arkos and nothing had come up. There was no reason besides a truth Chris didn't want to face—that he had misjudged the horse's potential.

Chris schooled him and then rode over to the in-gate. The Turf Tour was the anti-WEF. No crowds, no announcer, no vendors. It was a horse show on the DL.

I watched Chris go over the course and then enter the ring. It wasn't that warm out today and I wished I'd brought my fleece. I was getting goose bumps. The sun had permanently disappeared behind the clouds. At home fifty degrees would have felt balmy but I guess my blood had already thinned out.

Arkos looked great over the first few jumps. He had room to spare. Of course, this was only a 1.35 meter class, but still. It was good to see. He looked happy and rested and he breezed over the course without any rails down. Chris did the jump-off, not going all out, but pushing Arkos a little here and there. Again, he was clean.

I got out of the golf cart and headed to meet him at the in-gate. Of course I'd let him debrief with Dale first. Even before Dale's stern warning of the week before, I knew not to intrude.

When Dale and Chris had finished talking, Chris hopped off and gave Arkos a hearty pat. Dale led Arkos off and I met Chris. "That was awesome!"

"It's a start," he replied, reminding me with those few words that one simple course at the Turf Tour did not equal grand prix greatness.

"He looked really good. Really rested."

Before Chris could answer, a girl pulled up in a golf cart. It took me a split second and then I recognized her from the photos on Facebook, Instagram, and *The Chronicle*. After all the this time I'd spent thinking about her, it was Mary Beth in the flesh. I had expected to see her on the horse show grounds—for some silly reason I hadn't expected to see her here.

"He looked good," she said, her voice perky. "Maybe the time off fixed him."

"Maybe," Chris said.

I tried to make out whether he was feeling awkward. I couldn't tell. It was inevitable that I was going to have to meet her. And now the moment was here. Why did she act like she knew everything about Arkos's story, when she'd been in Europe most of the summer? How did she even know Chris had rested him? She wasn't looking at me. Maybe she had no idea I was his new girlfriend. She had to know he *had* a new girlfriend.

I was beginning to feel really uncomfortable. Maybe it was only a few moments that had passed but it had felt too long. I caught Chris's eye and he realized I'd never met Mary Beth.

"Oh, sorry, Mary Beth, this is Hannah. Hannah, Mary Beth."

She stuck out her hand to shake. Very professional. She gave me a beautiful smile—all white teeth and perfect candy-colored lips. "Oh my goodness, so glad to finally meet you," she effused. "I've heard so much from Chris about you, and I've been dying to meet you."

How much could she have heard from him about me? I mean, why were they even talking? It was like a backhanded compliment, one that got under my skin and made me para-noid.

"Nice to meet you too," I mustered.

I'd seen the photos and I knew she was pretty but in person Mary Beth radiated a kind of annoyingly genuine beauty. She didn't have any of the traits that twenty-first century people stereotypically associate with beauty. Her hair wasn't blonde—it was dark brown. Her eyes weren't blue—they were brown too. She wasn't tall and waifish—she was slightly short and average weight. But she had to-die-for tousled ringlet hair, now up in a high ponytail, apple cheeks, and smooth, unlined, evenly tanned skin. She was natural and warm, the type of gregarious, outgoing person that makes normal people seem like they're lacking social skills. I wanted to hate her so much but part of me was kind of developing a crush on her.

I tried to think, well, at least Chris had good taste. But how could I compete with her? She was so at ease in her own skin, confidently relaxed.

"So I have the horse here—the one I was telling you about," she said to Chris. To me, she explained, "I've got this amazing horse and I can't ride it to save my life."

She was humble too. Ugh. Could she appear more perfect?

"I really want Chris to look at the horse. If anyone can help me, it's him. You wouldn't mind, would you? I mean that kind of thing doesn't bother you?"

That kind of thing? My boyfriend helping his ex-girlfriend? What was I going to say? If I said yes, it bothered me, I was confirming that I was that kind of person—the jealous, clingy kind. I had no choice but to act like, of course, I wanted him to help her. Like I was the supremely secure type of girlfriend.

"Yeah, definitely," I said. "If anyone can figure him out, it's Chris."

"I know, right?" Mary Beth said. "This guy is one of our country's best riders. It's a crime he doesn't have better horses right now. He's got to get back into the big ring."

"That's what I'm working on," Chris said.

"Do you have time now to help me school?" Mary Beth asked him.

Chris gave me another look, checking to see if I really was okay with all this. I gave a subtle nod, like I was so perfectly cool with it. But underneath, I felt myself itching to start biting my nails. It felt like an urgent bodily need, like when you really drink a lot of water and need to pee.

"Let me get on Logan and I can watch you while I'm getting him ready," he said.

"Which one's Logan?" Mary Beth asked.

So she didn't know everything. "He's my horse," I said, a little too fast.

"Oh, neat. Can't wait to see him go."

"He's nice," Chris said. "He's got some potential actually."

"You do him in the amateurs?" Mary Beth asked.

"I'm not showing him anymore," I said.

"She used to do the children's with him, actually," Chris added.

If I could have kicked him, I would have. Why not let her think I could jump the big jumps?

"Oh, cool," Mary Beth said.

But I knew inside she was probably dying a thousand deaths. Chris, dating a children's jumper rider?

"You going to stay and watch?" she asked.

"Yeah, of course," I said.

"Great." She smiled at Chris. "Meet you in the schooling ring."

From the golf cart I watched them. I thought about standing by the schooling ring but I wanted to act casual. They flatted around and then took turns over the same jumps. I wished I could hear what Chris was saying. Mary Beth nodded a few times like she understood what he was suggesting. Her horse was strong, more like a thoroughbred than a warmblood. He had a canter like an egg-beater and she had to hold him back from the jumps. But at the jumps, he slowed down and jumped sky-high. I could see how it would be a hard ride, though, and different than a lot of the grand prix horses out there.

As they came up to the gate, Chris was explaining to her about trying not to hold him off too much at the front rail. To let him try to figure it out. He was saying the horse was careful enough and she had to trust him.

Mary Beth went in. Chris watched her round and I found myself feeling jealous and irrelevant on the side, like I wasn't even part of the picture. He watched MB intently, like he'd watched me in Vermont. He cocked his head to the side slightly and I could see he was earnestly trying to figure out what would help her with the horse.

She had eight faults—from what I could tell with my more limited knowledge she spent most of her time fighting the horse and then found herself on top of the jumps.

She came out and Chris told her he thought she needed a different bit. I immediately thought he'd suggest a more severe bit but instead he told her the gag she had on him was too much for him, that it only made the horse angry, and also made him curl up. "Have you tried a hack-a-bit?"

"No, I thought I'd die if I did."

"I think it's worth a try. He might respond to the pressure on the nose better."

"I still think I might die." She gave him one of her beatific smiles. She had an almost incandescence to her when she smiled. She was one of those women that are so pretty even other women stare at them.

"You won't. I really don't think you will."

"Will you come over to the farm and we can try it? So someone will be there to call the ambulance?"

The groom could call the ambulance, as far as I was concerned. But as much as I didn't want Chris going over to Mary Beth's farm, I also could understand how she would want someone to help her. It must be hard to be a professional like Chris or Mary Beth. You got help sometimes from more experienced grand prix riders, but you didn't exactly have a trainer anymore. I could see why a lot of the grand prix riders relied on their colleagues to help them.

"Probably," Chris said. "If I have time."

Mary Beth stayed to watch him ride Logan. Logan went so well. His stride stayed the same the whole time around and he never looked like he didn't want to jump. It was amazing what the months of training under Chris had done. I was so proud that he was my horse. He looked ride-able and smooth and he jumped super, easily clearing the course and the jump-off. I made a mental note to video him next time and send it to my dad.

I met Chris at the gate this time. Dale could deal with it. Logan was my horse after all.

I gave Logan a mint and told him how good he was.

"What a difference," I said to Chris.

"I know, he's going well."

Mary Beth rode over, still on her difficult horse. "What a nice horse," she said to both of us. Her horse was looking agitated, frothing at the mouth, and jigging. She couldn't get that close to us and called, "Chris, I'll text you later."

"Okay," he said.

"What are you up to now?" I asked Chris. I didn't need to be back right away. "Stay a little while if you want," Linda had said. "Tomorrow it gets busy and by the end of the day you're not going to know what hit you." I could go get a cup of coffee with Chris, hang out a little. I hadn't seen him much since lunch on Monday and I desperately wanted to reconnect with him. After seeing MB in person, I was pretty shaken.

"I gotta go teach Susan and Jon," Chris said.

Susan and Jon were a married couple who rode with Chris now. They showed against each other in the low amateur-owner jumpers. They were in their fifties, their kids had gone off to college, and they had decided to make their hobby horse showing. They lived close to Chris's farm in Pennsylvania.

"I'll catch up with you later?"

"Sure," I said. "Of course." I tried to act like I wasn't disappointed. Like the whole thing was just peachy—him helping Mary Beth, her being so annoyingly attractive, and now him having to go teach. But it felt anything but fine.

Chapter 16

THE FIRST WEEK OF WEF, I got used to the routine of showing there. A tremendous amount of time was spent coordinating bringing horses back and forth between Morada Bay and the stalls at the show grounds. Dakota had six stalls on the grounds—more than she needed really. While it was a temporary tent like those in Vermont, most people put more time into decorating their stalls since they'd be there all circuit. Some of the bigger barns that had twenty-plus stalls and took up the whole front or back of the tents nearest to the rings went all out. I'm talking beautiful landscaping complete with waterfalls and full-grown palm trees. Another nice touch was wood paneling installed onto tent canvas so the stalls took on an air of a real barn or maybe even a book-stacked library in someone's fancy house.

Linda said she refused to go crazy like that for just six stalls, but she did make an effort. She had hired someone to install paneling on the stall doors and she made a cute little sitting area outside the tent with wicker furniture. It had a carpet of fake turf and an adorable bathtub size pond with a tiny bubbling fountain and a few rubber duckies floating around.

If Dakota was showing a horse, it stayed at the show. The horse show schedule was available on your iPhone through ShowNet but part of my job was still to make copies of each day's schedule with Dakota's classes marked and have them available at Morada Bay and at the stalls at the show so the grooms, Dakota, Linda, or Dakota's parents, if they ever made an appearance, could easily grab one. When we weren't trekking back and forth between the barns, we were trekking back and forth between the different rings that Dakota showed in.

Dakota competed Thursday through Sunday, and fit in school with a tutoring service that came to the house. There was a less expensive option where you went to a place off the grounds for tutoring but, of course, it was too much to ask to make Dakota go to the tutor—the tutor had to come to her.

I was typically supposed to be at the ring with Linda when Dakota was showing, unless there was some pressing need for me to be back at the farm, like if the vet or farrier was coming. At the ring, I tended to Dakota, making sure she stayed hydrated, or getting her an energy bar if she was suddenly overcome by hunger. I also helped the grooms when I could, throwing on a scrim sheet, switching a saddle, or walking a horse. I was Linda's liaison with the in-gate guy, making sure everything was set with our slot in the order of go or repositioning if we needed to. I tried hard to make friends with the in-gate guys, knowing that if they liked me they'd go out of their way to move us up or down if we needed it, but I stopped short of plying them with money like some trainers did. I was grateful that Nick, the in-gate/budding announcer I'd kissed and then essentially dropped for Chris in Vermont, was working in Ocala.

The in-gate guys held a certain status at WEF. Some became good friends with the trainers, dated some of the riders, and generally were more important in how smoothly the days ran than their paychecks indicated. Some of the guys had been doing the same gate for going on a decade. Some chose to dress nicely, in a polo and chino shorts, others looked like they'd just rolled out of bed in wrinkled T-shirts and long-hair. The good ones knew everyone's names, seamlessly managed the day's entries, so the ring rarely stood empty, and consistently and accurately fed the judges the numbers on the riders' backs, and somehow managed to small-talk about the Super Bowl with the trainers at the same time.

Often, I stood with Linda in the schooling ring and helped set the jumps. I liked that part especially, listening to Linda and the other trainers. It was like Vermont, only many more different faces. But there were still the Big Name Trainers who walked around with an air of superiority and self-importance like they owned not just the schooling ring but also the entire show. There were the tough-as-nails trainers who screamed at their riders and made them cry. There were the sarcastic trainers who cracked jokes and traded disparaging looks with other trainers when their riders chipped. There were the psychologically attuned trainers who spoke just barely above a whisper and talked about things like "riding the whole horse" and "finding your happy rhythm."

From what I'd observed, Linda was a good trainer. She cared about the horses and did things the right way, so far not going for quick fixes or gadgets for instant results. Every horse got its Perfect Prep when they showed but I hadn't seen any horse getting something illegal. It probably helped that Dakota had really nice horses, some of the best horses that money could buy, so training them involved keeping them sound, fit, and in a solid program—not desperately trying to make them go well. She didn't yell at Dakota but she could be firm and raise her voice when she felt Dakota wasn't listening. For the most part, Dakota wasn't a bad student either. She was spoiled, that much was clear, and out of the saddle she wasn't exactly a joy, but she did seem to care about how she did in the ring and most of the time she even seemed to appreciate her horses, patting them when she came out of the ring.

At the rings, I often got to see Mike and I sometimes saw Zoe, although she was usually doing the professional hunter divisions. She was riding for Donnie Rysman, a well-known and generally detested trainer. He was from the Southeast and produced lots of winners in the hunter ring but he was also known for his shady deals, illegal training techniques, unsound horses, and for accosting judges when his horses didn't win. According to rumors, she was sleeping with him too, even though he was twice her age.

When Dakota did her hunters, it was the most relaxing because no one expected her to win. An amazing junior-pro,

Cassidy Rancher, rode a bunch of spectacular horses for a widowed older lady who had inherited all her husband's wealth. Cassidy owned the top ribbons. All the other riders competed for the whites, pinks, and greens.

On Saturday, I stood at the in-gate with Linda, watching Dakota on Midway. Midway had quickly become my favorite of Dakota's horses. He was a blast to ride and was so sweet around the barn, goofy, like the class clown of the barn. You couldn't have him anywhere without him getting into trouble, chewing on a leadrope, trying to nuzzle Fernando's dog, Rudi. Now, he loped around the course like an overgrown pony. He didn't jump incredibly round but his knees were always up and neat. Dakota put in good rounds on him and when the jog was called, he trotted in third in the second round, even beating out one of Cassidy's horses.

I gave him a few extra mints. Dakota handed me her ribbon as Fernando took Midway.

"He's done for the week," Linda said. "He can go back to the barn and turnout."

We still had the two low junior jumpers left for the day. I walked the course with Linda and Dakota. A few tiny birds were taking a bath in the liverpool. The course designer roamed around, repositioning a rail in the cups and switching the flags on a pair of standards. Linda said hello to him and then told me in a quiet aside how she wished he were single.

As we walked out of the ring, Dakota asked me to get her a drink from the coffee cart.

"I want a smoothie with light unsweetened almond milk, flaxseed, unsweetened cocoa powder, protein powder, banana, cinnamon, and honey and get it right. I hate it when it's wrong."

Yes, I wished she would treat me as well as her horses—it was only my first week and I could have used the occasional pat on the shoulder instead of being ordered around.

I pulled out my phone. "Wait, say it again so I can write it down."

She repeated her order super fast, before I had even been able to type in my passcode. Then she stalked off to the stands.

I should have followed her but I didn't want to be that type of person—the Hollywood handler following their movie star around like a servant. I decided to forget putting it in my phone. Somehow I'd remember. I said it once more in my head.

At the coffee cart, however, I began to question whether it was unsweetened almond milk or unsweetened coconut milk. And had she asked for honey or cinnamon or both? There was a big line and while I waited I texted Dakota to double-check. No response, which seemed odd for someone who was always checking her phone.

I felt my body getting hot—she was going to freak out if I got it wrong. Then I got mad at myself for getting worried. This was a smoothie for a kid for Godsakes. She was no Hollywood star or big-time CEO. I decided to stop stressing. When it was my turn, I ordered her completely overpriced drink and went back to the ring.

"I texted you," I said, when I found her with a bunch of her friends. "I was trying to double check your drink order."

"Does it have the bee pollen?"

"Of course," I said, automatically, although I definitely had not ordered bee pollen. Had she said bee pollen? Who could taste bee pollen anyway, though? She'd never know it wasn't in there. I held the drink out to her.

She made a disgusted face. "I'm allergic to bee pollen. It could kill me."

I pulled back the drink. I couldn't tell her I'd lied and there was no bee pollen. "Okay, well, I guess if you tell me your order again I'll go back."

"No," she said, like I was too dumb to take proper direction. "You know what, just forget it."

She turned back to her friends and I walked away, nearly bumping into a woman filming the rider on course with her iPad. I told myself to breathe and calm down. I sat on the fence at the end of the in-gate area and tried to temper my hostility. I took a sip of the drink Dakota wouldn't touch. Not bad.

"Thinking about quitting?" Mike said, surprising me.

He must have seen what happened. He had a lead rope tied around his chest like people in the real world wear one-shoulder sling backpacks and a hoof pick sticking out of his back pocket.

"The thought has occurred to me," I admitted.

"Maybe she needs you," Mike said. "Maybe you're just the one to help screw her head on straight."

"We need you, Obie-Wan-Kenobi," I goofed. "You are our only hope." Ryan had been the one who was into STAR WARS when we were young and I'd picked up a lot of it from watching with him. "I think I'd need a very big wrench to screw her head on right and I might just hit her over the head with the wrench instead."

Mike laughed. "Hang in there, kiddo."

I held Dakota's drink up like we were toasting and took another big sip. At the very least I was going to enjoy her drink.

* * *

Dakota informed me after she was done showing that she was going out to dinner with her friends and I leapt at the chance for Chris and me to go out. He had been pretty busy with Lily showing in the 25K 1.50 meter speed class, and Susan and Jon showing in the low ami classic, and riding his own horses. I really wanted to sit down together and I could hear about his day and tell him about the Dakota Drink Drama, as I was referring to it in my head. But when I suggested we go to Oli's, he said he couldn't.

"I have to go out with the Tellers."

"Oh," I said.

I guess Chris could hear the disappointment in my voice when I said that one little word because he continued, "This is part of the drill. I wish things were like when I was working for Harris and I didn't have to do this stuff but I have to try to make all these different people happy. It was easier when I just had to keep Harris happy."

I could tell Chris wished he hadn't said that last part because I was one of the main reasons why Harris had pulled his horses from Chris. He quickly continued, "I mean it wasn't easy keeping Harris happy either and that partnership had its definite downsides. I'm not saying I wish I had Harris back . . ."

"I understand," I said. I did understand, but I still wished Chris had more time for us. And I wished he'd asked me to go with him to dinner with the Tellers. Mom said Dad always wanted her to go out to business dinners with him but she couldn't because of her anxiety and she felt terrible about it. A few times she'd gone and drank too much to try to calm down and he'd practically had to carry her out of the restaurant. I had hazy memories of a few of those nights, his coming home and putting her to bed, while the babysitter sat uncomfortably with us in front of the TV, waiting to be paid so she could go home. Eventually it was clear that it was better if she stayed home.

"Are you going to ask the Tellers about a horse for you?" I said.

"That's the plan," Chris said.

Linda saw me in the barn after I'd hung up with Chris. I was in Midway's stall, just hanging out with him. We played this game where I stood next to him and he searched every pocket I had until he found a mint.

"What're you up to?" she asked.

"Nothing. I thought maybe Chris and I'd go out but he has dinner plans with a client."

"Wanna go to the food trucks?"

"Sure," I said, even though I had no idea what the food trucks were.

Linda drove us to a parking lot on Forest Hill Boulevard

over by the Wellington Amphitheater. The lot was filled with at least ten, maybe more, food trucks parked around the perimeter of the lot. Once we got out of the car, we did a loop, checking out what each truck had to offer. There was everything you could want—Mexican, burgers, grilled cheese, Chinese, plus several ice cream and gelato trucks.

A few girls I recognized from the show passed us still in their breeches.

"I guess a lot of people come here," I said.

"Yeah," Linda said. "Where was Chris going?"

"International Polo Club."

"Fancy," she said. "Who's the client?"

"Lily Teller."

"Right. The Tellers. Big money."

"Chris is hoping they might invest in a horse for him."

Linda clucked. "Not sure about that."

"Why not?"

"In my experience there are two types of wealthy parents. Those who only want to spend their money if it benefits their kid and those who are willing to spend their money not just to help their kid."

"And the Tellers are the first kind?"

"So far. Maybe Chris will make the difference."

"I hope so," I said. "He's so talented and he works so hard. It just kills me that he doesn't have the right horses."

"That's the sport," Linda said. "The best riders usually *don't* have the best horses. They have to do whatever they can, prostitute themselves out, to get mediocre horses and ride the shit out of them. Or then, every once in while, they get lucky and find a nice rich girl to marry and buy them horses."

I let out a deep breath.

"Sorry," Linda said. "Am I being too blunt? I have a reputation for doing that. I don't mean to depress you."

"No, it's nothing new. It just kind of sucks." I liked that Linda was candid. She seemed wiser than her years. I guess if you didn't have endless means this sport could age you quickly.

Linda stopped at the Mexican food truck. "I think I'm going to get the fish taco."

"That sounds good. I think I'll get that too."

We waited for our turn to order. The lines weren't insane but each truck had a nice little crowd around it. Some were regular non-horse show people who lived in Wellington. I thought about how it'd be odd to live here if you weren't into horses since so much of the town was all about horses. I saw grooms and riders too. I spotted a few DQs—discernible because of their full-seat breeches. Wellington wasn't just a hunter/jumper scene—there was dressage and polo too.

After we had ordered, I said, "Well, I'm unfortunately not the rich girl Chris needs. I don't have that kind of money."

"No, that would have been Mary Beth." Linda grimaced at me. "Now that was too blunt."

I made a dramatic show of putting my head in my hands. "It's kind of refreshing actually not to dance around it. I feel like she's this nemesis of mine." I didn't say that every time I thought of her I wanted to chew my nails and a few times I'd come close.

"Is Chris over her?"

"Yes, definitely." I said it so confidently and then wished I hadn't. Maybe I sounded like I was trying to cover up that he actually wasn't. But he was over her. He had said so.

"Well, that's good. So all he needs is for the Tellers to buy him a number one horse."

"Fingers crossed they're getting on board with that tonight," I said.

We carried our cardboard trays over to the group of pub tables. The tacos were delicious. I asked Linda about what she'd done before she worked for the Pearces. She ended up telling me her whole horse show history. It seemed like horse show people were like that, not just Linda. You got them started with a question about a horse or a time in their lives and they'd happily recount nearly every horse and show they'd ever ridden in. But I didn't mind with Linda. She was a good storyteller and regaled me with crazy times working for different trainers. She'd ridden as a junior, winning a lot in the jumpers, including a Gold Medal at Young Riders. Then, instead of college, she'd gone to work for a grand prix rider in California. She'd burned out and taken an eighteen month hiatus from horses, working in Hollywood as an assistant to an assistant to a movie producer—a job she'd gotten through a rider at the barn she'd worked for. She thought about going back to school but found she missed the horses too much and didn't want to spend her days in an office job. So she moved back East, bounced around with a few trainers before getting the gig with the Pearces.

"Do you miss competing?" I asked her.

Linda took her sunglasses from where they were propped on her head and repositioned them. I'd never seen her without them either on her face or on her head. Often, she wore them like a headband holding back her hair.

"Sometimes but I knew I didn't have it in me to kill myself to find sponsors. What Chris is doing—it's hard and I think it's only getting harder. When an eighteen year-old with family money can make it to the Olympics, why would you ever buy a horse for a professional instead of your kid?"

"You think the teams should be picked by experience instead of record?" I asked.

"I don't know what the answer is, but I know there are fewer and fewer owners wanting to support a grand prix rider. And then you have some of the ones that do backing European riders."

I was so glad that I'd come out with Linda. I liked her no-nonsense attitude and she really knew what she was talking about.

"What kind of parents are Dakota's?" I asked. "The kind that only do for their child?"

"Yes, but with a weird twist since they're never here to watch her and they spend their whole lives helping others outside of the horse world."

"They're never here?"

"Well, not often."

I had finished my taco. I twisted my napkin under the table, wondering how this was ever going to work. I would need to be around 24-7 for Dakota and Chris seemed like he was always going to be busy scrambling to make his business thrive.

"Is Dakota, well, as bad as she seems?"

"Yup." Linda smiled. "But you'll get used to her."

"Other people who've done this job . . . . They've quit?"

"They don't last that long. But you're only signed on for the circuit anyway, right?"

"Right," I said.

Linda put her napkin in her empty cardboard tray. "Just don't let her run you off before then."

"No way," I said, full of fake confidence.

After we tossed our trash, we hit the popsicle truck for dessert. It was hard to choose from the many different flavors—Oreo, chocolate, coffee, strawberry, mango, banana. I decided on a banana base. Then you could choose to have the popsicle dipped in milk, dark, or white chocolate and covered with sprinkles or Oreos. I went with just dipped in milk chocolate. Linda got coffee base with milk chocolate and Oreo sprinkles.

"Do you have a boyfriend?" I asked her. I was pretty sure I knew the answer from her earlier comment about the course designer.

She swallowed the first bite of her popsicle. "Not right now. I was dating a vet back home but it's hard to maintain a relationship in this business when you're both traveling different places."

"Is the only way it works if you can be at all the same shows?" I asked.

"That doesn't always work for people either. Look at Miranda and Jeff. They have a fabulous business and now they're getting divorced. This industry is just hard on love, period. But there I go again being all negative. Just shoot me, okay?"

I made a pretend gun and shot her. She threw her hands to her heart and faked a quick death. I was still laughing when I turned and saw Zoe with the saddle guy, Étienne.

Zoe waved at Linda and Linda called out, "hey," to her. Zoe didn't even acknowledge me. She looked her usual pretty self, but haggard too in a way I hadn't noticed the first time I'd seen her. Maybe I'd been too surprised and taken aback at Arouet. I looked closer at her now. Her eyes were heavy and lidded, and she looked rail-thin. My first instinct was to feel worried for her and then I tried to remind myself that she wasn't my problem. That she wasn't my friend.

As we ate our popsicles, Linda said, "Now there's a girl in a heap of trouble."

"Why?" I asked.

"That guy is bad news. Drugs."

"Really?"

"Big time. He's making some nice cash on the side of saddle commissions."

"People here do drugs? Like the riders?" I knew I sounded naïve. I'd seen plenty of riders getting sloshed in Vermont but I'd never seen or heard about any of them doing drugs.

"Some of them, yeah. Don't forget there are also polo players here. Lots of wealthy polo players." Linda made a show of wiping her nose and inhaling to indicate cocaine.

"And Zoe? She's not selling drugs, is she?"

"No, but she's clearly using them."

Linda's words hit me hard. As much as I hated Zoe for what she'd done to me in Vermont, she'd also been the first person to help me when my dad dropped me off alone and helpless. And I knew what kind of life she had—a rider orphan, Chris had called her. Maybe there was even a part of me that could see myself in her. What I could have become if instead of shutting myself in and never going to a party, I'd gone the other way to escape my mom's anxiety and hooked up with everyone and anyone, drank and done drugs.

"Zoe's doing cocaine?"

"Probably. Maybe pharmaceuticals."

"But not heroin or anything like that?" I'd read a memoir in high school about a girl addicted to heroin. The book was by her sister, actually. The girl died. The book made it sound like heroin was something hardly any people ever recovered from.

"Who knows?" Linda said. "It's a sad situation."

"Is anyone going to help her?" I asked.

Linda made a pained face. "Not much anyone can do really."

Chapter 17

A WEEK LATER I WAS at the coffee cart with Linda. "We should probably get Dakota a drink," she said.

I pulled a few bills out of my pocket. "You're nicer than me."

For the entirety of week 2, Dakota's main purpose in life seemed to be to figure out a way to make me quit, or incite me to do something that she could get me fired for. She constantly came up with things she needed from the tack store and sent me on wild goose chases to every tack store on the show grounds—and sometimes off the show to the Tackeria too—in search of said item. Sometimes it could be something as simple as a hairnet but when I'd return with the hairnet she'd requested from Beval's, it was the wrong shade of blond and I had to go back but then Beval's would curiously be out of 'ash blonde' and I'd have to go to Jods but then Dakota would say that she had changed her mind about the brand and then I'd have to go to Hadfield's and so on. There were as many as six or seven tack stores set up at the show and I became an expert on what each one carried so that when Dakota asked me to go get something from Kocher I knew she was sending me there just to make me jump through hoops and to head to Running Fox instead.

She also liked to send me back to Morada Bay from the show grounds for her favorite crop or favorite spurs that she had curiously forgotten to bring with her. In the first week or two, I must have made that trip on the golf cart back and forth from Morada Bay four or five times a day. On my many trips to and fro on horseback, via golf cart and even once or twice on foot, I had seen it all. Dogs of all kinds, donkeys, goats, even a Zebra turned out in a field. People riding Western, riding bareback, even a pony pulling a cart.

I finally smartened up—I searched Dakota's trunk for what she would likely send me back for and brought it myself. She also tried very hard to leave one of her saddles, or her show coat, at different rings so I'd be forced to go back and get them. She probably hoped that a saddle or show coat would be stolen and then I'd be to blame.

At night, in the house, Dakota avoided me at all costs. She had me get her take-out food but ate at the kitchen counter, her iPhone inches from her face, or with her ear buds in. She spent the rest of the night in her room. The first few nights I'd invited her to watch TV with me in the family room. I'd suggested we watch a series on Netflix or HBO together. She'd just coolly said, "No, thanks." She did her homework alone—so much for me being able to help her.

Sometimes Dakota had me drive her to meet friends for dinner, or she'd have friends over. It was crazy but on those nights I felt so left out. Dakota and her other horse show friends would roam around the food trucks and I'd eat a fish taco by myself. Or I'd drop them off at Sushi Moto and come back and get them later. On those days, I'd usually go to Chris's condo while they had dinner. I'd bring take-out or sometimes Chris would cook. Even then, our dinners were often interrupted by Chris having to take calls from clients to tell them how their horse had done that day, or send quick email reports. The Tellers had agreed to buy two shares of a horse—half a million dollars. To people outside of the international show jumping world that would have seemed like a ridiculous amount of money but sadly it wasn't anywhere near what Chris needed to get a top horse. When he'd told me about their offer I'd been insanely happy for him, nearly squealing over the phone. Not only did I think it was a lot of money, I naively thought it would mean he'd be less stressed out. In fact, it was even worse. Now he had some money, but not nearly enough. If he didn't come up with more funds soon, perhaps the Tellers would change their mind. He also still had to find a horse to buy.

Other times Dakota slept over at a friend's and I got to spend the night at Chris's. I was always so happy to be with him but it ended up feeling like he wasn't ever totally present. We'd have sex and it was always good enough, but it wasn't with the same kind of passion we'd had in Vermont. He would roll away from me nearly right after we'd finished and tell me he just remembered he needed to send an email.

I had generated this whole idea of what Florida would be like. Chris would be riding and winning but he'd have so much time to spend with me. Our relationship would strengthen and grow, with us becoming closer than ever. But instead, during the days I ran around after Dakota and he ran around teaching and riding and trying to subtly promote himself to potential sponsors. I didn't feel closer to him; I felt farther away.

Linda waved away my money and said she was getting this round of coffees. "Is Dakota getting to you?"

"Not too bad," I lied.

"The trick is to let it all roll off you," she advised.

The nice lady, Cindy, who always worked the coffee cart smiled at Linda. "What do you need? A Linda?"

"Yeah," Linda said. "And a Dakota too." Linda looked at me. "What do you want?"

I was too speechless to answer right away. Then I managed, "What's a Dakota?"

"Let's see," Linda said. "Light unsweetened almond milk, flaxseed, something else and something else."

Cindy picked up where she left off. "Unsweetened cocoa powder, protein powder, banana, cinnamon, and honey."

That little bitch. She could have just told me to order a Dakota. So I wasn't paranoid—she was working every moment to try to get me gone.

"Are you okay?" Linda asked, seeing my face lose its color. "Do you know what you want?"

I laughed a little, thinking about what Dakota had done. Did she think she could make me quit that easily? She didn't know the first thing about me, then.

"Yeah, one skim cappuccino, please."

* * *

By the beginning of week 3, I spoke fluent WEF. I tossed off words and phrases like DeNemethy ring, Magavero ring, $20 ring, Oasis, Tiki Hut, Riders' Lounge, Dever, and Global—things that had been completely foreign to me only a few short weeks before. I'd also started on a very nice farmer's tan. The first week I'd forgotten to wear sunscreen and had scorched the bridge of my nose and cheeks. I knew to wear sunscreen every day now, even if the sun wasn't super strong. Some female riders went so far as to wear sunshield brims around their helmets to keep the sun off their face. Even though they looked a bit like Darth Vader, it seemed like a good idea if you spent your career baking in the sun. At fifty or sixty, too many horse show trainers sported Yoda wrinkles.

I kept tabs on Chris like I had in Vermont. Of course, now I could be more open about it and ask him what he was riding in that day. Between asking him and checking orders on ShowNet, I tried to rush over to the DeNemethy or International Ring to watch him whenever I could. I always tried especially hard to watch Logan. He was doing great in the 1.35 meter classes.

During a lull in Dakota's show day, I headed onto the bridge to watch. The International Ring was so large it was almost hard to see all of the ring. Some trainers preferred to watch on the wide screen by the in-gate. The bridge was a pretty good place to watch if you were tall enough because you were looking down on the ring and could see more of the ring.

Chris was a few riders away. I watched some of the other

riders go before him. There were so many riders at WEF and I didn't know them all like I had in Vermont. It was kind of like going from a small high school where you pretty much knew everyone to college where, besides your friends, you could only pick out a few familiar faces in the crowd. There were people I'd never heard of mixed with those I knew from watching them in Vermont or from reading about them. Since I'd been dating Chris I kept tabs on the world of show jumping, monitoring blogs, reports, and the World and Computer Rankings. I knew the top ten on the Computer List and the top Americans in the World Rankings.

Jimmy Sharpe, a friend of Chris's went, and also McNair Sutter, a young wealthy former amateur with super nice horses who had recently turned pro.

While McNair was finishing up, Chris came into the ring. The ring was so large that the course designers made the courses such that the rider on deck could canter in while the rider just finishing up was on his way out.

Chris was riding one of Lily's horses, Monteverdi II. Lily was flying in Thursday night since she had a big test Thursday morning. Chris was tasked with preparing Monty. Monty was an incredible horse. A horse that if Chris had him to ride all year he could probably win at the highest level. Lily still won a fair bit with Monty, but sometimes her inexperience led to rails down.

The tone sounded and Chris started toward the first jump. I didn't notice that Mary Beth had come to stand next to me until she said, "I bet Chris would love to have him as his number one horse."

I glanced over at her as Chris made his way down the first line. Monty jumped so high, making it all seem effortless.

"Yeah, definitely," I said.

Standing side-by-side, we watched Chris. I wondered how it looked to people around us—Chris's current girlfriend and his ex-girlfriend. Would this make it onto HorseShowDrama?

"How's it going?" she asked me.

I wasn't sure what she meant. How was my job? The circuit? "Like just in general?" I said.

"No, you know, you and Chris . . . here together during circuit. Circuit can be a really stressful time."

I glanced at her. She was so authentically beautiful. No makeup that I could tell yet her skin was even and smooth. Nicely worn Parlantis, Animo breeches, polo shirt, her ringlet hair pulled back, and Maui Jim sunglasses. "It can?"

"Totally. All the pressure to do something big, get noticed, get a sponsor, a new client, sell horses. It's bad enough for any rider but this year for Chris, you know, since he's kind of back to not exactly square one, but close . . ."

Chris had finished clean. He patted Monty. I could only imagine how much of a tease it must be to ride Monty. To know what he could do with a horse like that.

"It hasn't been the easiest at times, I guess," I admitted.

"How's Dale treating you? He can be a tough one."

"I think he hates me," I said.

"Dale hates everyone . . . except Chris, that is."

"He's not like, *into* him?" I hadn't thought Dale might be gay. Nothing about him seemed to indicate that but now that it had occurred to me, you never knew.

"No, Dale's straight. But his whole world is Chris. I guess

it's a good thing, for Chris, but I think Dale would prefer if Chris became a monk. Like a show jumping monk."

I laughed. MB was pretty and outgoing and socially adept, and now I was finding out she was funny too. I certainly wanted to hate her but she was good at making that hard to do.

"Did Dale like you, I mean when you and Chris were dating?" After I'd spoken, I sort of wished I hadn't brought up when they had been a couple.

"*Like* might not be the right term. Tolerate, maybe."

I felt my shoulders relax. Thank goodness she hadn't said they were besties. I don't think I could have handled that. "I thought it was just me. That's good to know."

"Chris isn't always the easiest either. I know how he can be, believe me." She made a face. "Like he's there but he's not really present, right?"

"Totally," I said. "That's exactly what it's like."

"I used to be mid-conversation with him and he'd have to go send some text or email. It's like when it occurs to him, he has to do it right then."

I probably should have been upset that Mary Beth knew Chris so well. Probably better than me, actually. But it was such a relief to have someone understand what was going on between us and to know it wasn't me. It was him.

"That's exactly what he's like," I said.

"Believe me, I know. I've been there." She was quiet for a moment and then added, "And the sex, right? Is it going downhill?"

I stiffened. Did I really want to talk to Mary Beth about my sex life with Chris?

Her voice turned soft and sisterly. "I don't mean to get personal and I get it if you're like TMI but I just know with me when he got all distracted with his career, I had to work to get it going again in the bedroom."

I didn't want to seem like a prude either, the girl who wouldn't talk about sex. Zoe always made me out to be some total lame-o. I checked to make sure no one might overhear us. "I guess it's been, not as great as at other times."

"And part of that's natural, right, I mean, when you're first with a guy it's like you're doing it all the time and you can't keep your hands off each other. Of course that slows down."

God, I wished Mary Beth wasn't Chris's ex. I so needed someone to talk to about stuff like this. This was where Zoe had fit in my life. She had been my best friend—the one I opened up to about things. Right now I had no one. Who was I supposed to talk to about this kind of stuff? Ryan? No way. I could have called Van, I guess. She would have been the best person to talk to. I felt like Mary Beth and I could have actually been friends, if she wasn't Chris's ex. Could I still be friends with her? Maybe that would be the best outcome. We could all be so grown-up about it.

Mary Beth continued, "But I found it got better when I tried harder. He just needed a little something different, you know? Well, I'm sure you've starting taking measures on your own."

Measures—what kind of measures was she talking about? I hadn't been taking any measures. "Um, like what, I mean, do you mind me asking?"

"Of course not," she said. "You might be noticing about

me . . . I don't really get embarrassed. I'm kind of an open book."

That was the complete opposite of me, of course. So why did Chris like me? The question still plagued me. Did he like conservative-me, or wide-open-book MB?

Mary Beth lowered her voice. "Well, first of all there's personal grooming. I got a Brazilian and let's just say that was a big success."

I felt my cheeks redden. And my stomach turn. I didn't want to think of MB and Chris in the bedroom. What her lady parts looked like and whether it turned him on. But at the same time I needed to know, didn't I?

"And then there's positions and places. I tried to mix it up when I could. Surprise him. Like there was one time after a night class." She went to a whisper, "I gave him a blow job in the VIP tent." She made a *can-you-believe-it* face, her eyes wide.

I couldn't believe it. Or I didn't want to. I also couldn't believe she and I were actually having this conversation.

"I don't know," I said. "I'm clearly not as bold as you are."

She poked me playfully on the arm. "You'd be surprised at what you have inside you. Have a little fun. Shake things up a bit. I think you'll be glad you did."

I nodded. "Thanks—for being so honest with me."

"Of course," Mary Beth said. "You know, I wanted to hate you, but I actually like you."

I let out a half-sigh, half-laugh. "Me too."

"You wanted to hate me?" she asked.

"I guess so," I said. "Isn't that kind of natural?"

"Because you thought I was going to be all trying to win Chris back?"

"Well, that's what some people said," I admitted.

Mary Beth shook her head as if she was disgusted with the whole horse show scene. "Yeah, because my main goal of circuit is to win Chris back."

She said it sarcastically, but after it was out there I felt like the air was stuffy around us. Like the moment had kind of brought time to a halt. Was she kidding? Or actually dead serious?

"I'll see you later," she said, with an innocent smile. "I've gotta go get on."

Chapter 18

OKAY, SO NOW I KNEW what I had to do. Apparently, I had to get a Brazilian wax and then seduce Chris in some public place, where we'd end up doing it in some crazy Karma Sutra position.

Only, none of that was me. The rest of the week I couldn't get Mary Beth's words out of my head. Chris and I had sex on Sunday night and it was perfunctory at best. The whole time I was thinking how I should suggest we at least do it with me on top, or try with him from behind, but I couldn't bring myself to. I had to do something. I had to change things up. Things couldn't keep going this way. I desperately wished there was someone for me to bounce what Mary Beth had said to me off. *Zoe, damn you*, I thought. *I need you now.*

I'd read some disturbing things about Zoe on Horse-ShowDrama, which thanks to Dakota I now frequented way too often.

Re: *What's up with Zoe Tramell?*
By Love2gossip:
Is it me, or does Zoe Tramell look like complete shit?

Re: *What's up with Zoe Tramell?*
By Jumphigher:
Yeah, she is scary skinny. Meth-head skinny.

Re: *What's up with Zoe Tramell?*
By Ridingmyassoff:
That's because she is a meth-head. Or coke-head. The girl is totally strung-out.

Re: *What's up with Zoe Tramell?*
By Ellie:
She is such a good rider. I mean super-talented. Such a shame.

Re: *What's up with Zoe Tramell?*
By Ridingmyassoff:
She's been a disaster-waiting-to-happen for a long time now. She can ride, yes, but she also fucks anything and everything.

Re: *What's up with Zoe Tramell?*
By Love2gossip:
I thought she's with the sleazy saddle guy now?

Re: *What's up with Zoe Tramell?*
By Ridingmyassoff:

Him and five other guys including Donnie, whose horses she's riding. That girl hasn't met anyone she wouldn't get in bed with.

Re: What's up with Zoe Tramell?
By Jumphigher:
I feel bad for her.

Re: What's up with Zoe Tramell?
By Ridingmyassoff:
She clearly has serious self-esteem issues. I literally get sick to my stomach watching Donnie yell at her from the in-gate. He rips her a new asshole every day in public when he's not smacking her around back at the barn. I'm sorry but no amount of make-up is going to cover the bruises he gives her.

I sat reading about Zoe, feeling myself getting cold despite the fact that I'd turned the air conditioning to a warmer setting so it wasn't freezing in the house. I knew Zoe had problems but was it really true that Donnie was beating her up?

I didn't know what I should do with the information I'd seen on HorseShowDrama. It wasn't my place to be concerned about Zoe but at the same time I didn't feel like I could just turn a blind eye to hearing that she was doing drugs and in an abusive relationship. I was confused about what to do about Chris and what to do about Zoe.

At the show, things weren't much better. I saw them all around—babysitters who were beloved by their young charges. Like me, they took care of a wealthy girl while her mom and dad were back home in another state or even just in Palm Beach but off playing tennis or golf, meeting with their money manager, having a massage, or grabbing lunch at the club. These women sat close to the girls on their golf carts or rode double on their mini-bikes to and from the ring. They ate together at the crepe place and watched together ringside. The minder helped her charge with her hair, helped her go over the course when the trainer was busy, and knew just what to say when her charge won or lost. Flash forward years and she'd be invited to her wedding and receive hand-signed Christmas cards year after year.

But not me. Dakota detested me. She stayed as far away as possible from me and when I was near she gave me looks that could strip paint. Intellectually I got that Dakota was trying to get rid of me just like she had gotten rid of all her minders in the past in the hopes that it would force her parents to come home and pay attention to her. I knew I should have felt terrible for her. But emotionally, I couldn't help feeling hurt by all her conniving.

In the ring, Dakota's circuit was off to a good start. She was consistently in the ribbons in the hunters and had placed in the low junior jumpers and even won a class with Tizmo. She seemed to have more talent for the jumpers. She had no problem going fast and slicing angles. In the eq, she usually had one or two hiccups that kept her just out of the ribbons but she was still young and the ribbon-winners of the eq at WEF were a veritable Who's Who of the top eq riders in the country.

On Saturday of week 4, I was requested to take Dakota

and her friends to watch the grand prix from the VIP tent. Of course all I could think about was how this was where MB had given Chris a blow job. That girl had gotten into my head. And with it came a nagging feeling. Had she meant to?

Dakota and her friends were dressed up like they were mini adults going clubbing. Shimmery tank-tops, tight tooth-pick pants, high heels, and designer handbags.

Chris hadn't wanted to come watch the grand prix and honestly I couldn't blame him. It was one of the bigger classes, a CSI-5 with close to 400K in prize money. He didn't have a horse that could come anywhere close to being ready for a class like this and Lily hadn't qualified either of her horses. She'd had four faults with both in the WEF Challenge round that served as the qualifier. I understood it would be painful for Chris to watch tonight. He said he'd probably watch the Live Stream at home. After his clear round at the Turf Tour, Arkos's performances had been going downhill. Four faults, eight faults, four faults, twelve faults. Never any horrible jumps—just riding by Braille. If he couldn't jump clean at 1.40 meters, he'd never jump a CSI-5. Logan was consistently placing in his classes but he wasn't about to jump a CSI-3, let alone a CSI-5, so that left Chris with the promise of money from the Tellers, which still wasn't near enough to buy a legit 5-star horse. I would have preferred to watch the Live Stream with him but because of the other girls' mothers' and minders' schedules, here I was.

We got there early as the tent was just filling up. It was a good thing because soon the buffet line stretched to the entrance. Dakota's parents had shelled out for one of the tables in the front of the tent with the best view of the ring. A waiter came and took our drink orders. The girls asked for diet cokes. In the line for the buffet, the girls people-watched and whispered comments to each other. I couldn't help but look around too. This was the place to be if you weren't at the in-gate with a rider. Some of the juniors the girls knew blew them kisses or waved to them as they walked by us. Others were so important in horse show terms that Dakota and her friends just stared after them. The ones they stared at were the young grand prix riders and the top juniors in their last year. Cassidy Rancher types in terms of celebrity recognition. A host of a daytime talk show whose daughter was a junior walked by on the way to her table. So did the movie producer father and his grand prix rider daughter, who were doubly recognizable because they were one of the only two African American families at the horse show.

Of course the girls didn't really want to sit at the table with me, but they had no choice so I got the privilege of hearing their conversation.

It became clear that for them the class was less about the horses and the competition, and more about the guys. They paid attention to the young, hot, straight ones and disregarded the rest. Some of the guys they didn't know well enough, like some of the foreign guys, prompted heated discussions about whether they were straight or gay.

They also commented on the young women who they'd heard were hooking up with or might hook up with the young, hot, straight guys. How they'd been seen at JoJo's or The Players Club with a certain grand prix rider or leaving JoJo's or The Players Club with a certain grand prix rider.

When McNair Sutter came in the ring, they oohed and aahed. Straight, hot, rich, young, single. Apparently he was the catnip of young equestrians. I knew Chris disliked McNair and all he stood for. Unlike Chris, McNair came from wealth and so he had the best horses. He stayed an amateur for quite a while, so he could win in both the amateur divisions on his younger horses and in the professional divisions on his more seasoned mounts. Only after so many people slammed him behind his back and probably on HorseShowDrama did he turn pro. He was still a common topic on HorseShowDrama, though: McNair liked the ladies and had left many broken hearts in his wake.

"I saw him by the Tiki Hut before the class," Addie said. "He is so gorgeous it's not right."

"I heard he hooked up with Adele Bonderman last Sunday night at Players," Dakota said.

"Adele Bonderman?" Taylor nearly shrieked. "She's not even that pretty."

"He could have any girl on the entire show grounds," Addie said.

"Starting with me!" Dakota added.

"And me," Addie seconded.

"Not me," Taylor said. "I'm all about Jimmy Sharpe."

I couldn't help myself from butting in. Until then I'd been pretending I wasn't even listening, concentrating on my salad. "Jimmy Sharpe? He's twice your age."

"McNair's only like five years younger than Jimmy," Addie said.

Dakota gave me the evil eye. "Don't pay any attention to Hannah, she has no idea what she's talking about."

"Aren't you Chris Kern's girlfriend, though?" Taylor asked. Apparently this gave me status and authority on the topic.

"Yes," I said.

"Chris Kern's not all that," Dakota said.

"I think he's cute," Addie said.

"Whether I'm with Chris isn't the point," I said. "You girls are thirteen. Those guys are in their twenties and Jimmy's almost thirty."

"We're just talking about them," Dakota said. "You need to chill out."

Was it all just talk? I hoped so. But then that wouldn't explain Audrina's concern over Dakota's behavior.

Partway through the class, the girls said they were going to talk to someone and were away from the table for quite a while. When they came back, they seemed louder, their cheeks flushed. I leaned close to Dakota and could smell alcohol on her breath.

"How did you get a drink?" I asked.

"It's really not that hard," she said.

"No more," I threatened. "I'm not kidding."

After the class, the girls insisted on lingering by the Tiki Hut long after the class was over as spectators and families left the show grounds. There was a good crowd of riders and those associated with the riders—owners, significant others, friends—having a drink and rehashing the class. McNair Sutter, who had come in second to the young British phenom, Liam Halliday, was there and the girls spent most of the time giggling and casting sidelong glances McNair's way. There was also a large pack of riders and hangers-on from the State of Qatar, who had been snapping up expensive and experienced European show jumpers right and left of late.

By the time I finally got Dakota to leave, even the crowd at the Tiki Hut had thinned out. It wasn't that late since the class only had forty in it. Still, I was tired and I was missing Chris.

Dakota said her good-byes to her friends. Taylor's mom and Addie's minder came and collected them. Dakota and I walked silently to where we'd parked the golf cart. Only it wasn't there.

My first thought was that we'd forgotten where we'd parked it. But I looked up and confirmed we were in the right place, next to the Oasis Café. This was definitely where we'd parked it.

I turned to Dakota. "Very funny."

She held her hands up. "What do you mean? What are you talking about?"

"Oh, like you didn't have some friend of yours move the golf cart or steal it or something to get me in trouble."

"You're crazy." She took a step backward like she couldn't be near me I was so unstable. "You're certifiable."

"*I'm* certifiable? You've spent the last few weeks trying everything possible to make me mess up so you can tell your parents to fire me. And this one might actually do it. Congratulations!"

"I didn't do anything with the golf cart."

She sounded actually genuine. The most genuine Dakota had ever sounded. Was I losing my mind? Was everything with Chris and MB and now Dakota driving me over the edge?

"So you didn't tell someone to move it?"

"No, it was right here where we left it."

I let out a huge sigh. "This is not good."

The first thing we did was look around in the general vicinity in case by accident someone had drunkenly gotten into our golf cart, driven it a little before noticing it wasn't theirs, and then returned it to the wrong spot. But the grounds were mostly empty and there was no sign of our cart. The next thing I did was text Chris. When I got no answer, I called him. After several rings, it went to voicemail. I couldn't believe he wasn't answering. I needed him to come get us.

I paced the area where our cart should have been, phone in my hand, trying to figure out what to do next. I could call Linda but I'd seem like an incompetent loser. It wasn't that far to Grand Prix Village. We'd walk.

"Okay, let's go," I told Dakota.

"Go where?"

"Back to the barn. We're walking."

She stuck out an ankle in my direction, showing me her very expensive, strappy heels. "Not in these shoes, I'm not."

I paced again. I wanted to make her walk in those heels. She deserved to walk in them and get huge, fat blisters. I could easily walk myself, get the car, and come back and pick her up. But that was being too nice to her.

She must have figured out what I was thinking because before I could give in and tell her I'd go get the car and come back to get her, she said, "But I don't want to wait here alone either. It feels creepy."

It *was* sort of creepy being at the show grounds in the dark now that most everyone had left. The vendors' tents were tightly sealed up and the rings looked vacant.

"Who else can we call then?" I asked. "Call Addie or Taylor."

She gave me a sheepish smile. "My phone's actually dead, and I don't know their numbers."

"Too many selfies?" I said.

"Fine," she snapped. "I'll walk. Let's go."

"Okay," I replied.

I headed off, not moderating my pace to take into account her shoes. She stayed a few steps behind me through the show grounds but once we got onto the sandy path heading over to Grand Prix Village she lagged behind.

Feeling badly for her, I slowed down. "Are you okay?"

"My shoes are going to be completely ruined."

"Which I'm sure you'll tell your mom right away. That and how I lost the golf cart."

Silence. It was dark on the path with only the light of my phone to guide us. I thought we might come across some other people in a golf cart heading back from the grand prix and they might offer us a ride. But we saw no one. Only shadows of bushes and trees. I felt grass against my legs and startled.

"What is it?" Dakota said.

"Nothing. Just grass, I think."

"What if it was a gator?"

There were alligators in the canals and ponds along the grounds. Sometimes you'd see one sunning itself in plain day. But it was unlikely one would come out of the water and brush against my leg. And they weren't large enough to bother people—they stuck to the occasional Jack Russell.

"It felt smooth, not like an alligator would."

"How do you know what an alligator feels like?" Dakota said.

"I'm just guessing. They'd feel scratchy."

"I kind of want to take my shoes off. I'll be able to walk faster," she said.

"No, you better not. All the manure mixed in these paths . . . You could get ringworm or something."

"Gross," she said. "I'm probably getting it anyway. All the sand is getting in between my toes."

"We're almost there."

We made it onto pavement. Up ahead, I saw the barn. Dakota stopped and took off her shoes, emptying out the sand. I waited for her to put them back on and we walked together to the barn and into the house. Inside she took her shoes off again and held them up so I could see. "Trashed," she said. "I might as well just throw them away. Three hundred dollars—down the drain."

"It sucks," I said. I wasn't going to say I was sorry. This was not my fault. And plus I'd seen her closet when I was putting away her new show coats. She had fifteen pairs of designer shoes just like them. "Make sure you wash your feet off well."

"What did you think, I was going to just go to bed without taking a shower?" She gave me one last evil look and turned and walked upstairs.

I tried Chris again. Still went to voicemail. I needed someone to talk to so I called Ryan instead. I told him all about Dakota and her spoiled ridiculousness. He thought it was good for her that she had to walk home in the shoes. "Maybe it'll teach her not to wear slutty shoes," he said.

"Or maybe she's on the phone to her mom right now getting me fired," I said. "A golf cart costs thousands. What if I can't find it?"

Ryan spoke calmly. "If you get fired, you'll get another job. I'm sure they're other people like you who go to Florida with a job all set and then it doesn't work out the way they thought it would."

"You're probably right," I said. "Do you have to be so reasonable? It's like you're fucking fifty years old."

Ryan laughed. "I guess I have always been kind of ahead of my time." It was true. He was very popular in middle school and high school, much more popular than me, but he was always the kid who was so much further ahead of everyone else. He had studying down to a science so he could do the least amount of work and still get As. He threw mind-blowing parties that kids died to get an invite to and somehow managed to get away with charging a cover fee so in the end he came away with pocket money to last until the next party.

We talked about Chris and I told Ryan how he hadn't answered. I didn't tell him my irrational fear that he was with MB who wasn't showing that night either. I complained, "I just feel like he's not there for me."

"He wasn't going to Florida to be there for you," he said soberly. "He was going to build his business and you weren't even supposed to be there. Then, all of a sudden, there you are. You can't expect him to be there for you. Maybe you need to be there for him."

"You're probably right," I said. I thought I'd been trying, being understanding, but maybe I needed to do more. Mary Beth's words about my sex life with Chris resurfaced in my head.

"It's been known to happen." I could picture Ryan smiling on the other end of the phone. Maybe there would come a time that he'd need me for advice, or comfort, or something. So far our relationship had been the other way around—me always needing him.

"Thank, Ry," I said.

"Anytime, H."

Chapter 19

THE GOLF CART HADN'T BEEN found by mid-week and I'd learned that ours wasn't the only one that had been stolen at WEF this year. Apparently golf carts had been disappearing from rings, never to return, as had saddles. Another barn had also been hit by the saddle thief, as he or she was being referred to, and people were speculating that there might be a connection between the ringside and barn thefts. The biggest question, though, was with the barn thefts—how was the thief getting past some of the gates and the locked tack rooms and trunks? Was it an inside job? All around the show, people were hiring locksmiths to install additional locks or they were taking their saddles home for the night.

I called and spoke with Audrina and she was more concerned with how awful we must have felt to have been robbed than with the money she was out. "Is everything okay with Dakota?" she asked tentatively.

"Yup, it's going fine," I said.

I wondered whether Dakota had told her about the ruined

shoes but I guessed not when Audrina said, "Oh, thank God, Hannah, you are a lifesaver."

I wondered how much Dakota spoke or texted with her parents. My guess was not much. Audrina said she'd order a new golf cart. I asked when she and Winston would be coming to visit and she seemed to dance around the subject, throwing out phrases like, "Need to pin down Winston," "Get our calendars aligned," and "Find a workable date."

I found out why Chris hadn't answered his phone Saturday night when Dakota and I needed help. It had all worked out okay for us but it still bothered me that I had needed him and he hadn't been available. He had taken an Ambien and said he must not have heard his phone.

"Since when you do take Ambien?" I asked.

"I just haven't been sleeping well. I needed a good night's sleep."

"Where did you even get it?"

"Jimmy gave me a couple. He said I looked tired and I told him I hadn't been sleeping well."

With Valentine's Day coming up, I decided to ask Linda what salon I should go to for a wax. "Not super expensive, though," I said. "Not the salon of the stars. I'm on a serious budget."

It was true. My job had a decent salary as far as I could tell not having had a job before but life was expensive, especially at the horse show. I always thought I'd run back to the house for lunch but then I never had time and I ended up eating the overpriced food at the show. Too many times Dakota wanted to get take-out and I never wanted her parents to pay for my food too, so I always split the bill and paid my portion.

"What are you getting done? Hair cut, mani/pedi?" Linda asked.

"I need to, um, get a wax. Bikini."

It wasn't like I was wearing a bathing suit anytime soon but Linda must have known I was just taking care of some landscaping issues.

"You don't want to wax. Go get laser." She told me to see Irina at the spa she went to. I thought about asking her if it hurt more than waxing but decided I would sound wimpy. Instead I made an appointment and found myself a few days later in Irina's capable hands. I also found out that it did hurt. That it felt like someone stabbing you with sharp glass repeatedly. But I closed my eyes and held my breath and made it through. Irina asked me if I wanted everything off. "Is that what, I mean, like, most women do?"

"Depend," she said, "On what the boyfriend like. On what you like."

"I don't know what I like," I said. "And I don't know what he likes either." I could hear Mary Beth's voice in my head. "But a Brazilian . . . that's everything, right?"

She smiled. "Yes, all off."

"Okay," I said. "Go for it."

I decided I needed something radical to get Chris and me out of our rut. I felt like he was so busy with his clients that during the day I barely saw him. He'd even picked up two more clients since he'd been at WEF. That was good for him, but not good for us. I was busy too, but I would have found time to hang out if he had time. So much of his time revolved around Lily. Riding her horses, teaching her, walking the courses with her, strategizing and planning the show schedule with her and her father. If Lily weren't homely looking with dull, frizzy hair and a kind of unfortunate ill-proportioned nose, I would have been seriously jealous and worried. But, thankfully, there was nothing attractive about Lily. I'm sure she idolized Chris and fantasized about him but there was no way he was going to be interested in her.

Sadly, at night, Chris was more interested in getting a good night's sleep, a full eight hours, than sex with me, it seemed. Which was why drastic measures had to be taken.

Once the laser was over, it was over. It didn't hurt anymore. More like a dull hum in that general area. I drove straight from Irina's office to the mall to Victoria's Secret where I bought two pairs of skimpy, lacey matching bras and thongs. When I got home, I looked at Irina's work. My skin was only slightly speckled red but she said that would go away in a few hours. Was it sexy? I had no idea. Would Chris think it was sexy? Would he even notice? I took the underwear out of the bag and held it up. At least I'd done something. I'd taken steps to get him interested in me again. Now, I just had to get him alone and put my bag of tricks to work.

* * *

The end of each show day was a wonderful time. It was especially good if the day had gone well. But either way, it had a sort of slow-down charm that reminded me of stories of how people used to sit on their porch in the summer and have a cool drink and maybe read the evening news. The mornings at the show were rushed—racing around to put in orders with the in-gate guys, making sure the right horses were braided and at the show, putting the right bit on the right bridle. There wasn't much time to enjoy the sun rising over the show grounds, unless you found yourself at the ring for an early class with a few moments to appreciate the horse show coming to life. But the late afternoons and evenings were for sitting on a tack trunk or in a chair in the tack room either at the horse show or back at the farm and taking a moment just to breathe as the sun dipped in the sky, casting shadows all around. We'd plan for the next day, make up the white-board, discuss any changes to tack or preparation but there would always be moments to reflect on the day's performances and to gossip a little. Sometimes Linda and I sat on the comfortable wicker furniture on the portico at the farm overlooking the ring as the automatic sprinklers watered the footing. A hawk sailed overhead, perhaps looking for a tasty Jack Russell, and a mourning dove cooed. Rudi and Taffy collapsed at our feet, tired from a day at the barn too—or in the case of Taffy, a day riding shotgun in the golf cart.

Linda would take a beer from the fridge and we'd relax as the temperature in the air went down and the occasional birds flew by. Linda offered me a beer the first few times but now she knew I didn't like beer. (Even though I loved kissing Chris after he'd had a beer—that faint, yeasty taste.) I envied her as she tipped her head back and pulled on the beer. To my mind there seemed like nothing cooler than a woman who liked beer. And Linda wasn't the kind of woman who only liked beer when she was out at a bar so she could keep up with the men.

Watching her drink her beer, I thought about Chris and how I'd first met him at the bar in Vermont. He had been drinking a beer. My stomach pulsed with the knowledge that I still hadn't made my first move toward reinvigorating things between us. The underwear I'd bought still sat in a drawer and he hadn't seen the work of Irina. Valentine's Day had come and gone. We'd gone out to a nice dinner but then I had to go back to stay with Dakota. Chris had parked in the driveway and we'd kissed for a few moments but I'd felt a certain relief in his kisses, like he was grateful I had Dakota to look after and I wasn't coming back to his condo. It was like the complete opposite of how we'd kissed fervently in the car in Vermont. When I whispered in his ear, "I'm sorry this is it for tonight," he said, "Don't worry about it," and it felt like he actually meant it. Like he was happy to go home, take an Ambien, and sleep.

"Did I ruin your romantic little evening?" Dakota said when I came inside.

"No, it was nice."

"No nookie for Chris tonight, though."

Her crass words sent shivers down my spine. Maybe because Chris didn't seem to care about nookie anymore.

"That's just juvenile and uncalled for," I snapped at Dakota, maybe a little too harshly, and went to my room. I hoped there was nothing worse then calling a girl who yearned to be mature juvenile.

Now, sitting with Linda, an idea flashed into my mind. I

had to go over to his barn. Right now. He'd be winding down with Dale. Dale would head home and Chris would be about to. I'd stop him and jump him right there at the farm. In the office. On a tack trunk. My cheeks turned red and I worried that Linda might notice but she was staring out over the ring peacefully.

But the moment the idea took flight in my mind I was already tampering it down. *Don't be ridiculous. Like I could really do any of that. It isn't me. I wouldn't go through with it.* Then, my mind quickly turned to anger at myself. *Why couldn't I do it? I had to do it. I had to do it to save things between Chris and me, and I had to do it now anyway just to prove to myself I had the guts.*

I stood up and told Linda I forgot I needed to bring something over to Chris. I told myself not to think more about it as I drove over to his farm in the golf cart. I was doing it. But what if Dale and Chris were there talking for a while and my resolve weakened? No, it didn't matter. I had to go through with it. I kept reciting in my mind on the drive over: *I will do it. I will do it.* I wasn't even sure what *it* was yet. That part of my plan was unformed.

Dale's car was gone. Chris's was the only one there. It couldn't have been more perfect. My timing was exquisite. He was probably just packing up.

I barely parked the golf cart before I was out of it and on my way into the barn, Jasper by my side. A few horses had their heads over their stall doors but most were munching hay. Arkos saw me and tossed his head like he was saying hello. Chris wasn't in the aisle. I went into the office and found him sitting on a trunk looking at something on his phone.

"Hey," I said.

He startled slightly. "Hi."

"What're you doing?"

"Just looking at a few emails before I head home."

"How was your day?"

Chris shook his head like he didn't really want to go into it.

"You showed Arkos?"

"Yeah. Eight faults." He let out a heaving sigh. "I was talking with Jimmy. He thinks I'm wasting my time. That I should get rid of the horse. Cut my losses. Try to sell him as an eq horse just to get some of my money back. He said if I have Cassidy Rancher show him in the eq a few times some-one'll snap him up just because Cassidy was on him. He's probably right."

I was hearing Chris's words but emotionally I wasn't really processing them because my mind was on what I had come here to do. If I let that out of my sight, I'd surely give up.

I stepped toward Chris. We looked at each other and I could tell he was wondering what the hell I was doing. Why I wasn't responding with words like a normal person would or acknowledging anything about what he'd said. Instead I leaned down to his level and started kissing him. He kissed me back but it was weak, without much intention. I probably should have stopped right there but I had willed myself to keep going, no matter what. It was like riding a horse that might refuse—you had to go to a fence thinking the whole way that you were going to get to the other side. If, for one split second, you thought the horse might waver, it was over.

Chris stood up, I think to try to shake me off. "Hannah—" he said, his voice slightly annoyed but still trying to be delicate. "I don't think now is—"

"Shhh," I said. I kissed him again. I would take his mind off Arkos. I could do this. I put my hand on his chest and smoothed it down to his belt buckle. I started to undo his belt. I would unbuckle it, unzip him, and get down on my knees. I would do what Zoe did to the cowboy in the field at the rodeo. I would do what MB did to Chris in the VIP tent.

"Hannah, no." Chris pushed me away with his elbow. It was gentle, that push, but it reverberated all over my body. He did up his belt.

"Why not? What's wrong with you?" I said. "Aren't you interested in getting a fucking blow job?"

I hated the words as they came out of my mouth. But I was so hurt that he had rejected me. Wouldn't any other guy have loved this? A guy like McNair Sutter? Of course, Chris wasn't any other guy and that was why I'd fallen in love with him in the first place.

"For one thing, what if Lily comes back or her father because she left something here and walks in on us? I can't afford to lose a client like her, or have it be all over Horse-ShowDrama."

"But you let Mary Beth blow you in the spectator tent."

Chris's face blanched. "How the hell did you know that?"

"She told me." I held my hands up. "I didn't exactly ask

her. Believe me, I didn't want to know. But she told me anyway."

Chris's face turned angry. I had only seen angry on him a few times before and it was a little frightening to see such a usually composed person losing it. "I have no idea why you and she are talking about things like that. But regardless, that was when I was 17. I was a junior. I wasn't thinking about clients or my reputation."

"No, I guess you were just thinking about your dick. Which for some reason you don't seem to care about anymore."

"What the hell is going on with you?" Chris said. "I tell you that the horse I thought was something special I'm now going to have to dump for 150K as an eq horse and you're surprised that I'm not really in the mood for sex?"

I shook my head, disgusted with myself.

"I don't get this," Chris said.

"I'm sorry," I said, turning on myself. "I just thought I could take your mind off things. I just thought, I don't know, everything seems so much harder than when we were in Vermont. You're always busy. You're stressed out. I thought coming here would be so much different."

"Yeah, and I told you I didn't think it was such a great idea. Vermont was like this moment of my career where I had to make myself relax a little because I had no international horses and I was at a smaller circuit and that's not what the rest of my life is like. This is my life now and it's kind of stressful."

"So what we had in Vermont wasn't real?" I felt tears

pressing at the back of my eyelids. My breath was getting shallow. "Is that what you're saying?"

"No, Vermont wasn't real. What we had was real and I'm not saying we can't be together. Far from it. But we have to learn to be together in this reality. And it's different."

I nodded. I felt like such a fool. I felt horribly rejected by him, but more than that I felt dumb for not seeing how he needed an adult relationship, not a teen romance. "I'm really sorry," I said. "I don't know what I was thinking. Can we just forget this ever happened?"

"I guess." It didn't seem like he could forget it ever happened, though. He looked even less happy than he had when I'd come into the room and found him. "I guess I'm going home."

"Okay, I should go back to the farm anyway, see what Dakota wants to do for dinner."

Chris nodded. He seemed like he was out of the energy to speak, or out of words to say to me.

Chapter 20

THINGS RETURNED TO SEMI-NORMAL. Chris was busy, I was busy, and I think we both tried to pretend what had happened in his tack room hadn't happened. Anytime I thought of it, I burned with hot-faced shame. I felt no better than Harris's yoga wife who had come on to Chris in the stalls in Vermont.

We had sex Sunday night and it was mechanical, how-to-manual sex. Kiss here, feel there, insert Part A into Part B. After him pushing me away I certainly wasn't going to try any more wild tricks. It felt like something we had to do, not something we wanted to do or, even better, couldn't stop ourselves from doing. It felt like we were both trying to prove to each other that things were fine between us. But we both knew they weren't and the disappointing sex just made it even more obvious.

There was no great reveal of my laser-project. It was kind of by the by when Chris saw me naked after we had finished.

"Wow," he said, his voice tentative.

"Wow, good? Wow, bad?"

He pulled the sheet over us. "I guess just wow, different."

"That doesn't sound wow, good." I felt more shame creeping over me.

"You don't have to be something you aren't," Chris said. "I mean if that's what you want to do . . ."

"No, it killed," I said. "But I thought you would like it."

He ran his hand through his hair. I could see he was thinking how to put this delicately. "I don't know. It's a little dramatic. A little abnormal. I mean you're not an eleven-year-old girl, you're a woman."

My face flushed red. A woman. That wasn't exactly something that should make me blush but it sounded so adult, so mature. I didn't feel like I lived up to it in the bedroom or out of the bedroom with the choices I'd been making lately. "I'm sorry, it was stupid."

"I just don't get what you're doing," he said. "It's like you're trying so hard."

"I know, I *am* trying hard. I thought this winter would be like us spending all this time together and you just seem far away all the time."

"I'm just trying to get my career on track again." He looked sad—maybe that I didn't get it and that he had to keep explaining it to me.

It hit me that I didn't need sexy underwear or new moves in bed. I needed to understand what he was dealing with. I needed to be patient and forgiving. I scooted close to him and put my hand on his shoulders. I massaged his back. His muscles felt tight. "I'm sorry, I've been selfish. I get now more than ever what you're going through and I'm going to be there for you from now on. It's like I can finally see straight and I can see what's important."

He shrugged, moving his shoulders as I squeezed his muscles. Like maybe he didn't quite believe that things would change, or that I could understand what it was like to be him. But I knew they would change. Starting right now I had a new plan. I would stop listening to Mary Beth for Godsakes and start making everything about supporting Chris. I would listen to him tell me about clients and horses. I wouldn't ask him when he was free for dinner or put any other demands on him. I'd cheer him on at the ring. I'd bring him bottles of water and energy bars. Maybe I could help him by running part of his social media campaigns. Or there had to be other things I could do to lighten his load. Take his laundry to the cleaner, pick up Jasper's food. There had to be things I could do and I would do them. By God, I would do them and I would do them well.

* * *

I was in charge of scheduling and supervising all the people who worked on Dakota's horses. As with most A circuit hunter/jumper barns that meant a lot of service providers. If only people got treated as well medically as these horses did. There were the bread-and-butter services like the monthly visit from the farrier and the as-needed vet appointments. Then there was acupuncture, massage, and laser. Some of the treatments we did ourselves. I learned how to use the ultra sound machine to stimulate blood flow and each day every horse went on the vibration platform.

There were different kinds of personalities of the people who worked at this level with the horses and I enjoyed getting to know them and their stories. I found if you hung out with them while they worked on the horses, which I did, they were happy to tell you where they'd come from and how they got into what they were doing. Even the more buttoned-up people also let slip bits of gossip about the other clients they worked for.

Our farrier was the son of a farrier. He had gone into the family business right after high school, never really considering any other profession. He was the quiet serious type, focusing on his craft. At first I'd thought maybe he was mean, or didn't like me or Linda, but I came to learn he was just sort of socially awkward, maybe even on the autism spectrum. He didn't meet your eye when he spoke to you, and when he did say something it often came out of nowhere and it would take me a moment to figure out what he was talking about. He seemed more comfortable with horses than people.

The vet was more of a blowhard, who liked to name-drop. How he'd just been over at this or that Olympian's farm. He bustled in and bustled out with an entourage of assistants, suggesting injections and treatments, and always leaving an inconceivable bill in his wake. His name was Dr. Robb and I'd heard people call him Dr. Rob You Blind behind his back. I wondered if he knew people called him that.

The acupuncturist had been a lawyer in her first life but she had always had a love for animals. After the break-up of her marriage, she became disenchanted with the legal system and had gone back to school for acupuncture. She'd first practiced on people but had then become disenchanted with

people too and, since she always had a love of animals, offered her services at a barn near where she lived. Word spread
about her talents and all it took was working for one high
profile stable to set her on a course of working on the show
circuit. Now she spent her winters in Wellington. She had
never ridden a horse and before showing up at that first barn
she'd never spent any time around horses but she did fine
with them, knowing how to move around them and where
they needed help. She would talk to them in a whispery voice
as she inserted the needles. "I bet that feels good. I know you
hurt there, don't you, sweetie?" The first few times I found it
kind of annoying but I became used to her and sometimes I
almost felt myself relax at the same time that Midway or
Dudley let his head drop and his lip quiver.

Then there was Dede, the masseuse. She was my favorite
because she was a born teacher. She liked to work on the
horses and talk about what she was doing. She didn't just
have me sit there—by my second visit she was showing me
how to find a pressure point and hold it. She taught me how
to do stretches with the horses and not just the lame old
carrot-stretch trick. She taught me about their muscular
system and which muscles were used most in which disci-
plines. She worked on dressage horses and event horses too.
She had grown up riding, but locally, mostly Pony Club stuff.
She was in her early forties and had a daughter in middle
school. Her husband owned a construction company. She was
one of those attractive granola types—the kind that looked
good without make-up or fancy clothes. She wore athletic
tank-tops, loose-fitting cargo shorts, and L.L. Bean boots.

We became friends and I talked to her about how I left

school to be with Chris. I didn't tell her everything that was going on with Chris but she knew a little bit about how I was trying to support him as he rebuilt his business. I catalogued to her what I'd done to be helpful of late—brought him lunch at the show, stocked his fridge, picked up his laundry.

I felt like maybe the things I was doing for Chris were helping. He was appreciative but so far it didn't seem like he was much less stressed. And things between us were still slightly off. Chris had finally gone over to help Mary Beth with her horse, to be there in case he needed to call the ambulance. The hack-a-bit had worked wonders and MB had gone clean in the next class she'd shown in. She'd thrown her arms around Chris when she'd seen him next. The fact that I was with him didn't seem to deter her in the slightest.

"Be careful you don't just do things for him," Dede warned. "You have to take care of you, too." She pressed on Midway's neck. "Ooh, come here," she said to me.

She took my hand and positioned it on Midway's neck. "Now, with measured force," she said.

I hesitated. I swear Midway glanced at me like, *you're doing massage now?*

"You can do it," Dede said.

I pressed and Midway did a funny little sigh-groan. He lowered his head, looking dreamy. I kissed him on the little perfect white spot on his lower lip. I loved to kiss him there. It was like that spot was designed for being kissed. Right then horses felt easier than men.

"You just made his day," Dede said.

"If only I could make Chris so happy," I said.

Chapter 21

THE WINTER CIRCUIT WAS FILLED with charitable social events. Nearly every weekend there was one themed gala or another. The socialite riders and their wealthy parents donned their glittery frocks and turned out in droves for a night of cocktails, dancing, mingling, performances, and live auctions. All the causes were worthy—JustWorld International, Horses Healing Hearts, Polo for a Purpose, The Salvation Tree School etc. But to me it all seemed so tiresome.

Chris wasn't big on the social events either but he said he did need to be conscious of the fact that being seen at charity events raised your public profile, especially if your sexy smile got snapped and blasted out in a post-party press release. Also, it was at events like these that you met and chatted with potential sponsors. You networked and made connections that might just land you your next grand prix horse. Too many charity events and you became a social-slut—you had to pick and choose the right ones and make sure to present yourself well and never get sloppy drunk, which apparently was a problem for plenty of people at these events.

Chris had chosen two events to attend this season. The first was the Great Charity Challenge, which was a participatory event for him because riders competed on teams to raise money for a chosen charity. It was also fun because the riders dressed up in costume. Some riders took it really seriously and outfitted their horse too. I was fine with the idea of Chris doing the Charity Challenge. In fact, I thought it would be fun. Until I found out he was on the same team with Mary Beth.

"She put together the team, I didn't have anything to do with it," he told me preemptively because I'm sure he knew I wasn't going to be happy.

"That sounds great," I said, keeping my jealousy from bubbling up. It wasn't that I didn't feel jealous. I did. Super jealous. But the new me was supporting Chris. I was all about his career. I wasn't going to let him see how petty I really felt inside.

"Do you mean that?"

"Yes, this is good for your image. There'll be pictures in *The Chronicle* and all over. It's important."

And there were pictures in *The Chronicle* and all over. And it probably was great for Chris's image. But the night nearly killed me. To begin with, he hadn't told me that he and Mary Beth were dressing up in coordinated costumes. The theme of the night was superheroes. Mary Beth prepared this whole Batman costume for Chris and a Catwoman costume for her. I had to Google it to be sure, but yes, Batman and Catwoman were hot for each other. Chris asked me if he could ride Logan and, of course, I said yes. Logan looked great. He had a black saddle pad with a Batman logo on it, and a specially designed black hood that had the logo on it too. Mary Beth's Catwoman suit was skin tight and sexy, even on horseback. Lily was the third person on their team. She was dressed in a cute Batgirl costume. Now, couldn't Mary Beth have been the asexual Batgirl and Lily have been Catwoman instead?

I watched the class from the spectator tent, smiling at people around me and concurring with them how great Chris's and Mary Beth's costumes were and how yes, Mary Beth was a doll for getting the whole thing organized in support of the Helping Hands Assistance Program. Their team didn't win the grand prize but they did raise a fair chunk of change for Helping Hands. What a feel good night! Only, I didn't feel good at all.

Mary Beth and Chris came up to the tent after the class and posed for more pictures. They had drinks and chatted with sponsors of the class. My face muscles hurt so much from fake-smiling. But I couldn't let on how I really felt, least of all to Chris.

If the Charity Challenge wasn't enough, a week later there was the EQUUS event that Chris and Mary Beth were co-chairs of. EQUUS was a great umbrella organization that awarded grants to horse charities ranging from therapeutic riding programs to thoroughbred rescues to riding camps for impoverished inner city kids. I couldn't blame Chris for accepting to be a co-chair because it was such a great organization but I wanted things that kept him and MB apart, not brought them together.

"She asked me last year and I said yes and honestly I had

forgotten all about it until a few months ago and I couldn't back out."

"I totally understand," I said. "This is something you need to do."

This event felt a little better because at least I would be going as Chris's date. On a Monday, Linda went with me to the mall and I bought a very pretty dress and shoes at Nordstrom. Together they cost a week's salary but I didn't care. I had to look amazing at this event. More than anything, I had to look better than Mary Beth.

The day of the gala started out like any other. Put in the orders, get the horses to the ring, deal with Dakota's moods. Linda had said I could go home early to get dressed—she knew how important this night was to me. I left around 4:00 and started my preparations. Shower, blow-out my hair, actually apply make-up. Then put on my dress and the heels I bought. Linda had loaned me a clutch she bought at Skiffington's Boutique at the show.

I twirled in front of the mirror, waiting for Chris to come pick me up. I had to admit I looked good. I loved the dress I'd bought. It was a mesh, beaded fabric in a metallic gray color. The beads were frosty and sparkled a little and then the fitted waist tapered to a wispy, flared floor-length skirt. It was tasteful and a little sexy with a small opening in the back and a see-through part above my chest. I was ready.

I'd never seen Chris in a suit, let alone a tuxedo. Wow. He looked amazing. I hadn't gone to my senior prom and this felt like my chance to go back in time. If I had gone to the prom, I'd never have gone with someone so stunning. He didn't hand me a corsage, of course, but that was fine. He did tell me I looked beautiful.

"You look amazing too. Did you rent the tux?"

"I own it. Comes out a few times a year."

Of course. This was the life Chris led. I wondered how many times he'd put on this very same tuxedo and picked up Mary Beth instead of me. I tried to stop my mind from doing the whole jealous thing. What did it matter what parties he went to before we were dating? Only when it came to Mary Beth, it all mattered.

"Who's Mary Beth going with?" I asked.

"Andres."

"But he's gay, right?"

"Yeah, it's not a date, clearly."

Damn. Couldn't Mary Beth move on and find herself another man? No, apparently she had to do the bring-your-gay-BFF-to-the-party thing. Keeping her options open, surely.

The tent was beautifully decorated in the theme of farm-to-table dining. Each table was numbered with a rustic chalkboard and had votives in large ball jars. The center-pieces were a mixture of whimsical wildflowers. There were a lot of faces I didn't recognize. I guess they were mostly the older people who could afford the two hundred dollar ticket. I did recognize the wealthy, socialite mother of a former junior rider who had won everything a few years earlier, including the Maclay Finals. The mother must have had plastic surgery—I knew it was her, but her face looked distorted and off-kilter.

We arrived before Mary Beth and were enjoying our-selves, eating the delicious passed hors d'oeuvres of watermelon and chevre bites and tiny lobster clubs. It was one of the first times Chris and I had gone out together in a while and it felt good to be out of our barn clothes. Maybe this was just what we needed. He introduced me to a bunch of people as his girlfriend and that made me feel floaty. He also was introduced to several couples and each time I was pretty impressed by how good Chris was at making smooth, congenial small talk. People asked about the horses he had and he made them seem exciting and at the same time hinted that he needed to build up his string. With each wealthy couple he talked to, I could feel him hoping that somehow something he'd say would strike a nerve with them. That they'd be charmed by his manners and his determination and ask him more about his plans to buy an Olympic caliber horse. One older gentleman did give Chris his card, suggesting they meet for lunch sometime. "I'd love to hear more about your plans," he said.

When we had turned away, Chris said, "Do you realize who that was?"

I shook my head.

"Harborview Investments? James Carp?"

I was still drawing a blank.

"Ask your dad. He'll know. James Carp is one of the wealthiest men in the country."

"So he could totally buy you a number one horse."

"He could buy me five number one horses."

"Does he own horses, or have a granddaughter who rides or something?"

"No. His wife is very involved with the charity so they came tonight."

"Sounds promising," I said. "You're going to call him, right?"

"Oh my God, yeah." Chris was smiling more than I'd seen him in a while. And it was contagious.

I'd seen Mary Beth come in with Andres but they hadn't said hello to us yet. Andres was wearing a blue tuxedo with a shiny collar. On anyone else it might have looked ridiculous, but he was pulling it off. Mary Beth was wearing a coral colored halter gown with a jeweled collar. The two pieces of fabric that covered her fairly significant breasts crisscrossed at the collar while creating a peek-a-boo hole between her breasts. If I had been wearing said dress I would have been clawing constantly at my chest to make sure the fabric hadn't shifted, revealing a loose boob. But Mary Beth seemed utterly confident in her dress and herself as she and Andres made their way over, causing a few heads to turn as they did. Some of those heads might have been men ogling Andres, but still.

MB leaned close and kissed me on the cheek first, then Chris—thankfully on the cheek too, although I noticed she kissed him awfully close to his lips. She smelled wonderful. "What are you all smiling about?" she said.

"Chris just met a potential sponsor," I blurted.

"Oh, who knows." Chris's smile disappeared and I realized I shouldn't have said anything.

"Really? Who?" Mary Beth said.

"If it was James Carp, don't get excited," Andres said. "He loves getting people all hot and bothered, having them drool all over him, and then never gives a cent away. Perpetual blue-baller."

I wasn't going to speak up again and risk saying the wrong thing. I wasn't sure if we should admit to it being James or just brush it off.

"Whatever," Chris said. "It doesn't matter who it was."

"Your dress is gorgeous," I told Mary Beth. "Where did you get it?"

"This? Thank you," she said nonchalantly. "Oh, just foraged in my closet."

A photographer appeared and asked us to stand together. First the four of us and then Mary Beth and Chris alone. Andres and I stood back and watched as the woman took the photo. Chris was trying to smile but I could tell his hopes had been sunk a notch over James Carp. When I got him alone again, I said, "Andres might not be right. What does he know?"

"He knows everything," Chris said glumly.

"Well, maybe this time James Carp will come through. You should still have lunch with him, don't you think?"

"Probably not. Waste of time."

"You can't think like that. You have to stay positive . . . follow every lead."

"How do you know what you have to do?" Chris said. "I'm sick of following every lead. None of them are working out."

"That's not true. The Tellers have pledged."

"It's not nearly enough."

"But you'll get there, I'm sure you will."

Chris looked straight at me. "Hannah, your optimism is kind of killing me right now. Can we just grin and bear it, and get through this stupid evening?"

His response took the wind out of me. I had bought a four hundred dollar dress for this stupid evening, and I didn't look nearly as good as Mary Beth in what she'd apparently pulled out of her closet, if that was to be believed. I knew it wasn't Chris's fault that he felt down about his prospects but I wanted this one night at least to feel like it could be happy for us. I had been trying so hard. This was my prom make-up.

Feeling teary, I excused myself and went to the bathroom. For distraction, I took out my phone and was nearly pleased to see four texts from Linda, until I read them.

Tizz got cast.

Trying to get him out.

Sorry to interrupt your party but I'm freaking out.

Got him down but it's not good.

I stepped outside the tent and called her. I was in first responder mode now and it was a relief not to think about how the night was turning out. "How is he?"

"It's not good at all. He seems to have really hurt his back."

"Shit."

"Yeah. I'm sure he's out for a while. Dr. Robb stabilized him and gave him some meds to make him comfortable. Tomorrow we'll get X-rays and see what's what."

"Do you want me to come over there?"

"No, you're at the party. You should enjoy yourself."

"It's not been that great so far."

"Really, why not?"

I thought about unloading on Linda but it didn't seem like the time for either of us. "I'll tell you later. I guess I should get back."

"Okay, see you tomorrow."

At first I couldn't find Chris when I came back into the tent, having steeled myself to pull it together. I spotted Andres, who looked like he was flirting with an older gentleman. Maybe Chris wasn't the only person at this party hunting for a sponsor. Finally, I saw Chris with Mary Beth. Chris didn't look glum anymore. Quite the opposite. He was throwing his head back as he laughed in that way I had fallen in love with in Vermont. I wasn't loving it so much now since it was Mary Beth that was making him laugh. She was laughing too, holding her drink out to keep it from spilling she was guffawing so hard. I strode over to them and linked my arm through Chris's. It was very un-me, showy and possessive but I'd had enough.

"You were gone a while," Chris said.

"I had a bunch of texts from Linda and then I stepped outside and called her. Dakota's best jumper got cast and Linda thinks he's really hurt."

"Well, they certainly have enough money to get a replacement," Mary Beth remarked.

"Still, the horse is hurt."

"You're right," Mary Beth said, quickly correcting herself. It was like she had let her real, harsher self slip out for a moment and then caught herself.

I hated when people talked about horses "breaking" as in, "Oh, my jumper's broke so I had to go shopping in Europe for another." These were animals, not cars. Who knew what would happen to Tizz if he didn't recover enough to be a jumper again. Maybe Dakota's parents would retire him to some nice farm down South—they certainly could afford to.

But more likely he'd be passed on to someone else and passed on again and might end up at a not-so-nice barn getting poor care.

"What was making you guys laugh so much?" I asked them.

"We were remembering the first Nations Cup we ever showed in," Mary Beth said.

I raised my eyebrows at Chris. "Well, I want to hear about it."

"It's not really that funny," he said.

"I'll tell the story," Mary Beth said. "And it is funny. Okay, so we're in Bratislava. I think we were both nineteen, right?"

Chris nodded, looking uncomfortable with how this whole thing was going down. I hated that the story was all about them. Surely it would be about how they were such babies back at age nineteen—the age I was now.

"We're so excited to be riding for the U.S., we're out of our minds. It's our first time wearing our pinque coats. We have our white breeches on. We're thinking we look so good and we're the Americans and we're gonna kill it. I'm the lead-off rider so I go first and I trot into the ring thinking I am the total bomb. Chris is watching from the in-gate. Well, my horse stops at the second jump and I go flying. It's a grass ring and it rained the day before so the grass is still kind of moist and my white breeches are now brown-green. Disgusting. I limp out of the ring feeling like such a loser. Then Chris goes in and his horse stops at the third jump and he goes flying off and we now have matching brown-green breeches."

Mary Beth giggled and glanced sideways at Chris. "It wasn't really funny at the time. At the time we were pretty mortified but it got funnier over the years."

"That *is* so funny," I said, which is what someone says instead of laughing when something really isn't funny. Maybe it was funny. I couldn't have an objective perspective on it because I was so rattled by their shared history.

Chris added, "We both went clean in the second round though."

"And you won the grand prix that weekend," Mary Beth said.

"And you were second."

"So it wasn't really too bad for a first European outing."

I wanted to vomit at their cute patter.

"And we went out to a pub that night and drank with the Irish team and the Dutch team and got totally wasted," Mary Beth said.

I looked askance at Chris. "*You* got totally wasted?"

"That was a long time ago. Back then I didn't worry so much about, I don't know, about everything, I guess."

"I wish I had known you back then," I griped. It was mean-spirited and airing our dirty laundry in front of Mary Beth. I felt yucky after I'd said it.

"It was easier back then, wasn't it?" she said, as if I hadn't even spoken. "I mean we were just so happy to be riding for the team. We were on cloud nine about it. We weren't necessarily thinking about the World Cup or the Olympics. I mean, sure, if we made it, great, but it wasn't like that was all there was."

"Yeah, it was different, that's for sure. I wasn't worried about my business. I kind of just thought it would all work out. I'd ride well, sponsors would find me, and buy me horses. I guess I was naïve back then."

"I'm not sure you were naïve," she said. "We just didn't know the business enough. That comes with experience."

Chris turned somber again but it was different from before because Mary Beth shared the sentiment. They were on the same wavelength. They understood each other in a way I worried I could never understand Chris. Although, I wasn't sure exactly how Mary Beth understood it all so well since she had her parents' money to fund her career.

He continued, "Veteran riders talked to me about how owners were fickle and horses got hurt and one moment you were the top in the sport and then you had nothing to ride. But I never really believed that would be me. I thought somehow it would be different for me. I'd keep my horses sound. I'd keep my owners happy . . ." Chris trailed off.

A few tables over a handful of people burst out laughing as if it were designed on cue to make our group feel worse.

"Whenever I want a laugh I close my eyes and imagine our breeches that day," Mary Beth said. "Cheer up. You're a great rider. You have some promising horses. Your luck will change. You're acting like you're fifty and your career is dead."

I waited for Chris's response. I certainly had never dared say basically the equivalent of 'buck up' to him before and when I'd tried to be generally positive earlier in the night he'd shut me down.

"Thanks," Chris said, and he sounded genuine. "You made me think about when I loved this sport whole-heartedly and I needed that tonight."

Mary Beth held up her drink. "To many more Nations Cups and keeping our breeches clean!"

Chris raised his glass and I did too, even though it felt like the toast was more about them than me.

Chapter 22

ARKOS WAS ON THE CROSS TIES with ice-boots on. He'd just come from the show where he'd put in yet another poor performance in a 1.40 meter class. I'd come over to Chris's to visit Logan. Sometimes when I had a little free time, I came over to groom him or watch him in the paddock. A few times I'd come and flatted him when Chris had really busy days.

Eduardo had gone into the tack room and I was fussing around with Arkos. He was such a beautiful horse and sweet, too. It didn't seem fair that pretty soon it could be the end of the line for him. Well, to be honest, maybe his life would be better as an equitation horse. He wouldn't have to jump nearly as high, but then again he'd probably be drilled over three-six constantly. Either way would have its plusses and minuses. One thing was for sure, Arkos was lucky he was in Chris's barn. In another stable, he would probably have been coerced into being careful. Chris had used bamboo a few times with him but bamboo used correctly wasn't cruel, he told me. I had watched him school Arkos once using a bamboo offset and from what I saw I had to agree with him. But another trainer would have poled Arkos relentlessly, used capsaicin to make his skin sensitive, tried bell boots with carpet tacks sewed into them, and God knows what else. Chris wouldn't do any of those things.

I wished I could peek into Arkos's mind and see what he was feeling and thinking. Did he want to be a show jumper? Some people believed that horses didn't think about these things—but I believed that the best horses actually wanted to win. That they knew when it was a big night and a big class and they tried their hardest to leave the jumps up. That it wasn't just self-preservation when being thrown at a huge obstacle; that they knew on some level what clearing all the jumps meant. I'd even seen horses that seemed to be smart enough to know how much they could touch a jump and still leave it up. They were the horse-equivalent of the student who learns how to skim a book and still pull off an A paper.

Arkos had an intelligent eye. He seemed like he'd be one of the smart ones. So why was he knocking the jumps down? The only answer was that he was playing hurt but again and again the tests had come back negative.

I ran my hand across his neck, feeling the muscles underneath. He got acupuncture, massage, all kinds of treatments by experienced professionals. There was no way I could find something that they had missed. But I couldn't help myself from trying. I worked from his poll to his withers, using my fingers pressed together and leaning in at times to get the right amount of pressure. Arkos curled his head toward me and gave me a pleased look like he was saying, *I didn't know I was on the schedule for a massage today.* Some horses were less enthusiastic about being massaged but even the nastiest ones usually came around to enjoying it when they realized how good it felt.

I detected the usual knots and sore spots but nothing out of the ordinary. No Ah-ha moment. It didn't help that I had no idea what I was looking to find.

I gave up on his neck and worked around his poll. I used my thumb this time to palpate the areas behind his ears like Dede had shown me. He lowered his head happily but then when I moved to the spot right behind his eye it must have hurt because he jerked his head up, nearly smashing my nose in the process.

I withdrew my hand. "Did that hurt?" I ran my thumb on the same spot. Again, he jerked away. This time I was prepared and drew back so I wouldn't get hit. I took him off the cross ties and put a lead rope on him so he wouldn't end up breaking the cross ties. Once more time I pressed the same spot. This time he shook his head like he was trying to get me to go away. I tried the same spot on the other side. He flinched but it wasn't as bad.

Eduardo came out of the tack room and I put Arkos back on the cross ties for him. I patted his neck and told Eduardo I was just giving him a little massage.

As he took off the ice-boots, I sat down on a tack trunk and texted Dede. *What does it mean if a horse is really sore in the spot between eyeball and ear?*

How sore?

Whip head back and try to run sore.

Don't see that very often. But could be TMJ.

Like the jaw clenching thing?

Yup.

Horses can get that?

Yes. Teeth floated regularly?

I was sure Chris's horses had their teeth floated on schedule but I would certainly check.

I decided Chris wouldn't mind if I asked Dede to see Arkos in person. *Could you come look at him? He's at Chris's barn.*

Maybe later today. At the end of the day.

That would be amazing. That would give me time also to mention it to Chris.

Chris had stayed at the show with Lily so I decided to wait at the farm till he came back. I Googled TMJ and TMJ in horses. Of course Dede was right. It was a legitimate thing. I read that it was often hard to know what caused it in the first place but actually having the equine dentist come and use the oral speculum could exacerbate it and so could something as simple as eating a hard treat like a big carrot. I thought about the steroidal carrots that most farms had delivered from the landscapers in industrial size thick plastic bags.

When Chris came back, I explained how I'd been messing around with the limited massage techniques Dede had taught me and discovered that Arkos was really sore between his eye and ear, especially on the right side.

"When was the last time he had his teeth done?" I asked.

"Before circuit." Chris was looking at me like I was crazy and like he didn't have time for quackery.

"I know it sounds wacky that I'd find something that

might be wrong with him. But what if this is actually something? What if this is making him have all those rails? Dede thinks he could have TMJ."

"Like the thing people get from grinding their teeth?"

"Yeah, but that makes it sound like it's nothing. It can cause headaches and a lot of pain, even in horses." I motioned to my phone. "I've been researching."

"I don't know, Hannah. I'm not sure the reason why Arkos can't jump clean is because he grinds his teeth."

"He doesn't grind his teeth. It's not that. Well, just, I know it sounds crazy but you're about to give up on him and sell him as an eq horse so why not let me explore this one last crazy thing? Is it okay if Dede comes and checks him out later today?"

Chris looked up at the sky like he was so tired of everything. Of Arkos, of not having a top horse, of not having a good sponsor, of working hard every day and it not paying off for shit. "Sure, whatever."

Sure, whatever was a very un-Chris response. It told me all that I needed to know about his mental state.

"I've got Cassidy Rancher coming to ride him at the end of the week to see if she'd be willing to show him in the eq so go nuts. You've got till then to work wonders."

I wasn't sure I could work wonders but I wanted to at least try. "How did Lily do?"

"Double clean," Chris said. I knew he was happy for her and it was good for him as a trainer too, but I could tell it also chipped away at him a little to see someone with a fraction of his talent excelling because of her horses.

* * *

Dede texted me at the end of the day as promised and I met her back over at Chris's. Chris was at a wine and cheese party one of his sponsors, Equifit, was having. I wondered if they sponsored Mary Beth and whether she was at the party too.

I went to pull out Arkos and she said it would be better to look at him in his stall since he'd feel more comfortable there. She didn't go straight for the possible tender spot but instead worked around his body, getting him to trust her and relax. I stood there the whole time on pins and needles, my stomach churning, hoping what I'd found was something real. But even if it was TMJ, like Chris said, it didn't mean it was going to make him suddenly never touch a rail again.

She felt his poll and under his throat latch, then delicately palpated the area behind his eye. I'd learned it was in fact the joint where the jaw bones connected. Arkos shook his head hard.

"Okay, buddy," she said calmly. "Let's try again."

She tried again and he shook his head. She pressed harder and he threw his head up like he'd done for me. The other side wasn't as bad. I was proud that she was finding the same things I had.

"Good job, Hannah." Dede turned to me.

"I'm right?"

"Definitely. No question about it. This horse has got a bad case of TMJ."

"Chris said he was floated before circuit."

"So it's probably not the teeth that are the problem. We might never know what the problem is but the horse is clearly very sore and probably has been for a long time." She looked around the stall. "Chris doesn't use hay nets, does he?"

"No."

"How much turnout does Arkos get? Does he go out on grass?"

"He gets an hour or two a day. It's on grass. How do those things factor in?"

"Eating out of a hay net is unnatural for a horse. It can worsen TMJ. Grazing is good for them. Stress can be a factor too. Just the stress of showing can cause it. Maybe this guy is a sensitive soul?" She patted him on the neck and Arkos looked a little worried at us again like he might be poked and prodded some more.

"There's a lot we don't know about horses, like about whether they get headaches and about their vision. I think what we now know about ulcers and how they affect horses' performances, we're going to someday know the same kinds of things about headaches and how they affect performance horses."

"So what do we do now?"

"I can work on some pressure points that can help relieve some of the pain. I'm sure Chris's regular masseuse can too. Who does he use?"

"Riley Kagan."

"Riley can certainly do it too. I'd also call the vet and have him inject the area."

"Inject him behind his eye like that?"

"It's a joint like any other and it'll bring him a lot of relief."

"I don't know if Chris is going to go for that."

"That's something I can't speak to. But I can do a little bit now with him if you want?"

"That would be great."

I watched Dede work on Arkos. Of course I expected her to be rubbing and kneading his head area, especially around the TMJ joint, but that proved how little I knew. Instead she worked on five different pressure points all over his body that were tied to TMJ. Those pressure points included two on his front legs, one on his chest, one on his poll, and finally, one just beneath the center of his eye. She explained how each tied in somehow, relieving the pain.

I thanked Dede profusely. I was so happy I'd found something that might be the key to Arkos's success but I was wary too. What if this proved to be minor and wasn't some great watershed moment? I thought of Cassidy coming by the end of the week. Well, it was worth a try to get Chris to approve an injection.

"Are you not showing Arkos anymore?" I asked him later. "I mean since Cassidy's coming."

"No, not necessarily. I thought I'd just see how she rides him. See whether it might even work. I was still planning on showing him in the Speed Challenge on Friday but I guess at some point I do need to stop throwing entry fees away on him."

"Can we give him the injection and just see whether it makes a difference?"

Chris rubbed his jaw.

"Please?" I said.

"Sure, why not."

Chapter 23

Dr. Robb examined Arkos and agreed with Dede's diagnosis that he could have a severe case of TMJ. He injected the joint and said we'd have to see if there was any improvement. When Chris flatted Arkos, he said he felt pretty much like usual. Same for jumping him at home.

The entire week 8 was freezing at WEF, with temperatures dipping into the 30s at night and only reaching the high 40s during the day. People posted endless Instagram shots of the thermometer in their cars. At the show, everyone bundled up in down jackets, hats, scarves, and gloves and still shivered all day. Horses and dogs wore heavy blankets. Back at home in Boston, high 40s would have been fairly warm so Mom and I texted back and forth, comparing temps.

Don't complain! It's 23 here!

I know but we're not used to the cold. This is Florida!

On Thursday, Logan won the $2,000 1.30 meter class, which had seventy horses in it. I couldn't believe my once-crazy horse had beaten out seventy horses, including many ridden by the top professionals. Chris had given me the blue ribbon and I had hung it on the mirror in my room at Dakota's. Of course I'd also texted both my dad and my mom to tell them.

On Friday, Chris did Arkos in the Speed Challenge in the DeNemethy. Linda came with me to watch. She'd been following the whole saga and was interested to see what would happen.

We stood on the little hill sloping down from the VIP tent, crossing our arms for warmth. I had borrowed some clothes from Linda because I hadn't brought nearly enough warm stuff. I felt more nervous than I could ever remember. If Arkos went just the same, I'd feel like a fool who had gotten Chris's hopes up and wasted his money. Of course if Arkos went well, it didn't exactly prove anything monumental either. It would take more than one clear go to declare success.

"Breathe in and out," Linda said, noticing my clenched fists. "Christ, you're worse than a kid their first time in short stirrup."

Linda tried to distract me by telling me how the Pearces wanted her to find a replacement for Tizz as soon as possible and had given her a generous budget to work with. Tizz had sustained two fractures of his spine. He'd be sent back to the barn where the Pearces had their horses in Westchester to turn-out and rehab with hope, but no guarantee, that he would show again.

Chris entered the ring. I studied Arkos, searching for some slight difference in his gait or how he held his head. I couldn't find anything. He looked the same as he always did, impressive. But would he leave the jumps up?

He jumped high over the first fence, an oxer. The sides of

the ring were pretty empty. A few riders watched before their turn in the order. A man sat further down the long side talking loudly on his cell phone, complaining about how cold it was. Then I heard him mention something about the saddle thief and how everyone at the show was on edge. It was true. The thief had recently broken into another barn's tack room and now Linda had been making double sure to lock our doors.

Arkos cleared the next four jumps easily. "He looks like he's really jumping high, don't you think?" I asked Linda.

"He definitely looks good."

Chris turned to the double combination, oxer-vertical. He was a little deep into the oxer as far as I could tell and Arkos had no problem making the distance work. He always jumped in good form with his front knees and his ears were pricked straight ahead. He came around the corner by where we were standing and I swear I saw something in Arkos's eye. Like he was finally comfortable and able to perform like he'd always wanted to. Then I began to think I was crazy. Could a horse really look like he was feeling great, or was it all just about projecting my own hopes onto an animal?

He finished the course clear. Chris hadn't gone all out for speed but he'd been efficient and the announcer said he was in third place.

"Come on," I said to Linda, as I hurried to the in-gate.

I could tell Chris was trying desperately not to read too much into Arkos's performance. Arkos had gone clean before. He'd shown promise many times. But he'd never quite jumped like he just had.

"He looked great!" I said.

Dale moved in to take Arkos as Chris slid off him.

"He felt really good," Chris said.

I opened my mouth but Chris added, "No, no. Don't say anything more. Let's just leave it at that." He was serious but he was smiling too.

"Okay," I said. "You're right."

* * *

So we left it at that for a while and Arkos turned in clear round after clear round. It became our go-to line. Chris would come out of the ring and we'd look at each other and one of us would say, "Let's just leave it at that." When I couldn't be there to watch Arkos go in the 1.45 FEI Class because Dakota was trying a possible Tizmo replacement, Chris texted me, *Let's just leave it at that*, and I knew he'd gone clear.

After several clears, Chris did admit that he owed me big-time. "I don't want to jinx it or talk too much about it," he said. "But what you did with Arkos, how you figured out—"

I cut him off. "Shh! I thought we were leaving it at that."

"We are, but I feel like I just have to say something. I want to say thanks."

"It could have very well turned out the complete opposite."

"But it didn't. And even if it had, I hope I would have been able to see that you were trying to help me and think about why he wasn't going well and I hope I would have been grateful for that anyway."

"So I know we're not talking about it but what's next for him now?"

"I think I'm going to go crazy and jump him in the grand prix Saturday."

"Under the lights?"

"Yeah. Trial by fire. But I think he's up to it. It's never been about the courses or bravery or rideability or anything with him. It's just been about not leaving the jumps up."

It was what Chris had wanted all circuit—a chance to ride in the big class of the week. I was nearly giddy with the idea.

"I was thinking about seeing if my dad might want to come visit," I said. "Maybe that would be a good class to invite him to come watch."

I'd also been secretly hoping Chris would have a horse to show in a really big class so I could invite my dad. He might be so impressed with Chris that he'd consider investing in a horse for him. Or, at the very least, continue to support Logan. The grand prix this week wasn't exactly the half-million dollar CSI-5 that Chris was capable of riding in if he had the right horse, but it was still a big deal.

"Sure," Chris said. "I'd like to meet him in person."

I called my dad later that day and proposed the idea. It was a little bit last minute but sometimes last minute was better for Dad. Too far ahead and he got squirrelly about making plans in case something came up. He didn't care about the expense of last minute airline tickets. He was silent for a moment, which would have made most people think the phone had cut out, but I knew it meant he was thinking seriously about my idea. "I'll have Amanda check into flights," he said, meaning his assistant.

"Do you think Monica will come?" I didn't mind Dad's second wife. She was smart and pretty and nice. I didn't have the whole hated-step-mother thing going with her.

"I'll see," Dad said.

Dad texted me later that day to tell me that Monica had to be at a conference and couldn't come but that he'd invited Ryan and he was going to come. I immediately texted Ryan: *Yeah!!!!!*

Thanks for inviting me yourself, he wrote back.

I never thought you'd be able to take time out from your ultra busy life out there to come visit little old me.

Well, you're in luck cause I'm coming and I'm checking out this Chris guy to make sure he's good enough for you.

I'll warn him to be on his best behavior.

I was so excited to have my dad and Ryan coming. Well, most of all, Ryan. All week leading up to it I found myself smiling when I thought about them coming. I asked Linda and she said I could have three tickets to the VIP tent so Dad and Ryan could watch the class from there. Both of them had been to their share of fancy events. Dad constantly was being hosted by various companies at big-time sports events like the Masters or the MLB All Star Game. There were pre-parties and post-parties that were most likely more over-the-top glamorous than being in the tent at WEF but I had to hope that they'd be taken by the sheer power and grace of the horses and riders flying over five-foot fences.

Chris took me to the FEI Security office on Monday to get my photo taken so I could have my very own FEI pass. It was a simple plastic ID badge but it was the single most elite pass you could have at WEF. There were endless passes to be had—parking passes, passes to the VIP tent. But all those could be purchased by any old yahoo with money. The FEI pass, however, signified that you were either an FEI rider or one of the people most important to an FEI rider. Chris had an FEI pass for several of the weeks as Lily's coach and when he'd shown her horses, but this was the first time he was competing for himself. Chris explained that every FEI rider was given one pass for themselves, one for a companion (that was me), two for grooms, and two for owners. Wearing an FEI pass on a lanyard around your neck (backwards if you were really cool) screamed exclusivity to the rest of the horse show. Of course, I loved having mine. It was like a visible badge that said I was Chris's girlfriend.

The pass allowed you entrance to the FEI stabling tent, which was a temporary tent like the ones in Vermont. If your horse was going in an FEI class, it had to be in the tent from Tuesday after the jog till it was done showing in FEI classes. Depending on the week and how the horse did, this could mean Friday after the WEF class, or Saturday night after the grand prix.

Behind the tent, in the fenced-in FEI enclosure, was a schooling ring. It was the only place FEI horses could be ridden except for when they went up to the ring for their classes. Some of the European riders who didn't want to have their horses go through the mandatory three weeks of quarantine upon coming into the U.S. could have them stay in the FEI tent the whole time they were in the country. But that meant no turn-out, barely anywhere to hand walk, and maybe two small patches of grass to graze on, for however many weeks they were at WEF. It also meant certain scheduled times for treatments like injections of Legend or Adequan, which had to be done by a vet—and the official horse show vet also had to consent to additional treatments like massage or acupuncture.

The security was serious and I had to show my badge as I followed Chris in to see Arkos in the tent on Tuesday.

"How do you get carrots in?" I asked.

"Carrots are okay."

"How do people know they're not laced with NSAIDs?"

"I guess they could be, but they'd show up on the drug tests."

Arkos was looking over his stall door. "Hey," Chris said to him.

After scratching Arkos's neck for a little bit the way he liked it, Chris went out back to see how busy the schooling ring was. There were a lot of horses in the tent this early in the week for the WEF class.

I opened Chris's trunk to look for a treat to feed Arkos. I startled slightly when a man said in a heavy European accent, "Christopher around?"

Standing in front of me was Roger Berhardt, one of the most famous riders and trainers in the entire world. It took me a moment to answer him.

"He'll be right back," I finally said. "He went to check out the ring—see how busy it was."

I'd only ever seen photos of Roger Berhardt. Photos of him winning the World Cup Final and the Gold at the Olympics. During the past five years he'd been doing more training than riding—especially catering to young, wealthy American riders who spent months training and competing out of his farm in Belgium.

I sighted Chris coming back down the aisle.

"Christopher," Roger said. "I was just asking your groom where you were."

I shuddered. Apparently my FEI pass did not scream 'girl-friend' at all. Did one look at me say groom? Jeans, sneakers, T-shirt with a slobber stain from Midway when I'd gone to fix his magnetic blanket, baseball hat. I guess my attire did scream groom. I didn't really care so much that Roger thought I was Chris's groom but did it matter to Chris that I didn't look like girlfriend-material? That I wasn't one of those willowy women in animal-print tops and high-heels I'd seen on the arms of other grand prix riders? It seemed to me that the straight grand prix riders had one of two types of girl-friends or wives. Either the aforementioned beautiful arm-candy type, or the fellow-rider girlfriend in Animo breeches and Parlanti boots.

As if on cue with the thoughts in my mind, Mary Beth appeared in the aisle. I wondered if Roger knew her.

"Mary Beth," Roger said in his funny accent.

She threw her arms around him and kissed one cheek and then the other. She even knew the European customs. "Roger, so good to see you." She didn't say his name like I had been saying it in my head, plain old Roger. She said it the right way, Ro-ger, with a long 'o' and a soft 'g'.

"You as well, mon trésor. You are going to win this week?"

"I hope so."

"You and Christopher. First and second, that is how I like it. I'd also like to see both of you in Europe this summer."

"You and me both," Mary Beth concurred. She blew Roger a jaunty kiss and headed off down the aisle.

When Chris came back, he and Roger conferred for a few minutes. Roger did a lot of gesturing and shoulder clapping. All I could think about was how Roger thought I was Chris's groom. Should Chris have corrected Roger and told him I was his girlfriend? Should Chris officially introduce me to him?

Roger told Chris how he really had to show in Europe this summer. Since he wasn't an American, I wasn't sure why Roger cared so much. Maybe just because he liked Chris and thought he was a good rider. But that seemed rather uncomplicated in terms of a motivation, which did not aptly describe most things in the horse show world. Chris told him he was working on getting another horse.

"He's a fan of yours," I said after Roger had demonstrated another healthy shoulder clap and left.

Chris looked nearly forlorn—not the response I expected.

"It's nice to have people on your side. Rooting for you. Could you really go to Europe this summer?" The thought terrified me.

Chris shook his head sadly. "I wish, but the way it's looking getting a legit 5-star horse and having it ready for Europe this summer isn't going to happen."

I tried to disguise my relief. Chris would be around this summer.

Chapter 24

DAD AND RYAN ARRIVED on Friday afternoon. I offered to find a way to come collect them at the airport but Dad said his assistant had arranged a car for them. It was a good thing actually because the junior hunters went throughout the afternoon and I wouldn't have been able to cut out easily. Dakota was also trying more jumpers to replace Tizz, which meant a lot of running around to different rings to watch different horses go and then setting up going to various farms off the show grounds to try them. The only place you could try horses on the show grounds was the $20 ring and that place was crazy with horses going every which way. It was not where you wanted to try a horse, especially a high-priced animal like Dakota was trying. Linda had told me about a girl who tried a fancy hunter in the $20 ring and ended up colliding with a children's jumper. The fancy hunter got hurt, and the owners attempted to sue the family who had tried the horse. Whether that whole story was true was up for debate. WEF swirled with stories and rumors. It wasn't that

Linda was malicious in telling me the story. She didn't promise it was one hundred percent true. She just said she'd heard
it happened. I had learned, starting in Vermont, and even
more so here in Wellington, to take every story I heard with a
grain of salt. Usually there was always a part of the story that
was true but maybe not all of it. Like maybe the girl had
crashed the fancy hunter and the owners were pissed but they
hadn't actually gone so far as to seek damages.

A lot of the rumors that swirled around WEF had to do
with price tags of horses since the winter circuit was all about
sales for many barns and professionals. We were constantly
hearing numbers tossed about. This hunter going for 500K.
This pony sold for 250K. So-and-so was asking one million
for their jumper—could you believe paying that much for a
junior jumper? I'd heard my mom say once that rich people
thought that it was crass to talk about money but it seemed
like just the opposite here. At every possible opportunity, they
bandied about how much a horse, or a VIP table, or even
lunch, cost.

Dad and Ryan arrived at the barn after we were done for
the day. I could tell they were both immediately impressed
with the Pearces' farm, even coming from gorgeous Palo Alto.
And who wouldn't be?

"This is really something," Dad said, giving me a hug. He
held me close to him, despite the fact that I was dirty, and
didn't let go for a few moments and I soaked up the knowledge that even though my dad could be a total pain in the ass
the guy really loved me.

"A little crazy, though," Ryan said, giving me a hug too.

"It's like horse farm after horse farm. Couldn't some of them share barns or at least rings?"

"Share? Never. You haven't seen anything yet. Just wait till you see the show grounds," I told them.

I showed them around the barn and introduced them to Linda. Dakota had gone into the house. I could tell Linda thought Ryan was attractive, even though he was too young for her. He was medium height and had a thin build. Nothing that made him stand out so much. But his face was incredibly charming. He had dark hair and really blue eyes and a fantastic smile. I think he mainly got girls because of his smile. He also had a slightly stand-off-ish quality about him, especially when you first met him, which counter intuitively seemed to draw people to him. They wanted to figure out what he was thinking about. They wanted to get him to like them.

"So when do we get to meet Chris?" Ryan asked after the tour.

"Well, I thought we'd all get dinner together."

"Sounds good."

I should have been more nervous about my dad and Ryan meeting Chris but I just knew they would love him. What was not to love? A serious, motivated, centered athlete who was going about building his own business.

I was right that they hit it off. Dad and Ryan spent a lot of time asking about how the world of show jumping worked. They wanted to know how much the entry fees were and how much it cost to keep a horse and train it. Chris explained how the prize money in a class is divvied up percentage-wise among the top finishers. Ryan was surprised to learn that first place in a million dollar class didn't mean the winner walked away with a million dollars, but only $350,000. Of course there was talk about the price of horses, too. What it cost to buy a proven winner versus a green horse. How it cost less to bring a horse along in Europe so American breeding programs lagged far behind European ones.

"What about Logan?" Dad asked. "What's he worth today?"

Chris touched his napkin to his mouth and then repositioned it on his lap, probably just to give himself a moment to prepare his answer. "Logan's a good horse. Do I think he's a 1.45 or 1.50 meter caliber horse? No, I don't. I think he's a great 1.30 meter horse."

"Which means? Layman terms?" Dad said.

"He's not a grand prix horse. He's not an Olympic horse. He's a good junior or amateur jumper, or 25K-type grand prix horse."

"And those cost?"

"Two-hundred and fifty-thousand to five-hundred thousand."

Dad made a temple of his hands and rested them in front of his finished plate. "That's a big range. Where is he in that?"

"He hasn't won a lot. He doesn't have a proven record so I'd say if I were to market him tomorrow I'd put him at 325."

Dad let slip a satisfied smile. "Not bad."

"How much did you buy him for?" Ryan asked Dad.

"Fifty."

"Nice profit margins."

"Logan's a great success story," Chris said. "But that's pretty rare in this business. It's hard to make a lot of money on these horses and you can end up losing some too."

"I hope this isn't part of your pitch to prospective investors," Dad said.

I interjected, "Of course it isn't." I didn't want Dad to think Chris was that unsophisticated. But I realized after I said it that it wasn't my place to speak up and defend Chris.

"I'm being honest and open with you because you're Hannah's family," Chris said. "But actually I do tell prospective owners the truth because I don't want the relationship to sour if things don't all go swimmingly. Nothing ever goes like you thought it would, right? Nothing ever happens perfectly according to plan. I'm sure it's the same in your business, isn't it?"

"Yes, yes it is." Dad put his hand over mine and patted it, catching my eye quickly.

I could tell what he was thinking. He was thinking, *I like this guy, Hannah. You picked a winner.* I let my heart swell with pride.

Dad had to make a bunch of calls the next morning but Ryan came and tagged along with me at the show. He rode in the golf cart as I put Dakota's number in and went along to the coffee cart. Everywhere I went people knew me. They waved or said hi or asked how Dakota had done the day before. It felt great that Ryan was seeing me like this. In high school, he had been the one who walked the halls of our school with people constantly calling out to him. He was the one everyone knew and I faded into the background. But here at WEF, I had carved out my own place and identity. That identity might be tagged somewhat to Linda and Dakota and even Chris but still, people knew who I was and liked me and I could tell Ryan was noticing.

He was also noticing the pretty girls all around him. "Holy shit, this is like the seventy-two Virgins in Islamic afterlife," he said to me after yet another skinny young woman in breeches with beautiful hair pulled back in a ponytail walked by us.

I turned the golf cart toward the Grand Hunter Ring, making sure I didn't spin the wheel so hard as to make our coffee spill through its lids. "Okay, that's not really funny, and let me tell you most of these girls you are seeing are so not virgins."

"I don't care if they're virgins. They're beautiful. Can you even be ugly and compete in this sport?"

"You can but for some reason most of them are beautiful people. I don't quite know why. The ugly ones sort of stick out. So do the unwealthy ones."

"So they're gorgeous and wealthy. I think I'm gonna stay here for a few weeks."

"A lot of them are crazy, though," I said. "Comes with the territory."

"Okay, good to know."

Ryan wasn't the only one doing the checking out during the time we spent at the ring together. Plenty of girls were checking him out. One even came up to me at the in-gate when Ryan was taking a call in the golf cart asking all about him—who was he, where was he from, was he straight, was he available? I guess there were so few straight, available men in the horse show world that a cute new guy showing up on the grounds sent out a ripple of excitement.

I had so much fun being at the ring with Ryan. He got to see me in action and I definitely got the feeling he was impressed by the overall scene, how big the stakes were for all the classes, how throbbing with energy the show grounds were.

We had a few good laughs too, like when we saw a goat sitting in a golf cart.

"I'm sorry, is that a goat?"

I had gotten so used to the odd things you'd see around the show. One trainer even had a wolf. A legitimate real-life domesticated wolf. But Ryan craned his head at the goat in the golf cart and another golf cart filled with dogs, five or six dogs. It was hard to tell who was even driving what with all the tails and legs.

Ryan wanted to see Zoe for himself so we went over to the Grand Hunter Ring to find her. She was still riding for Donnie. I'd been so busy lately I'd put what I'd read about her on the back-burner but now I looked at Donnie and her for clues of what might be going on between them. The first year classes were finishing up and we got to see Zoe ride one horse of Donnie's. It was a spectacular mover and jumped very round, but a little drapey with its front legs. Still, Zoe gave it an amazingly accurate and nuanced ride. With any other rider, the horse wouldn't have looked nearly as good. She made up for its drawbacks.

"I'm not sure I really believe she's doing all these drugs if she's still here showing and doing well," I said quietly to Ryan.

"It's amazing how some people can keep functioning," he said. "Maybe not forever but for a long while."

My mind turned to her skeletal chest, the bones nearly popping out of her skin. Of course now she was wearing her show clothes so you couldn't tell as much how skinny she was.

We stayed around to watch the jog. Zoe jogged in first with another horse of Donnie's that we hadn't seen go. A groom jogged the drapey jumper in third. I wasn't really paying attention enough to the jog—I had been looking more at Zoe than at the horse she was jogging but apparently the judge had seen something because he called for the riders to jog again. This time, he motioned to Zoe to leave the ring.

Zoe walked the horse out of the ring slowly and with her head down. Maybe I was projecting emotions onto her but it seemed like she was dreading coming out of the ring and facing Donnie.

He was standing at the in-gate, his jaw set. "I told you not to jog him that way. Did you hear a fucking word I said to you?" He grabbed the reins from her, pushing her out of the way, and snatching on the poor horse's mouth at the same time. "You hold him up here." He demonstrated holding the horse up by the bit. "He's not lame. If you don't hold up here he looks lame. I've told you that again and again. Are you just too fucking stupid to remember that?"

His swears—*fucking stupid*—hung in the air. I shivered and leaned closer to Ryan.

"What an asshole," he said to me.

"Yeah," I murmured.

"He can just do that? Say those things? He doesn't get a red card or a technical foul?"

"I guess not," I said.

The other trainers around the in-gate didn't seem to take much notice of what was going on between Donnie and Zoe. I guess they were used to it, or didn't know what they could do to intervene. The whole complicity of the scene struck me as incredibly sad.

The horses that had remained in the jog came out of the ring. The second jog was called and I braced myself for what would happen next. Zoe got the top call again and this time I studied the horse trotting in. She held the horse's head tightly and Donnie clucked and shooed his arms from the in-gate. The horse looked a little funky behind to me but I was no expert in soundness.

The judge threw the horse out again. He pretty much had to, since he'd tossed him the first time. Donnie glowered at Zoe as she led the horse out of the ring but this time it was the judge that Donnie cursed from the in-gate. He tossed off a few expletives and finally stalked away.

"I don't know what to do," I told Ryan. "I don't know if it's even my place to do anything."

I wished we'd never come to watch Zoe. It felt like it had ruined my happy mood. Then I felt selfish for even feeling that way. Who knew what Zoe would be facing back at the barn with Donnie?

"After what she did to you I'm not sure you owe her anything," Ryan said.

"I know, but I can't help feeling like someone needs to help her."

Dad met us for a late lunch. We ate at the VIP tent and I could tell Dad was also pretty impressed looking down over the International Ring.

He spread his hands to encompass the whole show grounds. The riders waiting for their classes, the horses dutifully standing at the ready, the golf carts whizzing by, the trainers pointing and gesticulating, the vendors pushing for their next sale. "This is a huge operation the show management has got going on here."

Being a daily part of it, I had dulled to it all. But with them, for a moment, I saw it the way I had when I'd first arrived, fresh off the plane. It was like nothing else in the world. The constant motion, the vibrant sounds, the whirl of hopes, ribbons, and reality.

Ryan asked about Chris's routine before a big class. He seemed to understand that Chris really was a professional athlete. But unlike most professional athletes who made a living mainly from their own performance, Chris had to earn his money before he competed himself. I told Ryan that he would ride his horses at the farm in the morning and ride Arkos in the FEI schooling ring. He'd coach Lily, who was competing in the High A/O Classic. Then he'd go home in the afternoon, shower and have a meal packed with protein because he wouldn't feel like eating right before the class, except for maybe an energy bar or a piece of fruit.

He'd be back over for the course walk. The order had been posted and he went late in the class, thirty-fourth.

Dad said he had to make a few more calls and so I left

him looking very much at home in the tent. Ryan came with me while I went through the afternoon chores at the show tent and back at Morada. He watched everything I did with the kind of curiosity that made him who he was. He even helped me untangle the mess of polo wraps from the dryer. I taught him how to roll them. Fernando showed him some of Rudi's tricks. He held up a broom horizontal to the ground about waist high and whistled and Rudi jumped it from a standstill. Fernando raised the broom a few times. Ryan thought it was hysterical that the hunters wore fake tails and that part of my job was to wash them.

"You look happy here," Ryan said as I poured baby shampoo into a large tub to wash the tails.

"Mostly I am—when I'm doing barn stuff."

"But you and Chris?"

I shrugged. "It's not been what I imagined it would be."

"It never is," Ryan said.

I gently washed the tails, then rinsed them under clean water, careful not to get them wet close to the top where the glue held them together. "That sure sounds jaded. Are you seeing anyone?"

"Not right now."

"Sometimes I wonder if I'll ever be able to get married and be happy after watching Mom and Dad. Do you think they didn't stay together because they were like in two completely different worlds?"

"I don't know. Maybe."

"Do you ever wonder if Dad cheated on Mom?" I asked.

"I never really thought about it. I wouldn't worry about getting married, though. You're nineteen."

I made a face. "You know how I am—always thinking too much."

I sprayed the tails with a little leave-in conditioner and then hung them up in the shade to dry. Full sun wouldn't be good for them. When they'd dried fully, I'd bring them into the tack room.

"Yes," Ryan said. "Stop doing it. You'll be better off. Just stick to detangling your wraps and washing your strange fake tails."

Chapter 25

THE COURSE LOOKED BEAUTIFUL—a kaleidoscope of colors and shapes, many jumps with bright logos of sponsors like Ariat, Farm Vet, Arouet, Equifit, Adequan. Some of the impressive nature of the jumps had more to do with the open spaces between the rails and the panels that made the jumps airy yet formidable at the same time.

I loved the excitement before a big class. The tension and anticipation in the air. I pointed out the big-time movie producer to Ryan and Dad, and they both did their own double-take when they saw the software mogul whose daughter competed.

The course walk for any big class was always a scene. The pointing, the assessing, the striding, the standing around in clusters as a band covered recent Top 40 hits at the end of the arena. Whether they were trying to or not, the riders all looked very important and self-assured as they grabbed their show coats from the Riders' Lounge and headed onto the expansive course. Some riders liked to wear their show coats;

others wore their team windbreakers. Many riders wore base-ball hats bearing the name of their farm or advertising a sponsor. A few of the young men, like McNair, wore thin wool or cashmere V-necks over their show shirts. Several young riders were accompanied by their trainers. And what a group of trainers they were. They hailed from several different countries and sported strong accents. One of the older trainers wore a straw hat; another carried a little dog under his arm. The chef d'equipe for the U.S. Team was strolling around, chatting with various riders. Between them there were multiple Olympic medal winners, World Cup winners, and World Equestrian Game winners. It was rare these days if you were über wealthy and still retained a U.S. born, bred, and based trainer. Most of the wealthiest riders selected European luminaries as their trainers and based themselves at their European stables for parts of the year. Lily Teller was one of the few children of one-percenters who had an American trainer and whose trainer was competing against her in the class, no less, with only a few years separating them in age. I explained to my dad and Ryan how Chris coached Lily and pointed out where they were walking the course together. Ryan asked if it was weird for him to compete against her. I had asked Chris the very same question and he'd said maybe a little weird, but not really.

"What's weird is that she has much better horses than him," I said to Ryan and Dad. "She's not nearly the rider he is, but that's the nature of the sport."

We went ahead and got in line for the buffet early, so as to avoid the crowds. We were still finishing our meals when the class got underway. By that time the stadium seating was nearly filled with families from the area, thanks in part to the carnival-like atmosphere on the other side of the ring, which included a carousel, street-performers, and a petting zoo. Lily went tenth. The first six riders had faults. There was a big triple bar toward the end of the course and then right after it a vertical-vertical double combination. That seemed to be the trap of the course. Riders came in too forward to the double and ended up having one or both rails down. I explained my thinking on this to Dad and Ryan. When Lily came in, I could see Chris standing at the in-gate. He looked so professional and my heart leapt a little—could I really be dating him? I knew I was but it was moments like these that it hit me all over again.

Monty was a classic type. He was a beautiful bay with a white blaze and two white socks and he was a leaner warm-blood, almost a little thoroughbred-like. He jerked his knees up in perfect form and wore his ears well the whole way around the course, sighting in on each jump. He was the kind of horse that made it seem like horses liked to jump, that they liked to compete.

Lily was clean coming into the triplebar. She caught a long distance to the triple bar and instinctually I leaned back in my chair as if I was trying to get Monty to rock back for the ver-ticals. I knew from Chris he was a super adjustable horse but she didn't quite get him back enough. She was tight into the first vertical and any other horse would have had it down but he somehow managed to scrape over it. He cleared the second vertical too and then had just two more jumps left. I felt mixed about how I wanted her to do and wondered if Chris did too. If she went clean it would be good for him as her trainer; but as a rider it was frustrating to see her horse get her out of a not-so-optimal distance. She rode the last two jumps fine and did, in fact, finish clean.

"Our first to conquer the course tonight, Lily Teller and Monteverdi II, go clean," the announcer boomed.

By the time we went back to the buffet for dessert and coffee, three more had gone clean. Five riders before Chris was slated to go, Dad said, "I want to go down to the in-gate. Can we watch from there?"

"Wait, why?" I said, nearly knocking my fork off my plate I was so caught off guard.

"Just can we do it?" Dad said. "Are we allowed to? Or do we have to stay up here?"

"We can go down," I said. "If that's what you want."

Dad tossed his napkin on the table. I shared a look with Ryan like, *what the heck is this all about*? But we also both seemed to wordlessly know not to bother asking Dad to explain further or try to figure it out ourselves.

A quiet hush hung over the schooling ring as Chris jumped an oxer. Dale hovered next to the oxer to adjust it. A steward watched from the end of the ring, ensuring there would be no illegally set jumps. A few people stood on the rail looking in on the ring. Two other riders were jumping; two were flatting in preparation to jump. Another rider, the Princess of Sweden, trotted her horse on a loose rein, his head down low, just having come out of the class. This wasn't the schooling ring before a junior hunter or eq class where trainers shouted commands. It was almost eerily quiet since most riders at this point in their lives had done the preparation and the training and weren't trying to fix issues here. This was just a simple prep over as few jumps as possible—saving most of your horse's good jumps for the ring. This was perhaps about catching a slight convenient rub but nothing more.

The few words that we heard were, "Looks good. Ready to go? Let's go with that," and sometimes they were either said with an accent or in another language altogether.

Dad noticed Dale adjusting the jumps for Chris. "He doesn't have a trainer?" Dad asked.

"Up one and wider," Chris told Dale.

"Not really. Sometimes he has more experienced trainers or friends who'll come help him with a horse he's struggling with, or consult on a line in a course. That type of thing."

Dad nodded like he was processing all this and doing some sort of assessment.

Chris signaled to Dale that he felt good and they headed up to the in-gate. We followed behind. I wondered if Chris had seen us watching. If he had, he didn't let on. Perhaps he was too much in the zone to notice.

Nearby a foreign rider was talking to another fellow countryman. They talked in what seemed like incredibly fast bursts in their native language, every once in a while punctuating their sentences with an American turn of phrase. It sounded like: blah-blah-blah-blah-*seriously?* Blah, blah, blah, blah, *super careful!*

Dale double-checked Arkos's boots, bridle, and wiped Arkos's mouth. Chris stared into the ring almost like he was meditating. The rider before him was finishing up. I took Dad and Ryan onto the viewing platform to watch the class. Ryan followed me but Dad lingered, his eyes on Chris. Ryan and I stopped at the ramp to the platform. "What is up with him?" I whispered to Ryan, as Dad waited, still studying Chris.

"I wish I could say I knew," Ryan said.

Chris and Dale didn't speak. Some riders exchanged last minute words with their barn manager but not Chris. He didn't check his girth or fiddle with his reins. He just stared straight ahead.

The rider on course came out of the ring, letting her reins slip through her fingers. She blew out a big breath and threw her leg forward to loosen her girth.

Chris walked forward into the ring, sitting tall in the saddle.

Dad remained a moment or two longer and then caught up with us.

"Coming into the ring now," the announcer said. "We have Chris Kern aboard Arkos. Chris, a former winner of our country's equitation finals, has represented the U.S. on several occasions and placed at many top grand prix classes in the country. Arkos is a 16.2 hand Dutch Warmblood."

This was the biggest class I'd seen Chris ride in. I was in awe of how calmly serious he was. How focused. How he absolutely looked like he belonged on this stage, and on an even bigger stage. Maybe I wouldn't have seen him walk through the in-gate, or noticed how focused he looked, if it weren't for my dad asking to come down. Now I had seen it and I felt like I could also see the future—Chris going into the ring in the Olympics. If only he had the right horse.

Arkos jumped brilliantly. And Chris rode him brilliantly.

Whereas the other riders who had been clean had done so by having a few hard rubs and somehow also having the luck to have the rails stay up, or barely skimming over a jump like Lily had, Chris mastered the course. There was never a moment where Arkos looked anything but perfectly measured and in control. Arkos didn't come close to touching a rail. I didn't know if Dad or Ryan could tell how much better Chris and Arkos were than the other cleans so far—if they could see the difference. Probably not because of their uneducated eyes. I could, though, and goosebumps rose up my arms. Somehow I felt like I would always remember this moment in time. I looked down at my feet on the wooden deck. I would remember this: standing here, watching Chris and Arkos give a command performance. It felt like this was the beginning of something very big for them.

Maybe it wasn't just me that noticed because the crowd let out an enthusiastic cheer for Chris as the announcer blasted out, "And that's a clear go—we have another for the jump-off. Chris Kern and Arkos move onto the good list and will return at the end of the first round to try their luck over the shortened, speed course."

Chris walked Arkos out of the ring and over to the FEI inspection area, patting Arkos's neck heartily. Dale stood aside as the FEI stewards, dressed in blazers and jeans, took off Arkos's boots and inspected his legs.

Dad said we could go back to the tent for the jump-off.

"We can stay and watch from here," I said.

Dad didn't betray any emotion. "Nope, I'm all set."

I gave Ryan another look and we headed back to the tent.

Part of me wanted to go see Chris and congratulate him but I also thought maybe it was better to not bother him, to let him focus, *to leave it at that* for now. There were only a few left to go in the class and Chris would be getting on soon for the jump-off. I looked back one more time and caught sight of Mary Beth congratulating him warmly. She had four faults but of course she was conveniently still hanging around the in-gate. When I had pointed her out to Ryan earlier, I'd felt almost silly about how worked up I got over her but now I pulsed with jealousy again. Seeing her made me want to rush back down there.

"You coming?" Ryan said.

Reluctantly I followed them.

Five went clear—Chris had been the last clear so he had the enviable position of going last in the jump-off. The jump-off had a few tight turns to the same vertical-vertical combination and then finished over a line of what looked like seven or eight strides. Lily came back first in the jump-off. She rode efficiently and finished clear. Her time seemed good but beatable. Going first, it was probably just what she needed to do. She had done the eight strides in the last line and that was what the next two riders did. One pulled a rail and the other was slower than Lily so she was still in the lead. A rider from Argentina came in next and laid down a fast and clean trip, still doing the eight, though, and finishing just shy of Lily's time. To beat Lily you needed to do the seven and go clean. I wondered whether Chris would do the eight since he had clearly coached Lily to do the eight. I wondered if he'd play it safe for Arkos, or go for it. Going in a jump-off was all about measuring the stakes. You didn't always go as fast as you could. Your plan hinged on where you went in the order and what you were hoping to achieve in that class.

It was impossible to tell what Chris's plan was over the first half of the course. He was riding neat turns but there was only so much he could do. There were no shortcuts that Lily had missed. It was landing over the in of the last line that his intentions became clear. He was doing the seven and going for the win. I could feel the crowd lean forward, their breath catching in their throats. Even if, like Dad and Ryan, they didn't know how to count the strides or even what a stride was, they could see Chris urge Arkos forward, galloping at the last jump. Since I've never galloped at a huge jump before, I imagine it must take a lot of trust in yourself and your horse. You have to believe that you will make it happen and then it does.

The distance to the out of the line was long. Arkos stretched and cleared the jump. Chris galloped him through the timers and the crowd erupted. The announcer confirmed what everyone else had guessed—that the clock had stopped over a second faster than Lily. Chris had won.

We watched the award presentation from the tent. I couldn't stop smiling. Ryan leaned close and said, "Well, that was pretty fucking cool."

Dad overheard him and said, "Really fucking cool." It was the first thing Dad had said since Chris had gone in the first round. Ryan and I broke out laughing.

We met Chris down by the in-gate. He put his arms around me and hugged me extra tight. I hadn't seen him look this happy in forever. I hoped MB was watching us hug from somewhere.

"Can we say something now?" I asked.

He laughed, throwing his head back. "Yes, I think we can."

"That was really cool," Ryan said.

Lily Teller's dad came up to Chris and shook his hand. "Couldn't let her win?" he joked. Or at least I hoped he was joking.

Chris introduced Craig Teller to my dad and Ryan.

"She was right behind me," Chris said. "She rode great today. But going first and where she is at this stage she needed to do the eight."

I knew *The Chronicle* would have fun with their article about today's class—student and teacher going up against each other.

"Arkos looked good too," Craig said. "Looks like you have a keeper after all."

"He jumped great." Chris looked at my dad. "Did Hannah tell you she was the one who figured out that he had TMJ?"

"She mentioned a little about it," Dad said.

Mr. Teller left and Jimmy Sharpe came up to Chris and clapped him on the back. "Good go, man," he said.

"Thanks, Jimmy," Chris said.

Jimmy and Chris discussed a few details about how the course had ridden. Even though he was American born and bred, Jimmy seemed to have adopted a slight foreign accent or intonation to his words—as if he was trying to be foreign.

I guess foreign plain old ruled in show jumping. To be American was to be nothing.

Chris said, "Arkos jumped better today than he's ever jumped. I'm really excited about this horse again." Chris looked over at me and I could tell he was trying to tell me just how grateful he was.

"You stuck with him, though," I said. "You didn't give up on him."

"I was getting pretty close."

"And you were the one who picked him out, who saw something special in him from the beginning when others didn't."

"Well, either way, I'm excited. This was nothing for this horse. He always had the scope it was just the carefulness but now it's like he's back."

"It was fun to watch," Dad said.

Chris smiled. "I'm glad you were here to see a good class. Of course they're not all like this."

"I think I got a good sense for what it's like."

It was a kind of cryptic statement. How could Dad really get a sense of what show jumping was like from one class? But maybe he could. He was used to looking at companies and figuring out what they needed in a short amount of time.

One of the show's PR people came over and asked Chris to go speak to the media. "I'll catch up with you later," he said.

Chapter 26

AFTER THE EXCITEMENT OF THE grand prix and Dad and Ryan's visit, it was almost hard to go back to the routine. I missed having Ryan around the most. Chris jumped Arkos in the 85K 1.50 meter class the following week and he went clean again. His plan for the rest of the circuit was to do the CSI-3 during week 10, give him week 11 off, and then, if he really felt good, perhaps try to qualify to contest the CSI-5 the last week.

His happiness over Arkos trickled down to our relationship, making things between us feel better than they'd been. But still, I knew something lurked underneath the glow of Arkos's turnaround.

Chris was busier than ever and had little time to spend with me and all I could think about was how circuit was almost over. I couldn't believe it had gone by so fast and I felt like I hadn't come close to achieving what I'd set out to do. Chris's and my relationship wasn't more committed or defined than it had been back in December. In fact, it was shakier. I was still paranoid about Mary Beth. The urge to bite my nails was growing stronger every day and I felt like any moment I'd cave and chew them. Then there was the question of what I'd do after circuit. Linda had said they'd love to have me come back east with them and work at the farm. "I'm not sure Dakota would *love* that," I'd replied.

"Well, she hasn't exactly tried to mess with you lately, has she?"

"I think she's just waiting for the right moment. Plotting and planning."

Actually, while I wouldn't say Dakota liked me now, she had spoken to me once or twice out of her own free will. And she'd actually asked me to help her pick out clothes to wear when the photographer from The Book came to take candids of her with her horses. We had to get the horses looking as gorgeous as if they were going in the ring, only they didn't need to be braided. The photographer spent an hour doing a shoot worthy of a glossy fashion magazine. He was paid a hefty sum to follow Dakota at several shows throughout the year and then at the end of the year assemble a gorgeous coffee table book of her year of riding, including the candids. It was the super upscale version of a yearbook except it featured only one person, not an entire school, and only the wealthiest of riders could afford it.

I guess I could go back with them after circuit and continue to work for them. I liked Linda and the horses. But they didn't do all the same shows as Chris so it wouldn't be like I'd be getting to see him often. New York was a lot closer to Pennsylvania than Boston, though.

Dakota had so many horses that she never had to take a week off from showing. Linda and I plotted out which horses she'd do each week. Some weeks we just flatted and trail rode certain horses.

At the end of week 9, Dakota and her friends begged to go see WEF's Got Talent. I was a little tired and didn't want to go to another social event, even though this one did sound like fun. But Dakota said her parents told her it was okay to get the tickets and just to charge them to their credit card and that she had to go since all her friends were going. Of course they told her to charge it to their card—they were expert at throwing money at her. But they hadn't made an appearance all circuit and it didn't look like they would be as time was running out. I remembered how I'd been worried about sharing a house with the Pearces—I could laugh about that now.

I tried to get Chris to come with us to WEF's Got Talent but he didn't want to. Dakota got all dressed up. I just threw on jeans and a cute shirt. Despite not being very enthused about going, I actually ended up having a pretty fun time. Auditions had been held throughout the season and the top people from each audition competed in the final. There was a lot of talent. Most of the acts competing were solo singers. There was also one group of three young women, who called themselves the Jumping Janes. There was a dressage rider who did ballroom dancing and a ring crew guy who did a whole Michael Jackson dance impersonation. There was also a stand-up comedian who riffed on all things riding. Of course there was also the obligatory auction, although this one was live and included some pretty cool items including a package to go watch the Pan American Games.

I texted Chris a few times throughout the night updating him on what act I thought should win. At one point he wrote back: *Just had very interesting phone call.*

With whom? About what?

Jürgen. There's a horse that a British owner is selling. I've seen it go. It's a legit 5-star horse.

I couldn't imagine how said horse would ever be in Chris's price range. *Price tag?*

1M.

Isn't that low?

It took a while for Chris's response. I kept looking at the three dots on my phone indicating that he was typing. Then came his long reply: *Very. They don't want to sell it to anyone in GB or Europe. They want it sold to someone in U.S. The owner had a fight with chef of GB team and to spite him wants it sold to American, even if it means losing $$ on the horse. It's also not an easy ride.*

Wow. Sounds promising.

Dakota, Taylor, and Addie had gone off to the bathroom, or so they said. It seemed like they'd been gone a while and I worried that they were scoring drinks again. I searched the room for them. The last act was about to go on and then the winner would be announced.

Chris's next text came in: *I think I can ride it.*

So you just need the $$$.

Just need 250.

Just . . .

I looked up and saw Dakota on her way over to me, alone. "Can I sleep over at Taylor's?"

"Where is she?"

"She's already outside the tent. She's waiting for me. I'd said I'd ask you and then hustle out to her."

"Why's she in such a rush? You don't want to watch the end? See who wins?"

"Nah," she said. "So can I? You know my mom and dad would say yes."

"But they're not here and I'm in charge." Something in this whole thing sounded kind of fishy.

"Please?" Dakota said. "You can go over to Chris's."

Damn. That girl knew how to get me to say yes. I could go over to Chris's and watch videos of the horse and plot with him about how to come up with the 250K. There weren't all that many chances left for us to spend the night together.

Dakota gave me a quick hug, which seemed like overkill for just letting her sleep over at Taylor's, but the fact that she was offering me any kind of warmth totally made me melt. Maybe she was finally coming around to liking me. It had taken longer than I'd thought at first but maybe this was what I'd been waiting for all along.

"Have fun," I said. "But don't stay up too late."

"I won't!" she called back as she made her way to the front of the tent. I texted Chris to say Dakota was sleeping over at Taylor's and so I could come over and headed to the exit myself. Behind me the last act was introduced to the remaining enthusiastic crowd. My phone buzzed. *Cu soon,* Chris had written back.

I emerged from the tent and out of the corner of my eye I thought I glimpsed Dakota's long hair. But the head it was attached to belonged to a girl holding hands with a guy. All these girls had the same long, flowing locks, I told myself. They all looked alike, especially in the dim light of the tent. Dakota would have already been long gone with Taylor.

I speed-walked to my car, wanting to get to Chris's as soon as possible. I wondered who else he had told about the horse. Probably Dale. I wanted to be in on the ground level, one of the first to be there with him while he brainstormed how to somehow get this horse. Then later on, I could say, *oh, yeah, remember when you got the call from Jürgen and we stayed up all night trying to figure out how to make it happen?* This could become one of those big relationship moments that Chris and I could look back on, like the moments that he had shared with Mary Beth. This one could be all ours.

"This is so exciting!" I gushed to Chris when I got to his place.

"I know. I'm trying not to get ahead of myself but if I could somehow get this horse... You can't get horses with this amount of talent for a million."

"You really think you can ride it? I mean, of course you can. Can I see some video?"

We huddled around his laptop and he showed me the horse competing at a European show. His name was Athelstane and it was a big, powerful chestnut gelding. Chris said the hardest part was keeping the horse together. He had a huge stride and could get strung-out.

I knew if Chris could get Athelstane he could go far. But

somehow I got a dead feeling in my gut as I watched. I had the terrible sense that he'd go far with this horse, but without me.

"Mary Beth saw the horse go at Aachen and she said he has all the scope in the world."

"Wait, you talked to Mary Beth about him?"

So much for being in on the ground level. So much for this being our thing. MB had apparently gotten there before me.

"Yeah, I did."

"When? Did you call her, or did she call you?"

"What does it matter? This is about the horse. This doesn't need to be some big drama about her again."

I hated the word drama. No girl wanted to be associated with the word drama. This moment was turning bad and I needed to make things okay again so this could still be ours. Our exciting time together before we somehow cobbled the money together to buy Athelstane.

Chris's phone rang. "It's Jürgen," he said.

"Take it," I told him.

"Of course I'm taking it," he snapped.

He stood up and moved away from me, like he needed the distance. I felt my body heating up with anger and shame at how this night was developing. My own phone buzzed. A text coming in. It was from Mike and it was a photo of what looked like a girl at a bar. The image was grainy and I had to zoom in. Was that Dakota with a drink in her hand?

Another text came rapidly. *She's at JoJo's.*

"You've got to be kidding me," I said out loud. "That little—"

Chris motioned for me to be quiet as he talked to Jürgen. I heard him say, "What's the timetable?"

I glanced at the photo again. I couldn't believe her. She and Taylor had flat-out lied to my face. She had used the idea of Chris to manipulate me and worst of all, had hugged me, making me think she actually liked me when all she wanted was to fool me.

"I need to go," I told Chris.

He waved me away again. I grabbed my purse and stomped out. I drove over to JoJo's, getting more steamed with each passing minute. I went back and forth in my head about who I was most mad at—Chris or Dakota.

I strode into the bar feeling like a cop on a TV show. Or maybe like a mom or dad on a family sitcom. I would confront Dakota, tell her I was very disappointed in her, and drag her home. She'd sob in the car and beg for my forgiveness. Maybe I'd be kind and tell her I wouldn't say anything to her parents and then she'd owe me big-time and realize once and for all what a cool person I was and how lucky she was that I was working for her family. She'd be indebted to me for the rest of the circuit and be unendingly nice to me.

I saw Mike right away but I didn't see Dakota. He was at a table with an attractive assistant trainer I recognized from the show. *Good for him*, I thought.

The place was pretty full. There was an Irish contingent by the bar, talking loudly in their brogue accents and laughing uproariously.

I scanned the room with angry eyes for Dakota and still couldn't find her. I went over to Mike. "Oh my God," I said.

"You're a lifesaver for texting me. Do you know what that girl did? She said she was sleeping over at Taylor's house. Where are those girls? How did they even get in here? They're thirteen!"

"She wasn't here with Taylor," he said.

"What?"

"She was with a bunch of guys."

"Guys?" My mind flashed to the girl I had seen with hair like Dakota's. I started to feel more worried than angry.

"I didn't see Taylor."

"Shit. Well, whatever, where is she?"

"She went to the bathroom, then I kind of lost track of her. I'm sorry." Mike gave me a look that said he was a little preoccupied. "This is Sarah, by the way."

"Nice to meet you," I told her, casing the room again out of the corner of my eye.

I was starting to feel frantic. My thirteen-year-old charge was out with some guys at a bar and now she was gone. Her parents would kill me if they found out. I would kill Dakota first, when I found her.

"I'm going to go check the bathroom," I told Mike.

I charged into the bathroom, expecting to find her in there but the stalls were empty. One girl was fixing her eye-makeup at the mirror. I asked her if she'd seen a young girl with blond hair. She said she hadn't.

My heart beating too fast, I went back into the bar. My face felt flushed. I never should have let her out of my sight. This is exactly what Audrina had warned me about. I should have known Dakota might pull something like this. She probably went home with some guy and was about to have sex with him. She thought she was ready for that, but was she really? She had to be a virgin, right? Somehow it had never occurred to me until now. Dakota couldn't have had sex already? I mean, some thirteen-year-olds had sex. I'd never thought Dakota would be one of them, for all her snark and obnoxiousness.

I asked the Irish guys if they had seen her. They said they thought she'd been here but had left. "I think they were going to players," one of them said. "We're too low class over here for those types!"

They burst out in laughter again. Players. Well, it would be better than back at some guy's house. I just prayed they were right and she was really at Players. I told Mike I was going over to Players and to please text me if he saw Dakota again.

"Do you need help?" he asked.

I desperately wanted to say yes, but Mike had bailed me out so many times before and from what it looked like his date was going well. "No, I'm okay." Over my shoulder I called back to them, "Mike's a great guy!"

On the way over to Players I called Taylor. I'd gotten her number since the golf cart incident. She picked up, sounding half-asleep. "Do you know where Dakota is?"

"No," she said, like it was automatic and planned.

"Don't lie to me," I said. "Did you know she said she was sleeping over at your house?"

There was silence. "I'm telling you, you better be honest, or you're going to be in a world of hurt." I had no idea where these kinds of threats were coming from. I didn't know I had it in me, but I was desperate. I was worried for my job, but more than that I was worried for Dakota. It was like some kind of big sister or mamma bear instinct had been unleashed inside of me.

"Yeah, I knew she was saying she was sleeping over."

"But where was she really going?"

"Out to JoJo's with McNair and Demetrio."

"Well, I just came from JoJo's and she wasn't there. Have you heard from her?"

"No, I swear, I haven't. I'm telling the truth. I haven't heard anything from her since I left the tent."

I told Taylor to call me if she heard anything and to call Addie too and see if somehow she had heard anything about what was going on. No texts had come in from Chris—it wouldn't have killed him to find out why I'd hurried off.

I was still a few blocks from Players when the car started making a horrible noise. I had no idea what was wrong with it. I stared at the dashboard, hoping a warning light would pop on and tell me what the heck was wrong. It sounded like a grinding noise and the car started shaking, like when you drive too fast over a rumble strip on the highway. I slowed down to only a few miles per hour and the sound lessened but didn't fully go away. I pulled over and got out of the car to find that one of the front tires had blown. Seriously? This was happening now?

I was only a few blocks from Players, though, so I grabbed my purse, locked the car, and left it there on the side of the road. I'd call AAA later.

The atmosphere at Players was more subdued. No pack of uproarious Irish guys. More couples enjoying a night out and a cocktail. The European scene wouldn't be in full force till Sunday. Still, no Dakota. My face burned again and I felt like I was having bad heartburn. If she wasn't here, she could be anywhere in the town of Wellington. How could I ever find her?

Chapter 27

I TRIED TO SLOW DOWN my breathing. Okay, maybe Dakota knew exactly what she was doing. She was a sophisticated kid. Maybe she would be out all night and have sex and be just fine. I could go back to Chris's and let her fend for herself. Tomorrow she'd reappear and I could act like nothing had happened. She would know that I knew from Taylor telling her and it would be like this secret knowledge I would have that would shift the power dynamic between us. Or I could calmly tell her that I knew she lied to me and didn't sleep over at Taylor's and never to do that again or else I'd tell her parents.

I sat down to think it all over. That's when I saw McNair Sutter come out of the bathroom and pull up a stool at the bar. I jumped up and nearly accosted him.

"Where is she?"

"Who?"

"Dakota! Didn't you bring her here?"

"Whoa, calm down."

It is a proven fact that when someone is not calm the worst thing you can say to them is, "Calm down." I wanted to punch McNair, sitting there in his expensive, button-down shirt that was maybe blue, maybe purple. His hair expertly styled to look not-perfectly-styled. Most people probably never felt such hatred toward him. Most people probably only felt lust because he was devastatingly good-looking.

"Where the fuck is she? Tell me now!"

"She left."

"With whom?"

"With whom? Do you always have perfect grammar?" he said coyly.

"With whom, with who, whatever. Where is she?"

He twirled the straw in his cocktail. "So, Chris Kern, huh? How did that happen?"

"I want to know where she is. That's all I want to know from you."

"It's just that Chris is kind of serious, kind of driven. You're pretty but you don't really fit into his ten-year plan."

"What ten-year plan?" I said, letting him pull me off track.

"Oh, I'm sure he has one. You don't seem like you're conducive to his plan."

McNair was driving me crazy but I couldn't ignore that the things he was talking about were things I was interested in. "How do you know Chris so well?"

"We used to hang out."

I found that hard to believe. Chris and McNair seemed like different species and I knew Chris didn't like him. I waved my hand like I was shooing a bug and refocused on why I was talking to him in the first place. "Whatever. All I care about is Dakota."

"Seems like you care about more than Dakota."

"Just tell me who she left with," I said impatiently. *Please let it be a girl*, I thought. *Please let someone with half a mind have taken her home.*

"She met a nice polo player and he took her home."

"Nice polo player? Isn't that an oxymoron?"

"There we go with the impressive language skills again, Ms. English Major. And aren't we being quite judgy?"

"Did he take her to his home, or her home?"

"His, of course. You're not that naïve, are you?"

"She's thirteen. You know that, right? Where does he live?"

"I think somewhere over in Greenview Shores but I've never been to his house."

"Well, who has?"

McNair shrugged.

"You're despicable," I said, turning toward the exit.

"Don't you think that's a little harsh? I didn't take her home, after all. She wanted me to, by the way."

I didn't answer. I strode out of the bar, only to come out into the parking lot and remember I no longer had a car. Greenview Shores wasn't that far away but what was I going to do, jog there, and jog around the complex, screaming Dakota's name? I scanned the parking lot, not sure what I was looking for. My eyes fell on a white Land Rover with a Vineyard Vines sticker on the back. But I hadn't seen Zoe in Players. If she wasn't in the bar, where was she?

I walked toward the Land Rover and saw a figure in the

driver's seat. She was in there. Doing what—I had no idea. What choice did I have? I needed help.

I approached the car, wondering what kind of shape she was in. Maybe she was passed out. Nope, her eyes were open and she saw me and startled. I motioned to her to roll down her window.

Her hair hung into her face and she made no effort to pull it back. "What the fuck do you want?"

"What are you doing just sitting in your car?"

Her voice was hoarse, like she'd been yelling. "What does it matter to you?"

"I need your help. Dakota went home with a polo player and all I know is he lives in Greenview Shores."

"So what?"

"She's thirteen." In case that wasn't enough for her, I added, "I'm in charge of her and she lied to me. She said she was going over to Taylor's house to sleep over and if something happens to her, it'll be on me. My tire blew out. I left my car on South Shore."

Zoe laughed. "Pretty funny, you needing me."

"Well, are you going to help me?"

Zoe blew out a breath that moved her hair a little. "I guess."

"Should I drive?" I said. "I mean, are you drunk or high?"

"Maybe," she admitted.

"Come on, get out," I ordered.

Zoe opened the door and nearly fell out of the car. I wondered if I would need to help her around to the passenger side but somehow she made it. I jumped in and put on my seatbelt. In the light that the car door opening triggered, I saw her face: her left eye was swollen half-shut.

"What the hell?" I said. I hadn't wanted to believe Horse-ShowDrama but now here was the proof right in front of me.

"This is the least of my problems," Zoe said.

I swung out of the parking lot and over to Greenview Shores the whole time thinking how everything had changed so quickly for Zoe. This past summer she had been one of the country's most promising riders. Back then her personal life was a little troubled and she drank too much but as far as I had known she wasn't doing drugs or getting beat up by a man twice her age. Yet, now she claimed being beaten was the least of her problems. I wasn't sure how that was possible.

We pulled into Greenview Shores. "How the hell are we going to find this guy?" I said.

"Polo guy. He's clearly not a ten-goal player or he'd live in Palm Beach Polo but that doesn't mean he doesn't want to act like one. Look for the totally sparkling clean, beautiful BMW or Mercedes sedan."

"Really?" I eased by two driveways with dually trucks in them.

She said deadpan, like it should be obvious. "Polo players drive super fancy cars that go really fast. Not like horse show people. Also, look for Florida plates."

The dually trucks had Kentucky and Virginia plates, respectively. Next was an SUV with Connecticut plates. I began to think Zoe might know what she was talking about. We kept passing the same kind of cars.

"What if it's in a garage, not in the driveway?"

"No one parks in the garage here. They store their shit in it and they don't want to smash into the side of it when they come home drunk in the middle of the night."

I braked hard. There it was. The kind of car Zoe had described perfectly. A metallic gray sick-looking BMW with Florida plates. Ryan would know what kind of BMW it was immediately but to me it just looked like the kind of car a showy asshole would drive. "What do you think?"

"Pretty good bet."

I released my seat belt but Zoe hadn't moved. "Aren't you going to come?"

"Not so good on the walking, remember?"

I nodded. "Right." So this was on me.

I got out of the car and strode up to the door. I knocked lightly at first. What if this was the wrong house? Well, then I just woke someone up and it would be a big misunderstanding. I knocked harder. When I got no response, I knocked really loud.

Finally, the door opened on a guy with his shirt half unbuttoned. Yup, this sure seemed like polo player territory.

"Is Dakota Pearce in there?"

"Who are you?"

"Who the fuck are you?" I said. "Do you know she's thirteen? Thirteen!" This had become my refrain for the night.

His face turned white. Maybe he didn't know she was thirteen. She'd probably lied about her age. But still, he must have known she wasn't over eighteen. He hesitated a moment, like he was trying to figure out whether to come clean or try to lie too.

"Dakota?" I called. "You are so in trouble right now."

There was no answer, which seemed strange. "What the fuck did you do to her?"

He took a step back. "She wasn't feeling well. She's lying down."

I barged past him, into his house of dark colored walls and solid, masculine furniture. Dakota was splayed out on the prominent leather sofa. She looked asleep, or worse, unconscious. Her skirt was hiked up on one side.

My heart was going in my ears. Was she going to be okay? Did she have alcohol poisoning? Had she taken drugs?

I kneeled down by her side and shook her. "Dakota, Dakota!"

She moaned and rolled to one side. That seemed like a good sign. But still, she was nearly comatose. I wished I knew what do to, like take her pulse, check her temperature, or listen to her gut sounds like I would have if she had been a horse. I knew more about taking care of a horse than a girl.

"Like I said, she was fine and then she said she didn't feel well."

My mind raced with what I should do. Should I call an ambulance? Oh my God, it would be all over Wellington. HorseShowDrama would have a field day and so would the *Palm Beach Post*. Dakota's parents would fire me instantaneously. But I wasn't going to risk her life.

"You roofied her?"

It was Zoe's voice. Apparently the guy had left the front door open or Zoe had just let herself in. She looked like hell. Skinny, slightly wobbly, the swollen eye. But I was so glad to have her there.

"Roofie? Like date-rape drug?" I looked horrified at the guy.

"I didn't touch her. I didn't rape her."

I glanced at Dakota. Her skirt was up but her underwear seemed intact. Maybe we'd gotten there just in time.

"*Yet*," Zoe said. "You didn't touch her *yet*, perve."

"What do we do?" I asked Zoe. "Do we have to take her to the hospital? Should we file a police report?"

The guy's eyes bulged from his head. Before he could try to regain his speech and dissuade me, Zoe said, "No. Let's get her home. She just needs to sleep it off." Zoe turned to the guy. "What did you give her? Nothing crazy, right?"

He hesitated like he wasn't sure he wanted to incriminate himself.

"Come on, you shit-bag," Zoe said. "We're not going to the cops. We just want to know if she's in trouble."

"It was a tiny amount. I guess it just affected her really strongly. She was nearly out before I got her here."

"It affected her strongly because she's thirteen!" I said, going back one more time to my motto.

"You wanted her compliant, not totally lifeless?" Zoe said. "Guess that didn't really work out for you."

He held up his hands. "I was going to let her sleep it off, I swear."

"Well, now you can help us get her to the car," I said. I couldn't believe I would be taking help from this asshole but there was no way I could get her to the car by myself and Zoe still couldn't walk straight herself. He took her under the armpits and I took her feet in one of her many pairs of expensive designer shoes. For a skinny girl, she was heavy. We weaved and staggered out the door, with Dakota occasionally wriggling and mumbling as if she were having a bad dream.

The guy helped me lay her in the back seat. He tried to thank us before we drove away and Zoe growled at him, "Don't even."

I was so grateful for her. I'm not sure what I would have done without her. I probably wouldn't have even found Dakota in the first place. I'd still be walking around Greenview Shores and he might have raped her by then—I wasn't sure whether I believed him that he wasn't going to. I mean what kind of guy gave someone a date-rape drug but got all ethical and drew the line on how out of it the person had to be when you took advantage of them?

"Thank you," I told Zoe.

"At least I could help someone else since I can't fucking help myself."

My head hurt and I couldn't really deal with delving into all Zoe's messed up shit right now. In the backseat, Dakota moaned, as if seconding the thought.

"Is she really going to be okay? We don't need to take her to the hospital?"

"No, sadly I've been to this movie before."

"*You've* been roofied?"

I must have said it like I was in total disbelief because Zoe said, "You know, despite what everyone says about me, I don't fuck anything and everything. There are guys I've said no to, and some guys who haven't been so happy about that and haven't wanted to take no for an answer."

"So a guy roofied you?"

"Yup."

"That's awful," I said genuinely.

"Well, he got what he wanted. He got to say he wasn't the only one I wouldn't screw."

Automatically, I had driven to the Pearces' house. When I got there, I realized I was still in Zoe's car and had left mine on the side of the road. I'd deal with it tomorrow. I certainly wasn't going to let Zoe drive home in her condition. She seemed to have come down slightly from whatever high she was on, but I wasn't taking any chances. I also didn't really want to be alone with Dakota tonight. Zoe seemed to know what she was doing.

I pulled right up to the house and somehow this time Zoe was able to help me get Dakota inside. Dakota was coming to a little bit and we each positioned ourselves under a shoulder. She was still completely disoriented but she could stagger along and it was less like carrying a dead body. At one point she said, "What the?" but then she shook her head like she didn't even care.

I shushed her and told her everything was fine. She was home and I would take care of her. I took off her shoes and tucked her into her queen-sized bed.

"I'm not leaving her for a second," I told Zoe. "And I'm not letting you drive home so I guess you're sleeping here unless you have someone who can come pick you up."

"No, there's no-one," Zoe said pathetically, and she looked the most distraught she'd looked all night, even when she was talking about some of the awful things that had happened to her.

"I'm sleeping in here with her," I said. "Can you stay and watch her while I go put on some sweatpants?"

"Sure," Zoe said.

I changed and came back in with a set of extra clothes for Zoe to sleep in. When I entered the room, Zoe was sitting on the side of the bed close to Dakota, observantly watching her sleep it off. In the light from the hall, I could see tears glistening on Zoe's face. She wasn't making any noise as she cried. They were silent tears.

Chapter 28

DAKOTA CAME INTO THE KITCHEN looking sheepish the next morning. I wondered how much she remembered about what had happened.

Zoe and I were having coffee, like it was a usual thing we did together.

"Good morning, sunshine!" Zoe said brightly.

"What the hell happened last night?" Dakota asked, taking in Zoe's black eye.

Zoe put down her mug. "Well, let's recap. Do you remember being at Players?"

Dakota nodded. I noticed she was having a hard time looking me in the eye.

"That polo guy you were flirting shamelessly with roofied you and when you were starting to get woozy, he piled you into his car and took you home to his place."

Dakota put a hand on the counter like she needed to hold on to hear the rest. "Did I . . . ?"

"No, and you can thank Hannah for that. She tracked

you down from JoJo's to Players, then found the polo guy's place and got there just in time."

Dakota finally looked at me. I'd never seen her look so apologetic or humble before. "Thank you, Hannah."

"Lesson learned," Zoe continued. "Never drink anything unless you see the bartender pour it and watch it delivered to your hand. Did you see him pour the drink?"

She shook her head.

I spoke up. "I think the lesson learned here is not to go out to bars when you're underage and not to flirt with older men."

"That too," Zoe said. "But I'm just trying to be practical here. This girl needs to learn a thing or two."

Zoe didn't seem to think it was a little preposterous that the girl with the black eye was handing out advice.

"And your eye?" Dakota said. "That wasn't because of me?"

"No, sweetie," Zoe said. "That has nothing to do with you."

Dakota didn't ask more. She'd probably read all about Donnie beating Zoe on HorseShowDrama.

Zoe went on to instruct Dakota in post-Roofie recovery, which involved drinking as much water as possible to flush your system. After Dakota had slowly sipped—no gulping—twelve ounces of room-temperature filtered water, Zoe said she should go shower.

We resumed our coffee. Zoe's hand was jittery as she brought the mug to her lips. I couldn't help but stare at the concavity near her collarbone, visible under the T-shirt I'd leant her. Her skin looked like it was actually sinking in on her bones.

Then there was her face. In the morning light, pre-make-up, no sunglasses, her eye looked awful. I'd never seen a black eye in real life before, only in the movies, and it was actually black.

"What's going on with you?" I asked.

Zoe looked out the window. It was another beautiful Wellington day. Maybe Wellington in the winter was a little bit like L.A., kind of like a fake movie set. The harsh gray winter at home wasn't fun, but perhaps it was more real.

"Depends who you ask. Have you seen what they're saying on HorseShowDrama?"

"I'm asking you," I said.

I expected Zoe to give me some witty and sarcastic answer, to end up somehow emphasizing how lame and sheltered I was. I expected her to find a way to dodge the truth. But she didn't this time.

"I'm in big trouble," she said, sounding teary.

"How so? Is it drugs?"

"Yeah, and, of course, there's this—" She motioned to her swollen eye and the bruise that had formed around it.

"Donnie?"

She nodded and a few tears slipped out.

"Why do you stay with him?"

"He has nice horses. I'm winning on them. What else am I going to ride?"

"Someone else *has* to be willing to give you nice horses." As I said it, I realized it wasn't true. I had learned enough through Chris to know that talent didn't equal good horses being thrown at you. Plus, Zoe wasn't Chris. She had a tarnished reputation and so many trainers wouldn't want to touch her with a ten-foot lunge whip. I'm sure Donnie had emphasized that point to her regularly in his desire to hold power over her.

"But whatever, that's not the worst thing." Zoe brought her shaky hand to cover her eyes. "You know all the stealing? It's been Étienne and I'm a part of it."

"How? Like you've been doing the stealing?"

"No, but I've been telling him who to steal from. In some cases I've been getting him the codes to the locks and the gates. It's not just that I've known what's going on. I've been a part of it."

"Wait—did you tell him to steal our golf cart?"

"No, I swear I didn't. He might have swiped it but for once I didn't target you."

"Did you take any money from him?" I wasn't sure why that mattered but it seemed like it might be relevant.

"No, but he used it to buy me drugs."

I tried to listen if Dakota was out of the shower. I didn't want her to overhear this conversation. It was still quiet from upstairs—no footsteps. "What kind of drugs are you on?"

I watched Zoe's scarecrow chest as she inhaled deeply. "Painkillers mostly. Percocet. Oxy. A little Adderall mixed in for good measure."

"Cocaine? Meth?"

"Have I done them before? Yes. Am I on them regularly now? No."

"Not heroin, either?"

She shook her head violently. "Never done that."

"Well, that's something. I mean painkillers, that's not that bad."

"From your extensive knowledge of drug addiction?"

There was the witty sarcasm back again. "Just from stuff I've read online."

"What the hell am I going to do?" Zoe said. I didn't answer right away because I didn't know and she added, "Why am I even asking you? You don't owe me anything after I fucked you and Chris over. You're probably just waiting for me to leave right now so you can have nothing more to do with me again."

I softened my voice. "That's not true. I . . . We were friends. I was really angry at you but that doesn't mean I can't forgive you. If you're asking for my help, I'm willing to help you."

"Really?" Her face was pained, like she didn't believe me.

There was a part of me that worried that it was all an act. That Zoe was using me again somehow. That this would all come back to bite me in the ass. What would Chris think when I told him I was back involved with Zoe? By virtue of his relationship with me he could be associated with her and her problems, and his name, via mine, might show up about her on HorseShowDrama. But I kept thinking about how I'd seen her last night, looking over Dakota as she slept, and crying softly. And I thought about the good parts of the summer, how Zoe had been a really good friend to me at times. She was in a world of hurt and she needed my help. I couldn't turn her away. I just had to hope I didn't regret it.

"We'll figure out what to do," I promised her. "It'll be all right. But right now I need to call AAA and then you need to take me over to pick up the car."

Chapter 29

OF COURSE, I HAD NO IDEA of what Zoe should do to turn her life around. So I called Ryan, my go-to for any sort of big life questions. In Palo Alto, he was surrounded by young people with too much money, either inherited or earned themselves for some high tech startup. He *had* to know about drug problems.

And, in fact, he did. After hearing me describe what Zoe had told me, he suggested an out-patient center. He said it would be less expensive and she could keep riding. He said she would go to the center, probably daily at first, get on a program to fully detox, and get support and counseling. I went online and printed out a list of places I thought would be good for Zoe that were right in Wellington. Of course, the circuit would be over soon and I wasn't sure what her plans were for where she was going next. Thank goodness Zoe told me she was still on her parents' health insurance so that would cover some of the costs. I had picked places that specialized in dual-diagnoses, which I'd learned meant substance abuse and mental health issues, and were heavy on the therapy-part. Given the fact that she slept around, was being abused by Donnie, and had helped Étienne with his crimes, she needed more than just detox. I wasn't going to fool myself. Even if Zoe called one of the centers to find out about their program, it didn't guarantee she would follow through with going. And even if she followed through and went, it might not work. No matter what, she had a long road ahead of her if she actually was going to get clean and get her life back together.

I also asked Ryan what he thought she should do about being involved in the thefts. "Should she go to the police?"

"I think she has to," he said. "It's probably key to her recovery. Facing up to things."

"Poor Zoe," I said. "I don't know if she'll be strong enough to make it through all this."

"All you can do is be there for her," Ryan said. "What about you? Have you figured out what's next?"

"No, not in the slightest."

"How're things with Chris?"

I told him about the 5-star horse and how Chris needed the money to buy it. Chris and I hadn't ever talked about how dismissive he'd been of me the night Dakota was roofied. I'd decided to let it go and chalk it up to how tunnel-vision he was about getting Athelstane. I had vowed to make myself all about his career so I told myself I had to put aside how he hadn't been there to help me the night with Dakota. He knew what happened to her, though, and he'd been appropriately horrified, if not as apologetic as I would have wanted him to be.

"I think I'm going to ask Dad. Do you think he might go for it?"

"I don't know. He did seem kind of intrigued by it all."

"That's what I was thinking," I said, flashing back to Dad asking to watch Chris from the in-gate. My spirits lifted. I had expected Ryan to bring me down to earth and say no way was Dad ever buying a share of a horse. But now I harbored even more hope.

Dad had to have known I would one day approach him about helping Chris. He'd probably thought it would have come a hell of a lot sooner. I had asked him to pay for Logan's training and entries but I hadn't asked outright for him to invest in a horse just for Chris. The time had come. After I hung up with Ryan, I dialed Dad's number.

"You saw for yourself how dedicated and talented Chris is," I said after explaining about Athelstane and what the horse could mean for Chris's career. "It's an investment you'd be making."

He was silent.

"What do you think?" I asked eagerly.

"I'll tell you what I think—I want to, I really do, but it's not an investment, honey," he said. "There is nothing about buying part of a horse or a full horse that's an investment. Investments are smart decisions based on the long term viability of a business. Horses have no long term viability."

"But you have to admit that Chris is amazing, don't you? I mean, as an athlete."

"Yes, I think he's immensely talented and impressively focused. If he was a CEO, I'd back him. I liked the horses, the competition. But I can't quite wrap my brain around the sport and how much money it takes, how you don't get any of that back."

I felt tears pressing at my eyes. My dad always managed to make things so unemotional. He made everything about science and rational thinking. But when it came down to it, he had plenty of money. Couldn't he make a $250,000 investment in something part-emotional? And I hated that basically he was right. If Chris managed to buy this horse, he would want to keep it, especially if it ended up doing really well and being worth a lot. Why did show jumping have to depend on people having enough money to make non-investment investments? I had to dig deeper, to come up with a convincing counter argument.

"You'll be investing in an experience," I said. "In the privilege of watching a human and an animal perform in perfect harmony at the highest level. You will be investing in possibly going to the Olympics, in supporting our country, in giving young riders someone to admire and believe in. You'll be investing in memories. Memories don't have a price."

I paused, breathless, and proud of myself for what I'd come up with.

"I'm just not there yet," he said. "Maybe someday but I can't say yes today."

"But he needs the money now. Horses like this don't come around at this price."

"Then he'll have to look elsewhere. I'll keep supporting Logan, but that's it."

I nodded, even though he couldn't see me. There was no

use trying to change his mind. I knew my dad. Until I had some game-changing idea to add to my argument, I might as well save my words.

"It was a good pitch," he said. "The memories thing. Giving riders a hero. You were very eloquent."

Any other time I would have been thrilled by his praise. But not now.

Luckily, I hadn't told Chris I was asking my dad so I didn't have to disappoint him. I couldn't tell him how upset I was either, though. How all of a sudden I felt like I'd been knocked to the ground. How after the call I had put my pointer finger in my mouth and nibbled at the nail just a little before stopping myself.

The only place I wanted to be was with Logan, so I went over to Chris's barn, knowing that he was at the show with Lily anyway.

Logan and I had a different relationship now. I didn't toss him his morning grain, I didn't groom him every day, I didn't climb on his back and try to learn how to ride him. I missed those days. Especially right now they seemed so much simpler and I yearned to be back in Vermont, where I was consumed only by trying to find a way to get along with Logan and trying to figure out whether a guy like Chris could actually be interested in me. Now there was Zoe and her very serious real-life problems. There was Chris and the fact that he might not be able to get the last 250K and Athelstane would be sold to another American rider and he'd have to watch him win and witness on a regular basis what he'd lost. There was Dakota and the fact that she'd nearly been raped, and also the fact that her bleeding heart parents didn't seem to care about her at all. There was my dad, who refused to see what buying part of the horse for Chris would mean to me. I didn't want him to do it for Chris, really. I wanted him to do it for me. Would it be so terrible to make a less than wonderful business decision because it would mean a lot to his daughter?

Even though I wasn't taking care of Logan every day, we always picked up right where we had left off, like some people said about reuniting with old friends after years have passed. I pressed my face against his neck and inhaled. When life was getting too much horse people felt solace in the smell of horse. I rubbed my cheeks against his fine coat. I put my nose to his mouth and inhaled his sweet, grassy breath. The stubble of his trimmed whiskers felt nice against my cheek. He chewed a remnant of hay and I listened to the oddly comforting grind of his teeth.

I could have stayed there for a very long time, seeking harbor from the real world. I had come to Wellington to make life easier and clearer and it had only made everything more complicated.

I'm not sure if he was trying to sneak up on me and make himself seem even more intimidating or whether Dale just did everything stealthily, but my breath caught in my throat as I saw him looking over Logan's stall door.

"Did Chris tell you he could go to Europe with the team if he had a number one horse?"

So much for *hello*. So much for *how's it going, Hannah?* So much for, *what are you doing pressing your face into your horse's muzzle and looking like you're never going to move again?* Was Dale incapable of any sort of small-talk warm-up with everyone, was he just socially inept, or was it just with me that he refused to engage in the kind of niceties that make humans human? Even dogs seemed more subtle than Dale, the way they barked a hello or walked circles around each other when they met.

I decided I wouldn't try to be delicate either. "No, who said that to him?"

"The chef. He wants to see Chris on the team. Arkos is going well but he wouldn't be ready to jump solid 5-star classes this summer. It would be great if he could be Chris's second horse for the smaller international classes."

"What do you want me to do?" I snapped at Dale. I was tired of trying to be nice to him. "What can I possibly do? Can I break up with him? Will that somehow get him a horse? I don't think so. I already asked my dad to buy the last share and he said no. I don't know what you want from me."

Dale's expression didn't change. This guy seriously should have been a professional gambler or a politician. "Just wanted you to know."

"Okay, thanks, now I know."

Dale disappeared to whatever fastidious task he had been engaged in before, leaving me with Logan. Logan blew out through his nose and I swear it seemed like it was in response to Dale, like he was saying, "Jeez, that guy!" I laughed a little because it was the perfect response. But inside I still felt all tangled up with everything. It felt like everyone, now Dale included, was looking to me to figure things out, and I didn't have the answer to any of them, least of all myself and the question of what I was going to do at the end of circuit.

Chapter 30

"HOLY SHIT. NO WAY."

I was filling out the entries online for Kentucky Spring for Dakota. I had filled out plenty of entries for her and I suppose I'd seen her birth date many times before but this time my hands froze on the keyboard right after I'd typed it. February twenty-second. We had missed her birthday.

Chills ran through my body and I found myself crossing my arms and rubbing myself like I was standing outside on a freezing day and couldn't warm up. No one had known it was her birthday. As far as I knew, her parents hadn't even called her. Perhaps they had, or at least texted her. But there had been no birthday dinner, no presents, no cake, nothing. For a girl that people would say had everything, she hadn't even had a birthday.

I minimized the screen and rolled back from the computer. Of everything lately, this one had shaken me to the core. I didn't want to run to Logan this time, though. I wanted to tell Chris. I wanted to hear him say how awful it

was. I wanted to commiserate and plan what we could do to
make it up to her. Maybe throw an end-of-circuit birthday
party for her. Or buy her a really meaningful present.

I got in the golf cart and motored over to Chris's barn. I
didn't text him first. I just wanted to see him. I figured he
would be there since it was a Tuesday. I wanted to find him
alone in the barn and fall into his arms and let him hold me
and tell him everything. I wanted to tell him how complicated
everything had become and how I hated it and that I just
wanted it to be perfect again, like it had been between us in
Vermont. I could see the scene I had in mind playing out in
the movie in my head. He'd hold me tight and kiss me and tell
me he loved me. He'd say, yes, things were harder than we
imagined they'd be, but that love was what really mattered
and that it would all work out. Maybe he'd ask me to come
back to Pennsylvania with him after circuit. He'd say he
needed help running his business now that it was taking off.

The barn was quiet. No Chris. No Dale. Just Eduardo.

"Where are they?" I asked him. I felt unfounded anger
rising inside of me. How could Chris not be here right now
when I needed him?

"I don't know where Dale is. Chris went over to MB's."

My face felt hot and I could feel my pulse in my neck. I
threw myself hard back into the golf cart, banging my hip
against the steering wheel, and drove, this time as fast as the
cart would go, back to Grand Prix Village. Just the way Eduardo had casually said MB killed me. I couldn't believe Chris
was over there and hadn't at least told me he was going. I expected to see them out in the field or the ring. Mary Beth

riding and Chris helping her. But when I pulled up, I could make them out leaning against the fence of one of the paddocks. MB was smiling radiantly, her hair loose, half over her shoulder, the sun shining at the perfect height in the sky. Chris was standing close to her and looking at her like she was the only thing he cared about in the world. They weren't kissing or touching but somehow it looked more intimate than if they had been. There was more feeling in the look Chris was giving her than there might have been in a kiss.

I felt like I wanted to drop to my knees right there. I could actually see myself collapsing. I had fought this and fought this all circuit and maybe it was impossible to keep fighting it. It was like a super-powered enemy force that could not be beaten back. There was too much still there between them.

Instead of collapsing, I walked numbly forward. I wasn't sure yet what I was going to say or do. Then there it was: the truth, but not as I had expected. A photographer stood with an expensive camera pointed at them. A woman next to the photographer said, "Mary Beth, try looking at him this time. Kind of over your shoulder."

The scene came into focus for me. A photo shoot for Animo. I waited to feel silly and relieved at the same time. But instead I felt hollow and angry.

I turned and ran back to the cart, my feet feeling to my own ears like each step was letting out a giant thud that could have been heard for miles. I wanted to scream and it was all I could do to keep my feelings bottled up.

Chris must have seen me because he came after me. He caught me just as I was getting back into the golf cart.

"Where are you going?' he asked. I saw him take in my expression and I knew he was realizing how upset I was. "I'm sorry I didn't tell you this was happening. I didn't want you having to even think about it. I just thought it would be over and done and—"

"And then I'd see the ads all over *Horse & Style* with you looking adoringly at her?"

"I couldn't say no. They're a sponsor."

"I didn't ask you to say no." As I said it, I knew I would have wanted him to say no. If I had known, I might have even asked him to say no. "Couldn't it have been anyone else but her?"

"They sponsor both of us."

"Well, isn't that perfect."

"What does that mean?"

I held my head in my hands. "I don't know. The way you were looking at her . . . it was like it was real. Like you still have those feelings."

"Oh my God, Hannah, do we have to go through this again? I was acting."

"I didn't know you were such a good actor."

He shook his head, exasperated. "I don't know what else you want me to do. I have to do these things for my career."

"Because you can't buy your own breeches?" It was the meanest thing I'd said probably yet in our relationship but I was sick of him making everything about us also about his career. It was like the one thing he could always fall back on to trump any feeling I had, no matter how legit the feeling was.

"It's more than the breeches. It's the exposure. It's making me a recognized figure in the sport."

I wondered what the photographer and the person from Animo and Mary Beth for that matter were doing while we were having this fight. Our voices were loud and they could probably hear every word we were saying. Mary Beth was likely enjoying every minute of it, hoping that it spelled real trouble for Chris and me.

"If it was no big deal, why didn't you tell me?" I said.

Chris held his hands up in front of him, like he didn't know what else he could have done. His voice turned quieter, more serious, and sad. "You know what, I think we both need to do some thinking."

My stomach dropped. We had been arguing about a photo shoot, and I had been really upset, but I hadn't thought it would lead to this. "What are you talking about?"

"I just don't know that our relationship is working right now. I think we both need some head space."

"Head space? Are you breaking up with me?"

"I just think we need a few days, a week. I don't know how long. But something's not right. Maybe I should have told you about the photo shoot but the fact that I was scared to tell you, should tell us both something. This feels like more work than it should be."

I couldn't believe this was happening and I couldn't believe it was happening here in Mary Beth's driveway. My worst nightmare come true. He could turn from me and run into her arms with the sun perfectly aligned behind their shoulders. I knew he didn't mean to break up with me here but he'd clearly been thinking about it before now and that hurt me more than anything.

I didn't cry, though. Not until I had started the golf cart and was driving away. Then, I sobbed. Tears gushed out of my eyes, soaking my entire face and dripping onto my shirt. I made horrible mewing sounds—it was the kind of crying you only really do when no one can hear you.

"Let's just take a break and see where we are in a week or so." Those were his last words to me that day. I couldn't stop my face from contorting in ugly ways as I wailed. I was so mad at him too, for giving up just like that, like what we'd had wasn't worth fighting more for. And I was furious at myself for ruining everything with my jealousy.

Linda saw me as I staggered into the barn. I was still crying, but more quietly now. I told her about the photo shoot and how he was looking at Mary Beth. She acted like the perfect friend and blamed Chris. She said he definitely should have told me about the photo shoot and that he should have had the decency not to break up with me in the parking lot. He should have waited till later. As she spoke, I felt queasy that she didn't know the whole truth—how I was paranoid about MB, that maybe my behavior had pushed Chris to the brink, giving him no other choice.

She told me to go to the house. That she didn't need me for the rest of the day. I didn't know what I would do at the house that would make me feel better, but it wouldn't be right to have me sobbing the rest of the afternoon at the barn either.

On the way upstairs, I passed Dakota. She was coming down in her bikini, headed to lie out by the pool.

"What the hell happened to you?"

"Chris broke it off with me," I said, my voice thick with all my crying.

"Oh." Dakota grimaced. "I'm sorry."

She actually sounded genuinely sympathetic and it made tears flood to my eyes all over again. "I know it was your birthday," I blurted out. Suddenly the whole world seemed so grossly unfair and like both Dakota and I had been wronged, that we shared a common pain.

Dakota made a face and I could tell she was trying not to cry.

"Did your parents even call you?" I asked bitterly.

"Texted. They said I should pick out a new show coat or whatever else I want." She sucked in her lips, making her face look severe but I knew she was just holding it together. She was so pretty. Her Nordic features and skinny adolescent body in her tiny bikini. It killed me to think that she was almost date-raped.

"I was thinking I should throw you a big party or give you some really perfect gift, like something real, not something expensive but even if I found the perfect thing it wouldn't make any of it better."

Dakota said so quietly I had to pause to make sure I'd heard her right. "You gave me a good gift."

I knew she meant coming to find her and bringing her home, unhurt.

I wiped at my eyes with both my hands. "Why does life have to suck so bad at times?"

"I'm sorry about Chris," she said again. "He's making a big mistake."

Dakota was fourteen and had never had sex or been in love, for all I knew. But somehow those words coming from her meant the world to me.

Chapter 31

I TOOK MY PHONE WITH ME everywhere, intent on not missing any text that might come in from Chris. Surely, he would text to see how I was doing, or say he'd realized he had made a big mistake and couldn't go another day without me. I took my phone with me to the bathroom, left it on the counter while I showered, slept with it next to me in bed. But he didn't text or call. He'd said we needed a break and I clung to that statement, hoping for another chance. But as the week went on, I was sure it was just a nice way of his saying he wanted to break up for good.

I stalked Facebook and Instagram, looking at his page and Mary Beth's. Chris's accounts were silent. Even when he placed third in the CSI-3 with Arkos, he didn't post anything. Mary Beth posted: "Great photo shoot for Animo!" But that was it. I checked HorseShowDrama but miraculously no one had posted yet about our break-up. Maybe that was worse. I almost wanted to read what people thought about us, what our chances of getting back together were.

I gave in and chewed my nails down to the quick. The worst part was, it didn't even feel good to do it, and now I had to look at them and see what I'd done.

While everything with Chris was falling apart, things between Dakota and me were the best they'd ever been. Finally, she let me into her world. We ate meals together, we talked about horses, and also about life. She told me things I don't think she'd told anyone before like how she missed her parents all the time and often cried herself to sleep at night. She said she slept with a light on. She said she truly loved riding and she wasn't one of the kids pushed into it by hyper-competitive parents. She also loved that it gave her a life and a family, of sorts, because her parents were never around.

"They would be so much happier if they hadn't had me," she said, which made my heart ache for her. For everything with my parents, I knew they both wanted me. "It's like they had to check some box—have child—and I don't think they thought about what it'd be like. They would be so much happier if they could just dedicate themselves to saving the whales, feeding the poor, and fixing the ozone layer."

On Sunday, Linda said I needed to get out for the night. She wanted me to go to JoJo's with her. I knew she was genuinely trying to make me feel better. She also needed someone to go with her on her continued quest to find a man. She told me that she had decided, maybe too late for this year, that an Irish guy would be good. "The Irish guys come here and sow their oats but they're also really family guys at heart. They want to get married and have a family," she said.

I guessed these Irish guys might be different than Dermott, the dirtbag Zoe had slept with in Vermont.

It broke my heart a little that Linda was so honest about her hunt for a man to marry. The horse show world made it nearly impossible for people to have healthy relationships with guys in the real world. As I was painfully learning first-hand it was even hard to have a relationship if you were both in the horse show world. I was still very young but I could see how it was to be Linda—thirty-four and wondering if she was ever going to find a man to marry and have kids with, or whether she would become one of those lifelong single lady horse trainers.

I decided to go with her because I figured at least it would distract me from thinking about Chris. As I was getting ready to go out, I got more into the idea. I decided to put a little more effort into my outfit and appearance. I straightened my hair and put on makeup. Looking at yourself in the mirror when you're feeling mildly pretty can be dangerous. I checked myself out and vengeful thoughts spawned in my head. *Screw you, Chris Kern*, I thought to myself. *Just look what you're missing out on.*

Linda remarked on how hot I looked as we walked into the bar. She had her sunglasses on like a headband again—apparently she was even going to wear them in the bar.

"You are so right that I need to get out," I told her, shaking my hair over my shoulder and loving the way it felt.

But what I really needed was someone to tell me to think twice about what I was about to do. To tell me that when your heart has been broken by the first man you have ever loved and you don't know what the hell you're going to do with your life, you can make disastrous decisions.

JoJo's was packed, which only added to my careless,

quickly-turning-reckless attitude. We let the Irish boys buy us drink after drink. Linda could hold her liquor and knew how to space out her drinks. I had never drunk so much before and didn't know how to space out my drinks so I couldn't really tell how drunk I was getting before I was already sopping drunk.

It felt wonderful at first. It felt freeing and adventurous. A few of the Irish boys flirted with me and I loved every second of it. All I could think was how sorry Chris would be, how if he could only see me now, surrounded by guys who would love to take me home. I told myself he could have MB—that they deserved each other. I thought about how serious he was all the time—the opposite of the fun-loving Irish guys.

It probably would have been fine if I'd stayed with the Irish boys. I think I would have shut down any real attempts by them to get me to go home with them. I would have felt alive and sexy and gone home and cried again for Chris, who I was still very much in love with.

But McNair Sutter took the seat next to me when one of the Irish boys, Cormac, or was it Cian, had gotten up. McNair put his nearly finished drink on the bar next to my half-finished one.

"Chris know you're out like this?" He gave me the once-over, checking out my outfit. I could tell he liked what he saw.

"We're on a break," I said, getting close to him so he could hear me over the din.

McNair gave me an intrigued smile. "On a break, huh?"

"Probably means we're broken up for good," I said.

"Could be. Either way, no use crying over rotten milk. People come to bars to forget things." He nodded to the bartender to bring him another of whatever he was drinking and asked if I wanted a refill. I polished off what was left in my glass and said yes.

"So what are *you* trying to forget?" I said.

"My heartless, soulless social life."

"Social life? You call what you do a social life?"

"What would you call it?"

I had to think about that one. "Drowning yourself in conquest-sex?"

"Conquest sex?"

"Yeah, it's when—"

He held up a hand. "I think I can figure it out."

He looked into my eyes. There was no doubt he was incredibly hot but his attractiveness had never affected me viscerally before. Now, with too many drinks in me, I felt sucked into his stare. So this is what all the girls went crazy about. That's when I should have gone home.

"Does it get old? Sleeping with different people like every night?" I said.

"Every night might be an exaggeration. You know I have had longtime girlfriends."

"What's longtime to you?"

"Months, a year."

"What happened?"

He gave a terribly sexy shrug. He wasn't a big guy, but he was completely confident in his stature. And there were his green eyes and slight stubble.

"It just ran out of steam."

"Do you think you'll ever settle down? Do you think it's about meeting the right girl?"

"I don't know. I haven't figured that part out yet."

"And that doesn't bother you? Not having it all figured out?"

"It bothers me when it's a horse I can't figure out, but my life is pretty good. It'll sort itself out."

I envied him. He had the horses Chris needed. He didn't just have one great horse, he had a few so that he could manage their schedules and decide which horse would contest which big class and which would get to rest. He could decide which venue suited which horse—what would give him the best chance at the win. He had young horses coming along to take the place of his top horses as they aged. He never had to try to scrape together money just to buy a complicated ride like Athelstane.

So maybe it was that he was the anti-Chris. Maybe it was that I was drunk. Maybe it was that I just wanted to feel something, or that part of me wanted to hurt Chris as much as he'd hurt me. Or, it just happened, the way some things do. They aren't planned. They aren't thought out. They don't have reasons. But that doesn't mean those things don't shape your life for years to come.

Somewhere in that night, Linda went home with a nice Irish bloke, and I went home with McNair Sutter to his gorgeously decorated place in Palm Beach Polo with sleek modern, low, steel furniture and large framed black-and-white photos. On the way to his place I checked my phone one last time. Still nothing from Chris. Would a text from him have changed what I was about to do? Even if it just said 'hi,' the answer was yes. It would have changed everything.

McNair had a whole wall of his trophies and ribbons, all from the biggest classes. We kissed standing in front of the trophy wall and he greedily moved his hands all over my body. Then, in his bedroom, we started to take each other's clothes off. First my shirt, then his. My bra, his pants. My pants. He rolled down my underwear, twisting it in his grasp as he did so the fabric bit into my thigh.

"Very nice," he said when he saw the work of Irina, the laser hair removal queen.

That was when my stomach lurched and I knew it was all wrong. That what I was doing was a big mistake. McNair wasn't Chris. He could never be Chris, and Chris was what I wanted.

I wish I could say that I gathered my clothes back up, got dressed, and went home. I didn't, though. I stayed and had sex with McNair. He was gorgeous, even more gorgeous with his clothes off. His chest was tan and his stomach and arms ropey. He was absolutely amazing to look at but I didn't feel anything much beyond the recognition of his good looks. I didn't feel the heat and passion I felt for Chris. I didn't feel the connection. Perhaps McNair had never had such a connection and so he didn't know to miss it because he seemed perfectly satisfied with what we were doing. He told me how hot I was and how much he wanted me as he moved on top of me, his eyes wide open and staring at me the whole time.

I felt the sour taste of the liquor coming up my throat as he thrust into me. It didn't hurt but it felt hollow and sad. Perhaps it felt sadder since he seemed to be so turned on.

When it was over, I did gather my clothes.

"You don't like to cuddle?" he said.

"I guess not."

He lay completely naked on the satiny gray sheets of his upholstered, low platform bed. He wasn't self-conscious about himself at all, not even the fact that his dick was now flaccid and small-looking.

"Chris doesn't seem like the cuddling type anyway," he said.

I hated that he had brought Chris's name into this tarnished moment. And Chris *was* the cuddling type. He didn't have a dark heart like McNair.

I probably shouldn't have driven home because I was still fairly drunk. But I made it home on the mostly empty roads. I made it to the bathroom just in time to throw up. I slumped by the toilet, retching. I knew that what was happening was a simple physical process—my body had consumed too much alcohol in too short a time and was trying to rid itself of the poison. But somehow it felt more metaphorical, like my body was so disgusted with what I'd done it was trying to purge it all out or to punish me for what I'd done. A punishment I felt I keenly deserved. When I finished, I threw myself face first into bed. I pulled the covers over my head. All I could think was, *what have I done? What in the world have I done?*

Chapter 32

"Is it true?" Zoe woke me up with her phone call. I had nearly fallen out of bed trying to find my phone, which was still in my purse, thinking maybe it was Chris calling. If I hadn't been so hung over I would have known it wasn't Chris because it wasn't the MISSION ringtone, but in my still addled state my brain went straight from *phone* to *Chris*.

"What? Is what true?"

"Someone posted on HorseShowDrama that you went home with McNair."

"Oh my God," I said. My head throbbed and my tongue felt as big as a horse's. I needed water. Gallons of it. I made it to the bathroom with the phone still pressed against my ear. Somehow I was able to cradle the phone against my shoulder, fill a glass with water, and drink it while simultaneously pulling down the sweatpants I'd thrown on when I got home and sitting on the toilet.

"Are you peeing?" Zoe said.

"Yes. Please, give me a pass. I had a really bad night."

"So it *is* true? Did you sleep with him?"

I hadn't yet figured out what I was going to do about what had happened with McNair. Technically Chris and I were on a break and he hadn't called or even texted me in a week but I knew full well that none of that meant sleeping with McNair was permissible. I hadn't decided yet if I was going to try to lie and not tell anyone about McNair and just hope Chris never found out. I had basically just passed out but now it was clear that there would be no covering up what I had done. Unless . . .

"Do you think Chris will see it? He said he never goes on that site. But will other people tell him? Will he find out?"

Zoe's voice was impatient. "God, first, just confirm that you slept with him."

"Yes, okay? I slept with him. I slept with McNair. I was totally drunk and I made a horrible, horrible mistake. I knew it was a mistake when it was happening but for some stupid-ass reason I didn't stop it."

"I know. I've been there before. It's like you get to a point and you just wait till it's over."

Zoe's words were some consolation although I didn't really like the fact that she had faced similar sexual situations.

I started crying. "I'm so lost, Zoe. I don't know what I was thinking. I screwed up so badly."

"You weren't thinking. We already established that one."

"I guess I was also so pissed at Chris. Maybe for a second I thought I'd make him jealous. Oh God, it's over now. For good. He'll find out if he hasn't already and he's going to be so disgusted with me and he's never going to want to get back together. I mean—McNair?"

"Yeah, you probably should have picked someone else. Anyone really. You know what happened with them right?"

"No, I know Chris doesn't like him."

"He got their team disqualified from a Nations Cup because he had weighted boots on his horse. You can imagine how Chris felt about that."

Zoe was quiet on the other end. I was still sitting on the toilet, my sweatpants bunched at my knees.

"Maybe it wasn't meant to be between you two," she said softly.

I said through my tears, "I can't believe that. I won't accept that."

"Are you going to tell him? He *will* find out. If not today, then in a matter of days. No one in this sport keeps their mouth shut. I also wouldn't be surprised if McNair says something."

The idea of Chris finding out from McNair, of him bragging, made me feel like I might need to throw up all over again. "I have to go tell him myself." I knew as I said it that I had to, and that it would be the hardest thing I'd ever have to do. But if there was any chance he'd ever forgive me, it had to come from me.

* * *

Jasper greeted me outside Chris's barn. I kneeled down and he licked my face. Maybe it was salt from the tears I kept crying that he liked, but either way it felt so good that he was acting like he loved me. He had gotten used to me. He had accepted me. I was a friend now. He didn't know or care that I had betrayed Chris. In his dog mind, I was a good guy, and always would be. The knowledge that Jasper loved me, when I felt so rotten inside, made me achingly sad. *I'm not good,* I wanted to tell him. *You shouldn't like me. I don't even like myself right now. You'd hate me too if you knew what I'm about to tell your owner.*

Chris was surprised to see me. I studied his face and his body language to try to tell if he already knew. It was clear he didn't. In fact, he brightened when he saw me and gave me a hug, which nearly killed me. He would have never hugged me if he knew. When we pulled away he saw the pain on my face.

"What happened?"

I knew he thought something had happened to one of Dakota's horses like Midway. He knew how much I liked Midway. Or maybe he thought I'd had a falling-out with Dakota, that I lost my job. I don't know what exactly he thought but there was no way he thought I'd slept with someone else.

I cleared my throat. "I have to tell you something and it's awful."

He cocked his head at me and gave me a funny look, like, *what could you have to tell me that could be so awful?*

It was right then that I realized Chris was naïve too. So much of the time I felt like I was the young, innocent one when it came to so many things, like the pressures of the competition, the financial hardships, and the complications that came with love and sex. Finding Mary Beth with another guy should have made him jaded and skeptical but it hadn't. His heart was still pure and open to being in love. He had trusted me fully.

I think if I had never slept with McNair and I had come to him that day and told him how much I missed him and how much I loved him, we would have gotten back together. I felt it in the way he had put his arms around me and the way he had looked at me. Knowing as much made what I had to say even harder.

"I went out last night with Linda and I got drunk. Really drunk." In my head rehearsing what I was going to say to him, I had planned to give lots of build up and explain why I'd made such a bad decision, but it seemed worse to do that now. It seemed like Chris deserved me owning up to what I'd done, not trying to minimize it or make myself blameless.

"I went home with McNair," I said. "It was the biggest mistake of my life."

Chris stared at me, his eyes narrowing. It seemed like he was trying to understand what I was saying. He was trying to make sense of it. "You slept with McNair?"

"Yes," I said plainly.

"We weren't even broken up . . . and you . . . you slept with *McNair*?" Chris blew out a breath through clenched teeth. He took a step back from me, like he didn't even want to be near me anymore, like I was contaminated, and that was exactly how I felt. Toxic.

"We were on a break . . . you hadn't texted me in a week. I thought it was over."

"And if it had been over, would that make it okay?"

I shook my head. No. No, it would never be okay. "I am so sorry," I said. "I am totally, completely, undeniably, thoroughly, utterly, unconditionally, unreservedly sorry."

Chris brought one hand to his face and pressed his fingers against his right eye. He inclined his head further into his hand, and made a sound like he had just been punched in the gut. When he straightened back up, he said, his voice thick with tears, "When I first met you I thought a lot of things might happen, but I never thought you'd break my heart."

He turned and headed out back to the paddocks and ring, leaving me in the barn with a few horses with their heads over the stall doors, looking at me like they were trying to figure out what this human thing was that they'd just witnessed. I knew the horses would be a solace to him. He would throw himself into his riding and his business. I didn't have any such solace. No matter how bad it was for him, I had to live knowing what a terrible thing I'd done and how much I'd hurt him.

Chris didn't look back at me. Jasper did. He gave me one last, nearly mournful glance before following Chris.

* * *

I don't know how I got through those last two weeks. I guess by putting one foot in front of the other. Taking it moment by moment. I was glad I had to work and go about all the little details of getting Dakota ready to show. I only saw Chris from afar. His world in the jumper rings didn't cross much with Dakota's. I chose not to go watch him ride, but I did check online to see how he'd done.

Zoe texted me a bunch. It wasn't lost on me how in Vermont I'd been friends first with Zoe and then with Chris, and as I had fallen in love, I had lost Zoe's friendship. Now, I had lost Chris and Zoe and I seemed like maybe we were regaining our friendship. She said she'd looked online at the rehab places but hadn't called yet. She also was still riding Donnie's horses and probably sleeping with him too. I would have told her she absolutely needed to call, or offered to call for her, if I hadn't been simply distraught about Chris. I kept seeing myself with McNair only in my rewind of what happened I changed things and I stopped myself from going home with him from the bar. Or Mike was there and he saw how drunk I was and drove me home. Or I stopped myself from sleeping with him. In my retold story, I came to my senses and went home. Or I didn't go out that night at all.

I wasn't mad at Linda, though. It wasn't her fault that I went home with McNair. She had no idea I was going to do something so stupid. And the Irish guy she had met seemed promising—they had already been on a second date.

Zoe came over to the barn on Friday afternoon of Week 11. "Just thought I'd check in on you," she said. "Anything from Chris?"

I shook my head despondently. "Did you make any calls?"

"Yes, but not to rehab places."

"Zoe—"

She clasped her hands together and rubbed between her thumb and pointer with her other thumb. "No, just listen. One of Donnie's clients is a lawyer. I talked to her about turning Étienne in."

"Really? Good for you."

"I can't sleep at night. I think I have to go to the police."

"What does she say this'll mean for you?"

"I can probably get a plea deal. Maybe it'll include rehab. Community service. I keep seeing him around and I see people we robbed and I can't live like this. I'm not a bad person. I know lots of people think I am, but I'm really not."

"I know you're not," I told her.

"I've done some really shitty things. I don't have to tell you that." Zoe looked up and shook her head.

"And now you're going to try to make up for them," I said. "And get away from Donnie."

After Zoe left, I remained on the tack trunk, the radio playing in the background. MISSION came on and tears flooded my eyes. Zoe might be able to make things better, if not right, but I wasn't sure I could do the same. I wasn't sure I could ever win Chris back. I knew it would only make my heart ache more but I took out my phone and looked back through photos of us from Vermont and a few from earlier in the circuit. I thought about Vermont again, that wonderful summer, and what it felt like to ride Logan out to the far ring to meet him in those first early mornings.

Logan.

Just like that, I knew what I had to do.

Chapter 33

IT WOULDN'T BRING CHRIS BACK. At least, not now. In fact, it could push him further away from me but it would give him what he wanted most—what he needed—Athelstane.

I explained to Linda what had happened with McNair and Chris and how Logan would be perfect for Dakota.

"But we're about to set up the pre-purchase for Holly's horse," she said.

"Please, it's not a done deal yet and I can't sell him to just anyone. I know you'll take good care of him. Just have her try him. As a favor for me."

"Okay," she said. "I guess we can try him."

I called my dad and told him I wanted to sell Logan and that Dakota might be the one to buy him.

"You want to sell the horse?" he said.

"Yes, but, I want you to put the money into Chris's horse. I know you said it's not an investment but otherwise you keep spending the money on Logan's training. This is what I want."

"Why now? Why all of a sudden?"

I'm not sure I'd consciously thought it through but as I replied to Dad, I knew clearly what was next for me. "I'm going to be going back to school. I won't have time to ride him. He's become an incredible horse and I think Dakota will do really well with him. He'll have a good life with her."

"You and Chris . . . are you two still together?"

"It's not about that," I said. Because it wasn't really. I wanted this so badly for Chris, regardless of where things stood with us. I wanted him to have his number one horse and to get a chance to go to Europe this summer. I wanted him to have a chance to do the biggest classes and maybe go to the World Cup Finals next year. "Will you do it?"

"If it's what you want," Dad said.

"Yes," I said. It was the closest thing to what I wanted. What I truly wanted—Chris—I knew I couldn't have.

* * *

Dakota tried Logan on a gorgeous day. The perfect day. It was the kind of weather I'd dreamed about when I'd been stuck in Boston with all the grayness. I came and watched her try him. Chris was civil to me but nothing more. We put on a good front, saying hello and how-are-you, fake-smiling at each other.

It was nice just to see Chris. I hadn't seen him except from afar. He looked so good in his breeches and polo shirt. It made me hate myself all over again. It made the pain, which had hardly dulled, come back even stronger, nearly cutting off my breath.

Chris didn't know yet that if Dakota would buy Logan the money would go toward Athelstane. I just hoped the deal could still be made. I had Dad tell Chris he wanted to sell Logan, nothing more. Perhaps Chris thought I wanted him sold just to get him out of his barn.

Dakota rode Logan really well. I knew he went well for Chris but he was so rideable now that he was great for her too. A few times she got pretty deep with him and he found a way to make it work, and it didn't seem to bother Logan at all.

"He's really fun," she said, coming to a walk and patting his neck.

"Is there anything else you want to do on him?" Chris asked Linda.

"No, looks like a natural match. Maybe she could do a class on him early next week?"

"Sure, if that's okay with Hannah." Chris turned to look at where I was standing outside of the fence. "Okay if Dakota does him in a class?"

"Of course," I said.

Dakota did Logan in a low junior jumper class during the last week of circuit and was double clean. Linda arranged a pre-purchase exam. She had put the other people on hold and when Logan passed the exam with flying colors, she told them the other sale was off. Dakota's parents had agreed to buy Logan. I thanked Linda profusely.

"Does this mean you'll stay on working for us?" she asked. "Because you're the only person Dakota has actually liked."

I shook my head sadly. As much as I now too liked Dakota—something I never thought would happen—I knew I had to give up the horse world for a time.

I had Dad call Chris and tell him that he was putting the money into the new horse. It took a few days for the wire-transfer and then Logan was Dakota's and the money was Chris's. Dad told me Chris sent him official papers outlining the partnership and that Athelstane was still available. I heard Linda on the phone with Dale coordinating for someone to bring Logan over and I asked if I could go get Logan from Chris's. Linda said sure and she drove me over in the golf cart with tack and boots for him.

Jasper didn't come out to greet me and I felt my stomach sink. I had hoped that Chris would be there and I'd have an excuse to talk to him. I'd booked my flight; in a few days, I'd be going back to Boston. I wanted at least one more chance to see him. Maybe he'd say something to me about my dad putting the money into Athelstane. But Jasper not being there meant Chris probably wasn't either. His car wasn't there.

Dale had Logan on the cross ties. There was still no sign of Jasper or Chris. I helped Dale tack up Logan. Besides saying a curt hello, I was pretty sure he wasn't going to talk to me. I wondered if he was happy Chris and I were broken up, or if he was pissed at me for breaking Chris's heart. Probably both.

"Need a leg up?" he said as I started to walk Logan out of the barn.

"I can use the step-stool," I said coolly.

"Okay," he said. "I just want to say, you did a good thing."

I stopped Logan and looked back at Dale.

"Selling him so Chris could have the horse. He might not say it to you but it means a lot to him. This horse is going to make the difference. He's going to get Chris to Europe this summer."

"And now you have me out of your hair too," I said.

"Maybe you weren't all bad," Dale said.

"Let's not get crazy, now." I chuckled but then turned serious. "Keep an eye on him, okay?"

Dale nodded and it wasn't unkindly. "You know I always do."

* * *

Dakota and I went on a last trail ride. I rode Midway and she rode Logan. We talked about the summer of showing she had planned. She said she was really looking forward to showing Logan.

"I like the jumpers the best," she said.

"You're good at them," I said.

I looked around at the farms, the jump fields, the fence lines, and the canals. Wellington was a place unlike any other. It was strange and I would miss it. Maybe I'd be back someday.

"I'm sorry I'm not staying with you this summer."

"I get it," she said. "You have to go back to school."

"Yeah, I do. I kind of just ran away and that didn't make things better. You hang in there, okay? Don't go doing any more crazy things."

Dakota made a face. "Well, I'm not going to be boring my whole life."

I laughed. "I don't think you'll ever be boring. Just be more careful. You have to take care of yourself." What I didn't say was that she had to take care of herself because her parents weren't going to.

"Come visit?" Dakota said. "See Logan?"

I twirled a few fingers from one hand through Midway's thick mane. "I'd love to."

* * *

I thought I might not see Chris again before I left. I had watched him jump Arkos in the last grand prix of the circuit, the big 5-star class. Arkos had jumped amazing and had just one unlucky rail over a tall, skinny, airy vertical to keep him from the jump-off but it turned out the course was so tough there were only four clean and Chris finished fifth. It was very strange watching him because I kept feeling like we were still together but then reality would hit and I'd know we weren't. All I could think as I watched him was that I'd made the biggest mistake of my life and that nothing would ever be good in my life again. I left the tent sure that was the last time I'd lay eyes on him in a long time, but he texted me two days before I was supposed to leave saying I'd left some stuff at his place and probably should come over and grab it.

I hoped to God it was just an excuse for him to see me one last time.

He was dressed in jeans and a gray T-shirt. He stood aside to let me come in and I wanted more than anything to brush up against him, pretending it was by accident to at least feel his T-shirt against my skin.

"I'm not sure where everything is. I just thought you should take a look around before you head home."

"How long are you staying?" I asked.

"A few more weeks. Athelstane is coming and needs to go through quarantine so we'll stay here until he's all clear and then go back to Pennsylvania."

"It's exciting," I said, spotting a purple FEI horse passport on the dining room table. Chris was likely getting Arkos's paperwork in order for Europe.

Chris offered me what seemed like a genuine smile. "Yeah, it is. And I owe a good part of it to you, so thank you for selling Logan and convincing your dad to invest."

"You're going to have a great summer and I'm so happy for you," I said. The crazy thing was that I *was* happy for him. I had seen online that both Chris and Mary Beth were expected to get invitations to go to Europe with the team this summer. The whole circuit I'd tried to keep them apart and I had essentially been the one to send them off to Europe together. I'd realized that by trying desperately to keep them apart I'd only pulled Chris and me apart. I also knew that I needed to figure out my own life before I could be a part of Chris's. I still wanted to be a part of his life, but whether that could ever happen again remained to be seen. I had to figure out who I was without him.

"What are you going to do this summer?" he asked.

"I'm going to take some classes. I can make up some of this semester. It seems like that's what I should be doing—being a college kid."

"Sounds right," Chris said.

I found a few of my magazines in the TV room and a hair elastic. Nothing I couldn't have lived without. In the bedroom, I opened a few drawers and seeing Chris's clothes made my chest hurt. In one of the drawers I found my T-shirt, a pair of underwear, and a pair of socks. In the bathroom my hairbrush sat on the counter. I liked that Chris hadn't moved it. That he hadn't packed up these things the day I'd told him about McNair and thrown them straight in the trash.

I came out of the bathroom and found him standing in my way.

"Well—" I was going to say, *I guess this is good-bye*, but the words stuck in my throat.

Chris reached for me and pulled me to him. I pressed my face into his neck and he held his arms around my back. I don't think either of us could have planned it, but something told us we needed each other one more time. Maybe in some Darwinian way, Chris wanted to be the last one to be with me. I wouldn't be able to forget what I'd done with McNair but it was comforting to move one more step away from it. Being with Chris couldn't wipe away being with McNair, but it would be so much better to remember Florida this way.

We didn't say a word. It was completely silent. We were desperate as we pulled off each other's clothes and climbed on top of the covers. We did it with him on top, and I put my hands on his triceps, pressing hard so I could see his skin turn white. The whole time we were doing it, I knew this wasn't a reunion. This wasn't us getting back together, or him forgiving me, no matter how much I wished it could be. This was us saying good-bye. He needed to go to Europe and ride his heart out while continuing to reestablish his career. I needed to go back to Tufts and figure out who I was away from him and the horse show.

After, we lay in bed together for a while, but still didn't talk. Finally, I said, "I am so sorry this is the way it ended."

"Me too," he said.

"Maybe it won't be forever," I said hopefully.

"Maybe," he replied.

About the Author

KIM ABLON WHITNEY lives with her husband and three children in Newton, Massachusetts. In addition to writing fiction, she is a USEF 'R' judge in hunters, equitation, and jumpers and has officiated at the Washington International Horse Show, the Capital Challenge, the Winter Equestrian Festival, Lake Placid, and the Vermont Summer Festival. As a junior, she placed in two of the equitation finals. She later competed in the A/O jumpers on her self-trained off-the-track thoroughbred.

Keep in touch with Kim on Facebook, Twitter, Instagram, and at www.kimablonwhitney.com.

Also, stay tuned for *Hunter Derby*, Book 3 in The Show Circuit Series. Here's a sneak peek at the first chapter.

Hunter
DERBY

Chapter One

IF A HORSE WENT IN one spot in the stall, it made it easy to clean it out. But it also made it stink to the high heavens. Zoe liked a lot of horse smells but the acrid stench of urine was not one of them. The dark pee-soaked shavings weighed a ton as she pitched them into the wheelbarrow that was jutted halfway into the stall.

Beyond the smell, there was the absolute indignity of the fact that she was here, in this small, no-name barn, mucking stalls. Okay, at first she had been thrilled to avoid any larger consequences than probation and community service. It had been undeserved, like when someone gets you a gift that's much too generous and you don't know what to say or how to thank them. People she rode horses for as a junior used to do that. Since they couldn't pay her in money, they gave her expensive gifts like a new riding coat, a beautiful cashmere sweater, or once a gorgeous Hermes belt with the pretentious H for the buckle. Now, though, she hadn't ridden a horse for anyone besides Linda Maro in weeks and she was stuck spending her mornings at Narrow Lane, a therapeutic riding center, cleaning stalls. But the fact that she'd gotten off with her this as punishment was a true gift. After helping Étienne steal thousands of dollars in saddles, she could have easily found herself as an inmate starring in *Orange Is The New Black*.

When she had gotten her assignment, she had assumed she'd be leading mentally or physically handicapped people around, or doing whatever they did in a therapeutic program, but it turned out that she apparently wasn't even good enough to lead kids around. Instead, she had to muck out the stalls of a motley crew of horses that in no way even came close to resembling the athletic animals she usually spent time around. She swore these horses' piss smelled worse than that of horses on the circuit.

There was Daisy, a ridiculously feminine name for what was actually a squat so-ugly-it's-cute, Fjord. Danny, a black quarter horse. And Pepper, a leopard appaloosa, perhaps the ugliest kind of appaloosa there was, which was kind of like discussing the grossest kind of throw-up. Appaloosas were all gross; to Zoe it just was a matter of degrees.

As Zoe lifted the plastic pitchfork, all that ran through

her head was, *Zoe Tramell is cleaning a crappy appy's stall.* She didn't usually talk or think about herself in the third person but somehow whenever she was at Narrow Lane, that kind of thinking took over her brain. There was a lot of time to think because she was left alone to muck all the stalls, sweep, and make up the grain. The second day she'd put in her ear buds, content to lose herself in Pink's music but Kirsten, the director, informed her that she couldn't just "space out." That this wasn't a regular barn and they might need to get her attention. And for that matter Kirsten had to put in that wearing ear buds in any barn wasn't a good idea because you wouldn't hear things happening around you and you might miss a loose horse or another person calling for help. Like that stopped anyone on the show circuit from mucking with music pumping in their ears. Or riding with ear buds in for that matter.

Zoe filled the wheelbarrow and maneuvered it out to the manure pile. She was sweaty. At least doing the stalls would keep her skinny since she wasn't riding more than two or three horses a day. Pepper was the last stall of the morning. She put in new shavings and pulled the banks down. All that was left was sweeping the aisle, thank the Lord. She did the aisle, wishing they used a leaf-blower like most normal people. But they probably believed that it wasn't good because all the shavings and dust went up to the ceiling or something.

She said a quick good-bye to Kirsten and headed to her car. One good thing about coming early was she had yet to see an actual lesson. Usually when she was pulling out, the first minivan of the day would be pulling in and a tired-looking parent would be getting out and letting down the motorized back ramp. Today was no exception and Zoe sped out before she saw who would be coming down that ramp.

She braked at the end of the driveway and a horse and rider caught her eye directly across the road. She'd noticed there was a horse farm there too but assumed it was some backyard place like Narrow Lane. Or at least not a fancy show barn.

But the horse and rider that caught her eye looked legit. A bay warmblood with an impressive trot. A man who knew how to ride. It was amazing how in a split second a good rider could tell if another horse and rider were A circuit material, or not. She couldn't tell how old he was exactly but he looked to be in her general range for guys—somewhere between twenty and forty-five. But if he was anybody, she would have known he was here in Bedford, New York. She knew everyone who was anyone. Which meant he was a nobody. Of course, maybe he was a small step down from the professionals she was used to. Maybe he showed in the Northeast but didn't go to WEF or win at Indoors. It was possible. Unlikely, but possible. She felt a small dash of hope flutter somewhere inside of her. Could something good come out of this terrible assignment at Narrow Lane? Her mind raced to preposterous fantasies. Not so much about falling in love with him or anything, but about his having really nice horses and wanting her to ride and show them. She would show up at Old Salem and everyone would be in total disbelief that she'd put her life back together, found a great job, and was back in the show ring. She'd win every class that mattered in the professional divisions. Zoe nearly shivered a little thinking about herself winning again. She envisioned landing off that last jump after she'd nailed a course and all the clapping and whooping. She could feel the reins in her hand as she led a horse in on top for the jog. She heard the announcer's excited voice saying she'd scored a 94 in the handy round of the hunter derby. All of a sudden, it would be like she was a top junior again, but even better.

Of course that was her fantasy. Her reality was that her shoulders hurt from cleaning all the stalls and now it was time to hustle over to Linda's to ride a few of Dakota's horses.

Made in the USA
San Bernardino, CA
11 December 2015